"What do you remember about Lynx Lake?" Rainwalker asked.

Kendra swallowed, her throat suddenly dry. Lynx Lake? Even as a child she'd been afraid of the lake. And for years afterward she'd had nightmares about being back in the gloomy old stone house, alone in the dark and afraid, with something terrible stalking her, slithering closer and closer and closer....

"I'm sorry, Mr. Rainwalker," she said firmly, "but I can't help you."

"You seem upset."

Would he never stop probing? "I don't want to remember the past!" The words burst from her. "Stop trying to make me remember!"

He pounced. "Remember what?"

She stared at him, anger mixing with her rising anxiety. "Goodbye!" she snapped.

"Wait," he said.

She hesitated, poised to leave.

"I don't know if you plan to return to your family estate, Ms. Tremaine," he said softly, "but my advice is—don't...."

Dear Reader,

The nights are getting cooler now that fall is here, and that means it will be even easier for you to shiver as you read the wonderful new Shadows novels we've got for you.

In *Footsteps in the Night,* Lee Karr tells the story of a heroine whose trip to Ireland turns frightening as she keeps finding herself trapped inside another woman's body, another woman's life. No matter where she turns, danger seems to beckon, and the only man who can save her may be the one man she doesn't dare to trust.

Jane Toombs offers *What Waits Below,* a story of a family with dark and terrifying secrets, and a link to the past that may prove fatal—especially to the heroine. Only the mysterious new groundskeeper seems to have an idea what's going on, but even if he's on her side, will their united efforts be enough to save her from the tentacles of the family curse?

In months to come, we'll chill you even further with books by favorite writers, such as mainstream's Patricia Simpson, as well as the new authors we'll be bringing your way. So be sure to look for your reading pleasure in the shadows—Silhouette Shadows.

Yours,

Leslie Wainger
Senior Editor and Editorial Coordinator

JANE TOOMBS

WHAT WAITS BELOW

SILHOUETTE® Shadows™

Published by Silhouette Books New York

America's Publisher of Contemporary Romance

SILHOUETTE BOOKS
300 East 42nd St., New York, N.Y. 10017

WHAT WAITS BELOW

Copyright © 1993 by Jane Toombs

ISBN: 0-373-27016-X

First Silhouette Books printing September 1993

All the characters in this book have no existence outside the
imagination of the author and have no relation whatsoever to
anyone bearing the same name or names. They are not even
distantly inspired by any individual known or unknown to the
author, and all incidents are pure invention.

® and ™:Trademarks used with authorization. Trademarks
indicated with ® are registered in the United States Patent and
Trademark Office, the Canada Trade Mark Office and in other
countries.

Printed in the U.S.A.

Books by Jane Toombs

Silhouette Shadows

Return to Bloodstone House #5
Dark Enchantment #12
What Waits Below #16

JANE TOOMBS

believes that a touch of the mysterious adds spice to a romance. Her childhood fascination with stories about shape changers such as vampires, werewolves and shamans never faded, leading to her present interest in supernatural influences, not only in Gothic romances but in the early cultures of all peoples.

A Californian transplanted to New York, Jane and her writer husband live in the shadow of Storm King Mountain.

PROLOGUE

Kendra Tremaine's steps slowed as she neared the Egyptian temple. She'd chosen the Metropolitan Museum of Art as a safe place to meet the stranger who'd called her earlier in the week, but the closer it had come to Saturday, the more she'd doubted the wisdom of agreeing to talk to him at all.

Not only did she have reservations about disinterring the past, but she really didn't know much about the Tremaines, despite being one.

He'd identified himself as Dewolfe Rainwalker, an anthropologist from the University of Michigan interested in the relationship of Celtic myths to Native American mythology. Because of this interest, he was trying to interview members of the Tremaine family. She'd done her best to put him off, claiming she knew little if anything of interest to him, but he'd been so persistent she'd finally agreed to this meeting.

"You'll have no trouble recognizing me," he'd told her. "I'll be the one wearing a beaded headband."

In New York City anything went, so that didn't automatically classify him as weird—a tad unusual, maybe.

She paused by the pool, staring up at the two massive columns in front of the Temple of Dendur. A man stood between the pillars, dwarfed but not diminished by them, a colorful headband with an intricate thunderbird design setting off his raven-black hair and bronze skin. His gaze crossed hers and he held, examining her. He smiled, raising a hand in salute, and strode down the steps to her level.

"Ms. Tremaine, I presume," he said. "I'm Dewolfe Rainwalker."

"How did you know me?" she asked as they shook hands, curious because she hadn't given him any description of herself.

He smiled at her. "The same old woman in Tremaine's Wold that told me how to find you also mentioned that all the Tremaines have hair the color of wild mustard. The plant's in bloom in the foothills now—field after field of intense yellow-gold."

She smoothed her shoulder-length hair with nervous fingers. Tremaine's Wold was the mountain village close by the Tremaine estate. She'd had no idea anyone in the village knew where she lived.

He gestured toward the seats lining the glass wall, but she shook her head, saying, "You told me you were interested in the Tremaines, specifically their estate in the Adirondacks, but I left the estate when I was eight years old and I've never been back. I really can't remember much about the place, and it's not clear to me why you think the estate has anything to do with Celtic or Native American mythology."

"Tremaine is a Welsh name, therefore probably Celtic. And various tribes of Algonquins roamed the Adirondacks in the early days. Several clues—one being the name of the lake on your family property—lead me to believe there may be a possible connection."

Kendra swallowed, her throat suddenly dry. Lynx Lake? As a child she'd been afraid of the lake.

"Do you remember anything about Lynx Lake?" he asked. "Any idea how it acquired the name?"

An unwelcome memory snaked into her head. She wasn't supposed to go near the lake unless her mother was with her, but Collis, her older half brother, had coaxed her to the lake with him the month before her mother took her away from the estate, never to return. Though Collis usually ignored her, she had no other companion, and so when he did pay attention to her, she put up with his teasing, grateful to be noticed.

She'd never told anyone, not even her mother, how Collis enjoyed frightening her, and she certainly didn't mean to reveal childhood sibling problems to this stranger.

Although she tried not to let them, details of that frightening experience continued to crawl through her mind—she at eight standing beside her fifteen-year-old half brother at the lake's edge, staring, terrified, toward the small wooded island at the lake's center.

"There's something that lives partly on the island and partly in the water, you know," Collis had told her, pitching his voice low and scary. "When I call, he'll come. And when he comes he'll leap from the water and gobble you up in two bites."

Kendra hadn't waited around to see what, if anything, might appear from the depths of the lake in answer to the call. The one advantage she had over Collis was that she could run faster because he was lame. And so she'd fled, hearing his laughter following her.

The memory still had the power to disturb her, and her resentment at being forced to relive it spilled over onto Dewolfe. "I really don't believe I can help you." Annoyance tinged her voice.

"No one ever mentioned anything about the lake's name?" he persisted.

A vague recollection surfaced and, since it seemed harmless, Kendra saw no reason not to mention it.

"My mother once told me that Ezekial Tremaine, who built the estate, translated an Indian name for the lake into English."

Dewolfe smiled triumphantly. "I thought so! It fits right into the Mishibezo myth." Apparently noticing her puzzlement, he added, "Mishibezo is an Algonquin name for one of their most feared enemies, an amphibious monster. The word doesn't translate well, but in English it means something like 'the great and evil lynx.'"

She stared at him. "A monster? I always assumed 'lynx' simply referred to the animal."

"In this case, I don't think so. Are you aware that many of the people in Tremaine's Wold believe something lives in Lynx Lake? Something monstrous?"

Kendra stiffened. Was Dewolfe some kind of a weirdo? "Are you suggesting there's something like the Loch Ness monster swimming around in Lynx Lake?"

"I'm not suggesting anything. Myths of half men, half monsters are common to many lands and peoples. My Algonquin ancestors, as well as the ancient Celts, believed water was a supernatural dwelling place. The home of evil creatures."

Firmly pushing away the memory of Collis's teasing—a boy's joke, that's all it had been—she raised her eyebrows. "Monsters in Lynx Lake? I can understand inhabitants of an isolated mountain village conjuring up superstitious nonsense, but you're an anthropologist. Are you telling me you actually accepted what they told you about monsters as the literal truth?"

He corrected her. "Monster. Only one, from all accounts."

His seriousness took her aback but in no way convinced her. "One or twenty, I'm still skeptical. More than skeptical. I simply don't believe it. Actually, I'm not the person you should be talking to. My half brother, Collis, lives on the estate. Why haven't you contacted him about these wild stories of the villagers?''

He shrugged. ''No luck there. Your brother and his lawyer refuse to speak to me or let me inside the gates. That's why I'm trying to jog your memory.''

She wondered briefly at his mention of a lawyer before saying, ''I have very few memories of my childhood on the estate. I certainly remember nothing about any monster or monster myths, if that's what you're interested in.''

They'd been walking slowly about the room, but now he halted by the pool and looked down at the water. ''Some of the families who live in Tremaine's Wold came at the same time as old Ezekial,'' he said. ''They don't much like talking to strangers but I'm the persistent type and I finally convinced a few of them to trust me. One ninety-year-old woman insists her great-grandmother handed down a story about how her oldest son 'got took and et' by something in the water when he and a friend climbed over the estate wall on a dare and went swimming in the lake.''

Kendra shook her head. ''You seem to believe there's some kind of impossible hybrid creature living in Lynx Lake. Really, Mr. Rainwalker!''

''Yes, really. I think it's possible something dangerous lives in that lake and I'm determined to find out what it is. You lived on the estate for eight years. Are you sure there's nothing else you recall? Stories you might have heard? Childish nightmares, maybe?''

A shiver ran along her spine. Until she was in her teens she'd had recurrent nightmares about being back in the gloomy old stone house, alone in the dark and afraid, with something terrible stalking her, slithering closer and closer and closer.... She'd wake up screaming from the nightmares, frightening Aunt Meg, who'd raised her after her mother died. The nightmares had finally stopped, thank God, and she hoped they'd never return.

Kendra had no intention of trying to lift the veil surrounding her early years and, in the process, raise specters of the past better left buried.

"This is getting neither of us anywhere," she said firmly. "I'm sorry, Mr. Rainwalker, but I can't help you."

"You seem upset."

Would he never stop probing? "I don't want to remember the past!" The words burst from her. "Stop trying to make me remember!"

He pounced. "Remember what?"

She stared at him, anger mixing with her rising anxiety. He was so intent on his precious research he didn't care if he turned her inside out.

"Goodbye," she snapped.

"Wait," he said.

She hesitated, poised to leave.

"I don't know if you ever plan to return to your family estate, Ms. Tremaine," he said, "but my advice is—don't!"

CHAPTER ONE

Kendra watched the tall and massive metal gates swing inward, gates of barred iron decorated with grotesque gargoyles, gates protecting the Tremaine estate from easy access. They were set into a ten-foot-high wall of mortared stone, an old wall that had enclosed the thirteen-acre grounds for the past one hundred and eighty years, built by her paternal ancestors at the same time the house was. She knew little more about either the estate or those ancestors.

As she drove her bright yellow sports car through the opening, heading toward the house, she heard the gates clang behind her, shutting her in, and felt a momentary tremor of guilt. By coming here she'd broken a promise made only months ago.

"Don't ever go back to the Adirondacks, to Tremaine's Wold, to the estate," her dying aunt had begged. "I promised your mother before she died I'd keep you away from that terrible place, and I have. Now you must keep the promise I made."

To soothe her aunt's agitation, Kendra had agreed then never to return to these mountains, to the town of Tremaine's Wold and the house of her childhood. After last week's phone call, though, she'd had little choice. Gregory Morel, identifying himself as the Tremaine attorney, had told her that her half brother, Collis, had been killed in an accident, leaving the estate to her.

She'd listened with numb disbelief to the lawyer's bleak news. Morel had given scant details, saying only that because of the circumstances there'd been no funeral and her brother was already buried. He understood that she hadn't been back to the estate since her childhood but he hoped she'd be able to come now. As soon as possible.

He'd given her no chance to ask why there hadn't been a funeral or anything else, telling her that he'd answer any questions she might have after her arrival.

She did have questions. Those about Collis's death Morel would be able to answer, but she doubted he or anyone else could tell her why, as a child, she'd been so abruptly taken away from the estate. Or why her mother had been so insistent she never return.

Return she had, though, and here she was, shut like a prisoner inside the massive gates. Kendra shook her head at the thought. She would *not* be morbid or fanciful. She'd always been a take-control person.

She left her car parked under the porte cochere and stepped from under its roof into the sunny late May afternoon. Coming as she had from the clamoring bustle of New York City, she could hardly believe how quiet the Adirondacks were. As she stared up at the stone house, her hair was ruffled by a cool breeze carrying the fragrance of roses mixed with the scent of pine, and she breathed deeply, savoring the combination.

The house was built of gray stone quarried from a massive barren plateau to the south of the estate, a wold—Tremaine's Wold, named after her Welsh ancestor, Ezekial Tremaine, who'd been the first to settle here. To her knowledge, the village had never numbered more than a few hundred people. The estate, maybe a half mile north of Tremaine's Wold, included in its enclosed grounds a good-sized body of water—Lynx Lake. The lake Dewolfe Rainwalker had been so interested in.

When she'd passed through the village, the streets and buildings had seemed as familiar to her as though she'd gone away yesterday, instead of eighteen years ago.

No one had smiled or even nodded, and it seemed to her that response also was familiar. She could be wrong; she'd been away so long no one would recognize her. Why should she expect them to smile at a stranger?

Kendra walked toward the front of the house. As she reached the steps, she heard the creak and groan of the heavy chestnut door opening and she stopped, waiting, her heart beating a little too fast. The door swung inward. A tiny white-haired woman peered at her, blinking as though the light hurt her eyes. The housekeeper? Whoever it was, Kendra felt sure she'd never met her.

"I'm Kendra Tremaine," she said when it appeared the little old woman wasn't either going to speak or open the door wide enough for her to enter. "You must have been the one who let me through the gates."

The gap widened by a few more inches, enabling Kendra to ease past the woman, who promptly shut the door. "I'm sorry you came," she whispered so softly that Kendra could hardly hear the words.

"So you're here at last," a hearty man's voice said. "Welcome to Lynx House."

Kendra stared past the old woman to the stocky auburn-haired man striding toward her in the gloom of the spacious entry.

"I'm Gregory Morel," he said, taking her hand. "So we meet at last—we're cousins, you know."

"Cousins?" she echoed, amazed. "I wasn't aware I had any."

He shrugged, releasing her hand. "Fourth or fifth, something like that, but sharing Tremaine blood, all the same. I see you've met my mother."

Taken aback, for she'd supposed the old woman in her old-fashioned, high-necked, long-sleeved gray dress to be some sort of housekeeper, Kendra managed to say, "Actually, I haven't, exactly."

Gregory put an arm over his mother's shoulders. "I'm sure she'd like you to call her Leda. Wouldn't you, mama?"

"If she likes." Mrs. Morel's voice was thin and reedy.

"I'm afraid we're short of help at the moment," Gregory said, "so I'll bring in your bags myself. I assume they're in the car?"

"Don't bother," Kendra said, "I can—"

"No trouble at all." Gregory went out through the front door, leaving Kendra alone with his mother.

"I didn't know you and your son were staying here," Kendra said to her.

Leda stared at her. "I thought you'd been told. I'm the mother of your father's first wife, Beth, dead for many years, poor child. My son and I have lived in this house going on eighteen years."

Kendra flushed. "I—I'm afraid I know very little about my—my family."

"If you weren't told anything about us, like as not you don't know anything else about the place, either, or you wouldn't have come."

Puzzled and confused, Kendra said, "But your son told me to come here."

"I hoped you wouldn't."

Uncertain how to respond, Kendra glanced about the dark-paneled foyer, her gaze touching the curving staircase with its ornately carved banisters. She noticed the prisms of the chandelier sparkled even in the dim light, so evidently the departure of the servants had been recent.

Deciding to be frank about how little she knew, Kendra said, "I suppose you're aware I was raised by my mother's sister. I'm afraid my Aunt Meg knew almost nothing about the Tremaines. I've never even heard the name of the house before. Lynx House, didn't your son say? After the lake, I imagine."

Without replying, Leda turned away abruptly. "I'll show you to your room."

Kendra followed Leda up the stairs, confused by the woman's behavior and unsure of her own feelings. She'd never expected to return here. Not once in the years before he died had her father contacted her. Aunt Meg, following her mother's instructions, had made Kendra promise not to call or write to her father or brother.

As a teenager, she'd grown curious about the father and brother she scarcely remembered and sometimes had been tempted to break her promise: One Friday night she'd actually made up her mind to make a call during the weekend, but after she'd fallen asleep, she'd dreamed she was back at the old stone house and had the most horrible nightmare of her life. After that, she gave up the idea. Why should she call her father? He knew where she was, and evidently he didn't want any part of her.

When he'd died, her aunt had waited to tell her about it until three weeks after he'd been buried, so she hadn't been able to go to his funeral.

After that she'd had an occasional daydream about coming back to visit her brother, but had never followed through. Perhaps because her few memories of Collis were unpleasant. Now, too late to see either her father or her brother, she'd finally come home.

Home? Kendra shook her head. It really wasn't her home, even if Collis had left the entire estate to her in his will. Why had he? Wouldn't it have been more natural to will it to Leda and Gregory Morel?

She and Leda reached the second floor and started down the corridor to the west wing, the faded but still beautiful floral carpeting soft underfoot. Kendra drew even with Leda. "Are you taking me to my old room?"

"Your brother said it was. You'll find nothing's changed."

Nothing's changed. The words rang in Kendra's head after Leda left her at the door to the bedroom she'd had as a child. Entering the room, she recognized familiar pink-and-white furnishings—the frilly curtains, the ballerinas on the wallpaper—and it was as though she'd never left, as though the years of living in New York had never been.

Kendra drifted around the room, touching a ballerina music box, a fluffy white unicorn, a book of Hans Christian Andersen's tales with an illustration of a mermaid on the cover. As she stared at the mermaid, a terrifying memory swam into her mind. How many nights had she huddled in her bed trembling, certain something was waiting for her, something unspeakable slithering up from the vaults, up, up, up to claim her for its own?

The vaults. Not for years had she used that word as the Tremaines used it—to mean basement or cellar. When they were children, Collis had bragged to her about exploring the vaults, hinting of exciting secrets, but she'd been too afraid to ever go with him, no matter how much he coaxed her. As a little girl, nothing in the world could entice her through that door in the kitchen that hid the steep stone steps leading into the vaults below.

Kendra shook her head to rid herself of childish fears, then crossed to the window and looked out. The rose garden was immediately below, and the pines beyond cast an afternoon shadow over the bushes. Lynx Lake glimmered between the trunks of the pines and, over the tops of the trees she saw distant mountain peaks. Peaceful and serene. Where had her childhood fears come from?

And yet, if Dewolfe Rainwalker were to be believed—not that she put any credence in what he'd told her—Lynx Lake hid something fearful in the depths of its shimmering waters. *Don't go back,* he'd warned her.

Despite herself, Kendra shivered and turned away from the window so abruptly that she brushed against the stand holding the music box, jarring loose a tinkle of silvery notes that seemed to hang like ghosts in the air after the sound faded.

Stop it, she warned herself. You're no quivering wimp, nor are you the helpless child you used to be. Neither the past nor any strangeness here can undermine the strength within you.

If she shivered, it was because the room held the damp chill of disuse. If only her mother had told her aunt the reason why she'd fled with Kendra from her husband on that June night, the past wouldn't be so much of a mystery. But Aunt Meg had sworn she knew no more than she'd told Kendra, and that was very little.

Deciding a walk in the fresh air would clear her head of lingering childhood ghosts, Kendra turned toward the door just as Gregory entered with her two bags. He set them on the floor and smiled at her.

"Except for that molten gold hair, you really don't resemble the Tremaines," he told her.

Aunt Meg had always told her she'd inherited her mother's looks, especially her large brown eyes. "Just as well," she'd always added.

"I noticed at your mother's wedding that your half brother's eyes were the strangest shade of gray—almost silver. Thank God you didn't inherit eyes like that."

Gazing at Gregory, Kendra realized what her aunt must have meant, because Gregory's eyes were an unusual shade of gray and they seemed to have an odd, iridescent sheen.

"Thank you for bringing up my luggage," she said.

"I've put ads in the city papers for a grounds keeper and maids. I expect some responses soon."

"Why the city papers?" she asked. "I'd think it would be easier to recruit people from Tremaine's Wold."

"Them!" His voice held contempt. "They're an ignorant, superstitious lot who believe it's bad luck to work on the Tremaine estate. And no amount of money changes how they feel."

"That's a shame. I'll be glad to help your mother until you're able to hire someone. And, if you like, I'll try my hand at finding a maid."

"It's kind of you to offer to help Mother, but she's not one to welcome anybody in her kitchen. I doubt if you'll have any better luck in digging up servants than I've had, but you're welcome to try. Actually, you can do whatever you like about hiring help since you're now the mistress of Lynx House. Or will be after Midsummer Eve."

Concealing the frisson that shivered along her spine, she said, "That's the night of June 23, I believe. I looked it up after your phone call. Is there any significance to the date?"

"Apparently Midsummer Eve meant something to Collis, or he wouldn't have insisted on adding that codicil to his will. He was interested in old pagan celebrations, and I do believe Midsummer Eve is one of them. I take it you plan to remain here until after June 23?"

She nodded, thinking but not saying there was little choice. In order to meet the terms of that codicil, if she wanted to inherit the estate immediately, she must live here until after Midsummer Eve. If she chose not to, Gregory Morel was to administer the estate in trust for her for the next thirty years, and she'd be denied the right to sell for that period of time.

On the other hand, if she remained here through the night of June 23, she could sell at any time after that if she decided to. Though she might have thought the restriction odd, it wouldn't have alarmed her if she hadn't known that eighteen years ago, on the very same day, her mother had fled clandestinely from the estate with her.

If only she knew why!

Gregory smiled. "We're delighted to have you here. It seems strange we've never met before but, of course, the kinship *is* distant."

"Your mother mentioned that my father's first wife was her daughter—your sister. That would make you Collis's uncle and your mother his grandmother. I didn't realize he had any relatives except me."

"After my sister died and your father married your mother, we didn't want to intrude. But I don't for a moment mean to imply that your mother wouldn't have welcomed us."

Kendra hadn't the slightest idea how her mother might have felt about relatives of her father's first wife—she'd never mentioned any.

"I only hope you won't be bored with just the two of us for company," Gregory went on. "The estate is rather isolated, and I fear Tremaine's Wold doesn't offer much, if anything, in the way of entertainment."

"I'm looking forward to walking in the woods."

"One caution about that. During the day, the estate grounds are perfectly safe, but not at night. There are wild animals about—bears and bobcats—and they're night hunters."

"I certainly wasn't planning to roam the grounds at night."

"A wise decision. As for the lake, I'm afraid we'll have to forego swimming in it this summer. Because of a problem with algae, I was forced to have the lake treated with a herbicide, and they recommend we not even wade in the water for at least six months."

She hadn't believed everything Dewolfe Rainwalker had told her about the lake, but now Gregory was warning her away from the lake as well, if for a different reason. Though she had no reason to accuse Gregory of lying, it did make her wonder exactly what the truth might be.

"I'll remember," she said.

"Good. If you've any questions at all about the estate, please ask. As you know, I'm an attorney, but unless it's necessary for me to go to court, I work in my office off the entry—in what used to be the reception room. Don't be afraid of interrupting me—I'm always available to you."

"Thank you." While Gregory's words, attitude and looks were pleasant, something about him made her wary. Or maybe it was the chilly gloom within the house that made her feel so uneasy that she felt she had to get away. "I have some questions, but they can wait," she said. "What I'd like to do right now is take a walk outside."

"By all means, please do. I have a few things to attend to but I'll try to join you later."

Kendra watched him leave before unpacking the clothes that needed to be hung in the closet. Deciding the rest could wait, she slipped on a cotton knit jacket and left the room.

She saw no one when she went downstairs, her gaze lingering on the bizarre carvings of the banisters—reptilian animals with human faces, humans with animal bodies and other unsettling combinations. As a child she remembered being afraid of going up or down the front stairs alone—mostly because Collis told her stories of how the banister animals came alive at night and roamed the halls, searching for prey. No matter how many times she assured herself he was making up his eerie tales, they'd still made her fearful.

Was it because she'd had a mother and he didn't that her half brother had been so cruel to her? Or did he resent his being lame? Kendra sighed. She'd never know; he was dead, this brother she hadn't loved. Though sorry he'd died so young, she couldn't pretend to mourn someone she'd hardly known.

As she let herself out the front door, she heard a blue jay scolding in the pine grove and smiled, recalling her mother telling her as a child how jays were the sentinels of the woods, warning of intruders—anything from an animal to a human.

There'd never been any cats or dogs on the grounds, though. Perhaps her father hadn't liked them. She wished she had memories of him to conjure up and ponder over, but the truth was she couldn't recall him clearly enough to form any kind of a mental picture.

She followed the path into the trees, delighted when a chipmunk skittered across in front of her to disappear behind a fallen log. Breathing in the aromatic scent of the pines, she told herself there was nothing like this in the city, no private wilderness that could be enjoyed in safety. Her spirits rose as the pines closed around her, their needled branches filtering the sunlight so that she felt she'd entered a hushed and shadowed sanctuary.

The trees insulated her, protected her, making her lighthearted despite the gloom. As she relished the sensation of the brown needles slithering under her tennies, she decided she wasn't going to mind remaining here for a month—no, not at all. She might even stay longer, stay on her estate. *Hers*. It was hard to believe she owned all this.

When she reached a clearing beside the lake, Kendra paused and shielded her eyes against the westering sun glinting redly on the water. How inviting the lake looked, despite what she'd been told. Not being a fool, though, she meant to abide by Gregory's warning.

But suddenly the hair rose on the nape of her neck and a chill shot along her spine. This was no nebulous fear to be dismissed as a ghost from the past. As surely as if she'd sensed an assailant stalking her along a dark city street, she felt eyes on her. Someone or something was watching her. Watching and waiting.

Unable to bear the tension, Kendra whirled in time to see a four-legged gray shadow slip between the pine trunks. A dog? She couldn't be sure. As she stared into the gloom under the trees, a man strode toward her.

"If you're thinking of wading in the lake," he said as he approached, "I wouldn't recommend it."

She was surprised and disconcerted—why hadn't Gregory mentioned he was here? As he emerged from the darkness she cried, "Dewolfe Rainwalker! Don't you ever give up?"

He halted abruptly, his dark eyes narrowing. "I'm afraid you've got me confused with someone else," he said. "My name's R. W. Hartzell—they call me Hart."

She gaped in disbelief. Though it was true she'd met Dewolfe only once—a month ago—this man looked exactly like him: bronzed and handsome, with the same thick raven-black hair and eyes so dark they looked black. He wore jeans and a denim shirt just as Dewolfe had and carried himself with the same cool arrogance. One thing was missing—Dewolfe's beaded headband.

And one thing had been added. An excitement bubbled within her at the chance to renew her acquaintance with him. Surprising, since she hadn't been drawn to Dewolfe in any way whatsoever at their first meeting.

"I'm here to apply for the grounds-keeper job I saw advertised in the Albany paper," he said.

"You're not Dewolfe Rainwalker?"

"I told you my name."

She found it hard to believe him. Because she couldn't decide what to do or say next, she snapped, "Is that your gray dog I saw in the pine grove?"

He blinked. "I don't have a dog." No sooner had he spoken than he whirled to face the trees.

Startled, Kendra turned to look, too, and saw Gregory hurrying toward them.

"Is he the one who's doing the hiring?" Hart asked her.

Kendra nodded, her mind in a turmoil. Should she tell Gregory her suspicions about this man? Before she came to a decision, Hart was introducing himself to Gregory and explaining why he'd come.

She noted that Gregory didn't seem happy to see an applicant for the job. Or was it this particular man he mistrusted? As far as she could recall, though Dewolfe had told her he'd spoken to Gregory on the phone and been refused a visit, he'd never mentioned meeting him.

"I don't like strangers wandering around on the grounds," Gregory said to Hart. "He isn't bothering you, is he, Kendra?"

Before she could answer, Hart said, "I'm sorry if I've been a bother. I followed this young woman, thinking she might know who I should talk to."

Gregory frowned. "How did you get through the locked gates?"

Hart eyed him coolly. "I left my truck outside and took a walk around the walls to see what size the grounds were so I'd know what I was letting myself in for. I imagine you know how badly the rocks have crumbled over there." Hart nodded his head toward the west. "I climbed over with no effort at all. If you hire me, I'd make fixing that break in the wall my first priority."

Kendra could see that Gregory, though still displeased, was impressed by Hart. Finally he said, "I'll hire you on a trial basis and decide after two weeks whether to take you on permanently or not."

"Suits me," Hart told him.

Realizing she'd missed her chance to speak, Kendra bit her lip. Had she been right or wrong in remaining silent? What she'd actually done was give Hart the benefit of her doubt. Temporarily. Tomorrow she'd put in a call to the University of Michigan at Ann Arbor and see if Dewolfe Rainwalker actually did teach there, as he'd claimed. She'd describe him and see if her Dewolfe matched theirs. If he did, she'd ask them where he was now and, depending on the answer, go on from there.

"There will be certain prohibitions," Gregory said to Hart, "but I'll tell you about them later. When can you start?"

"Right now," Hart said. "The ad mentioned that an apartment went with the job, so I brought my things along in the truck, just in case."

Gregory nodded, fished in his pocket and handed Hart a set of keys. "The apartment's over the garage. You can open the gates with the apartment remote control to get your truck. I'll meet you at the house."

Hart nodded at him, then at Kendra, and hurried off without a backward look.

"Now if we're lucky enough to hire at least one maid," Gregory said as he and Kendra started toward the house, "we can begin to live halfway decently again. It's impossible to keep up the estate without help."

"I noticed you didn't ask him for references," Kendra said.

Gregory shrugged. "I'll ask when he comes to the house, but the ad's been running for well over a month and he's the first applicant. You know what they say about a bird in the hand...."

Hart climbed into his battered pickup and drove through the open gates, congratulating himself. He'd gotten inside. It'd been a fluke, seeing that ad in the

Albany paper. If he hadn't stopped in that doughnut shop and sat next to the guy reading the classifieds, he wouldn't be here legitimately, which was by far the best way.

But who the hell was Kendra? No one in Tremaine's Wold had mentioned her.

He was pretty sure she didn't live on the estate because he'd watched her arrive and had seen Gregory Morel carry in her bags. Since she'd called him Dewolfe Rainwalker, obviously she knew Wolfe. Where in hell had they met?

Her greeting—*Don't you ever give up?*—could be taken several ways, none of them helpful to him. He had to find out how well she and Wolfe knew each other.

Kendra was damned attractive with that corn-colored hair and those big brown eyes. To say nothing of how well she filled a pair of jeans. He had to admit he was drawn to her—and not only because she was physically appealing. Weird as it seemed to him, as he'd walked from the pines toward her, he would have sworn he'd heard his long-dead grandfather speak to him, saying as he so often had in the past, *"Pay attention, boy!"*

That aside, she was an unexpected complication, and he had enough trouble on his hands without a pretty and desirable woman being dumped into the mess. He didn't dare risk distraction.

He was well aware of the peril he faced. What about Kendra? Did she have any idea how dangerous the Tremaine estate was? Or was she a part of the danger? Until he knew, he couldn't trust her.

CHAPTER TWO

Hart jerked awake from a nightmare where he'd fallen endlessly down, down, down into dark water, into the icy, chilling depths of death itself. Attempting to free himself from the sinister threads of the dream, he took four deep breaths to slow his pounding heart, noting with wry amusement how he automatically used the magic number of his ancestors. Four.

In the predawn grayness he heard a chickadee's five-note call. The birds were up—time he was. Since he was now the Tremaine grounds keeper, he couldn't spend every hour of the day on his own pursuits. In effect, he now had two jobs. Vital as his purpose was, he also had to perform well for his employer or be fired, and he couldn't risk that. He desperately needed to remain inside the estate gates.

No one had ever kept him from finishing what he set out to do; no one ever would. His way wasn't to bull-doze through, seeking to squash all opposition, but to infiltrate, to watch and wait. Not that he was a coward. Like his warrior ancestors, he took the precaution of first discovering, if he could, exactly what he was up against.

He'd tried all his life to follow the true path, but he wasn't certain how much of his grandfather's Mide teachings he still believed. Since he was on enemy ground, though, as a precaution he felt he ought to greet the morning in the way of his people.

He padded down the stairs from the grounds keeper's apartment and slipped into the pines, pausing in a small clearing where he had a view of the lake. A thin mist floated above the silver water, a mist that Hart knew would dissipate with the rising sun.

He cleared the forest debris away until he exposed a small area of bare ground, then built a tiny pyramid of dry twigs with brown pine needles at the base. After placing a few dead branches within reach, he set the needles ablaze. When the twigs caught, he added the larger sticks until he had a fire the right size and quality—small and quick-burning.

Feeling slightly foolish—he hadn't greeted the rising sun in years, he filled his palm with pipe tobacco, tossed a pinch in each of the four directions and scattered the remainder on the fire, then faced the east, waiting. He chanted under his breath, unable to bring himself to intone the ancient words aloud.

Why was he going through the ceremony when he no longer followed Mide ways? What use was it performed by a non-believer? He knew he shouldn't be asking himself questions; ideally he shouldn't be thinking at all during the chant.

Do it right, he told himself, or don't do it at all.

Though he tried not to notice the slight breeze from the north, cool against his face, nor the aroma of the pines mingling with the tobacco scented smoke from the fire, nor the chatter of awakening birds, he'd lost the trick of closing off his senses.

Finally, as the first ray of sunlight broke through the morning mist, he sank cross-legged to the ground beside the fire, facing the lake. He closed his eyes, rolling them upward, recalling an old trick of his grandfather's.

"Turn your eyes inside your head," the old Mide shaman had urged him. "What you see there is more important than anything you'll ever see outside."

He sat in darkness. Time passed. At last a tiny glow began to pulsate in the center of the darkness. Striving to keep his mind blank, Hart shoved away the thought that he probably was seeing a blood vessel on the retina of his eye. The glow faded, returned, grew.

He imagined he heard a familiar voice saying, "Open your eyes."

He obeyed.

He saw the blue flash of a kingfisher flying low over the water of the lake, a dark object in its long, sharp beak. He blinked and the bird was gone, leaving him uncertain whether or not he'd seen a real bird or a vision. Did he still believe in visions? And yet hadn't the bird vanished too quickly to be real?

Dread weighted his heart as beliefs from the past surfaced. Real or vision, the kingfisher was a bad omen, for the bird played a sinister role in Chippewa myth.

Finding his throat dry, Hart swallowed, a thrill of recognition mixed with bitter anguish rippling through him as he realized what his seeing the bird must mean.

He sprang to his feet and took a deep breath, staring out over the lake as the sun rose and telling himself he was an educated adult who'd replaced myths with logic. There was nothing sinister about a bird flying over a lake.

But he failed to banish his gut feeling that, logical or not, what he'd seen had been a vision of death.

* * *

Kendra woke early, listening. Had she been dreaming or had she actually heard a dull clang? The muffled noise had sounded like a huge far-off gong being struck with a padded hammer. Now that she was awake, though, she heard nothing except the chirping of birds outside her window and the weary creaks and groans of the old house.

The sun hadn't risen; it was too early to get up, but she knew she wouldn't sleep again. Sighing, she rose and dressed in a raspberry-pink jogging suit. When she crept quietly downstairs, no one seemed to be about. Reluctant to either disturb Leda's sleep or forage for herself, Kendra unbolted the front door, stepped into a crisp dawn and took a deep breath of the mountain air.

What was that she smelled? Smoke? Looking up, down and around, she noticed a thin wisp of gray rising above the pines. She didn't believe there was any danger— May was not the month to worry about forest fires, especially following on the heels of New York's wettest April in years. Nevertheless, feeling she ought to trace the smoke to its source, she jogged into the pines.

Hurrying through the trees, for a moment she had the odd illusion that a shadowy animal—the dog she'd seen yesterday?—ran with her, just beyond the edge of her vision. But when she looked, there was nothing near her but pine trunks.

Learning to navigate in the city by herself at an early age had given her a fair sense of direction. That, plus the increasingly stronger scent of smoke, made her sure she was homing in on the fire. Yes, there in the clearing up ahead....

Kendra stopped abruptly, staring.

Standing in front of a dwindling fire, Hart or Dewolfe—or whoever he was—stared at the lake, his back to her. She couldn't imagine why he'd built the fire. Obviously there was nothing to worry about, though, since he was there to control it. The fire was almost out, anyway.

She gazed at his broad shoulders and lean hips, admitting to herself that she liked looking at him, though, oddly enough, she hadn't felt that way when she'd met Dewolfe in the museum.

Deciding to retreat silently, Kendra had taken one step backward when he whirled with the same suddenness she'd observed yesterday.

"Good morning, Ms. Tremaine," he said, advancing toward her. "Greeting the dawn?"

"Actually, I saw smoke and came to check on it," she said, gesturing toward the fire.

He stopped several feet away from her. "Sorry to worry you. I won't build any more fires unless I notify someone at the house first."

Her gaze flicked over his tall muscular body, noted the snug fit of his jeans, then switched quickly to his straight black hair and dark, dark eyes. He *had* to be Dewolfe.

"Where's your headband?" she asked impulsively.

His eyebrows rose. "Headband? I don't own a headband."

She frowned. "What happened to that beaded thunderbird headband you had on when we met in the Egyptian room at the Metropolitan."

"Egyptian room? What are you talking about? I didn't meet you at any museum. The first time I ever set eyes on you was yesterday, here in the woods."

"You keep saying that. But I can't believe you're not Dewolfe Rainwalker. The resemblance . . ." She shook her head.

"I am *not* Dewolfe Rainwalker." His voice rang with sincerity. "My name is Hart."

Is it? she wondered. Or are you masquerading for some mysterious purpose of your own? Or maybe not so mysterious. What you—or Dewolfe—wanted in New York was information about the Tremaines. And Lynx Lake.

Which reminded her. "Why did you warn me yesterday not to wade in the lake?"

"Because of its name," he said.

"Do I have to listen to that Algonquin monster nonsense again? Be reasonable—admit you're Dewolfe."

He seemed to freeze into position. Something about the way he stared at her reminded her of a predator about to leap at its prey, and she was tempted to edge away. Instead, she squared her shoulders and stood her ground. She was on her own property and had no intention of being intimidated.

"What Algonquin monster?" he asked, his gaze holding hers.

How dark his eyes were, she thought. Black and hard as obsidian. Revealing nothing. She didn't know what to make of Dewolfe/Hart. Why did he fascinate her? Why was she standing in the woods at this inconceivably early hour of the morning arguing with this man whose identity she wasn't sure of, a man she didn't trust?

"You know perfectly well!" she insisted.

"If you mean Mishibezo, yes. I learned about him from tales I heard as a child on the Chippewa reservation. He's one of my people's mythic monsters. Where did you hear the name?''

She clicked her tongue in exasperation. "From Dewolfe—you."

"Not from me." He turned from her and scattered dirt over the few surviving embers of his fire. When he'd finished, he said, "We seem to be at an impasse. If we're going to go on arguing, I feel the need of a cup of coffee. I switched on the coffeemaker before I left my apartment. If you don't mind sitting at the table of an employee, Ms. Tremaine, there's plenty for both of us."

Though he spoke without inflection, she caught the hidden challenge and fumed. He'd deliberately put her in a position where she couldn't refuse without sounding like a snob.

"If we're going to have coffee together," she said tartly, "you might as well call me Kendra. Be assured that it's my *real* name."

His smile didn't quite reach his eyes. "I'll do that if you'll drop the Dewolfe once and for all and call me by *my* real name—Hart."

Kendra nodded. She'd call him Hart but reserve her judgment as to who he really was.

As they walked through the woods, she caught glimpses of the stone turrets and towers of the house through the pines.

"It looks to me like your ancestors built a fortress rather than a house," he remarked. "How old is it?"

Deciding to behave for the moment as though he really was a stranger named Hart, she said, "I haven't been back here since I was eight years old, so I'm no authority on the Tremaines or Lynx House. As far as I know, Ezekial Tremaine had it built about one hundred and eighty years ago.''

He grinned at her, a teasing light in his dark eyes. ''Then it couldn't have been built for protection against my ancestors. They were long gone from these parts by then. Even my ancestors' enemies, the Iroquois, were pretty well fragmented by that time.''

Surprised and intrigued by his change of mood, she took a moment to reply. ''If not Indians, I don't know who those long-ago Tremaines would need protection against. Maybe Ezekial simply built a replica of a castle in Wales so he'd feel more at home in his new land.''

''And then again, maybe he knew something we don't. Maybe he needed a stone fortress because of Lynx Lake.''

She scowled. ''Are we back to that? Do you actually believe that monsters live in lakes? That's the stuff of myth.''

Hart shrugged. ''In the words of my grandfather, 'One man's myth is another man's truth.' Maybe there actually is a monster in the lake.'' All trace of amusement had vanished from his face. ''Gregory Morel warned me I was not to set foot outside my apartment at night, saying it was dangerous. Why?''

Kendra sighed. ''He mentioned wild animals—bears, bobcats. After all, this *is* a wilderness area.''

Hart stopped and turned to face her. ''I've camped many times in far wilder spots than the Adirondacks without any problems. The chances of meeting a bear or a bobcat face-to-face at night on these estate grounds is close to zero. Wild animals try to stay clear of humans if they possibly can. They rightly consider us more dangerous than we do them. No, I can't buy that reason, Kendra.''

"You're going to ignore Gregory's warning?"

Hart resumed walking. "I'm not a fool. If he claims there's danger prowling the grounds at night, I accept that the man's speaking the truth. It's the bears and bobcats I don't believe."

"You refuse to accept the possibility of bears and bobcats, yet you're willing to put a mythical monster in Lynx Lake. Come on, get real."

He shot her a dark look. "The lake's off-limits according to Mr. Morel. Herbicide, he said. Don't all these warnings and prohibitions strike you as odd?"

She waited until they'd climbed the stairs to his apartment to ask, "Why did you take the grounds keeper's job?"

"Because I needed this job at this particular time." Again, he sounded completely sincere.

His words, though, could be interpreted in more than one way, Kendra told herself. For her own peace of mind she must find out exactly who he was. She'd make that phone call to the University of Michigan as soon as possible. Not from the mansion—she'd rather no one knew what she was up to—but from a pay phone in the village.

He poured two mugs of steaming coffee. Ordinarily she took hers black, but after one sip she asked for milk. "Your coffee's strong enough to walk on," she commented.

"Separates the women from the girls," he said, the teasing glint back in his eyes.

"Meaning, if I were a real woman I'd take it straight and undiluted?" she challenged. "I've got news for you. Real women take it the way *they* prefer."

"Oh?" His look seemed to say, *we'll see about that.*

She quelled her impulse to react. Since she had no intention of becoming emotionally involved with him, whoever he was, it was best not to go any further with this double-edged conversation. In fact, she really shouldn't even be in his apartment. Why *was* she here?

"I have to run," she said, rising. "Thanks for the coffee."

"Next time I'll let you make it," he said. "I'll be interested to see what kind of brew you turn out."

As she hurried down the stairs, Kendra told herself there wouldn't be any next time and that he had a lot of gall to think otherwise.

When she returned to the house, she found Leda in the kitchen, stirring up a batch of oatmeal muffins. "I didn't know what you'd want for breakfast," the old woman said. "From what I read, it seems young women don't eat much at all these days."

"Muffins are great," Kendra said. "But until Gregory's able to hire a maid, I want to help with the cooking. I simply can't let you do all the work."

Leda turned to face her, wooden spoon in hand. She wore a none-too-clean white apron over her high-necked, long-sleeved gray dress, a dress that almost reached her ankles. "It bothers me something awful to have another person around me when I'm working in the kitchen," she announced.

Noting the firm set of her chin, Kendra said, "Then I'll set the table and clean up afterward. I insist."

Leda blinked. "I suppose that might be all right," she admitted after a pause. "These days I do seem to get tired sooner than I used to. It's a nuisance to carry the food in and out of the dining room, but my son doesn't like us eating in the kitchen. I wish we hadn't lost that last woman who worked here. She was a real help with the cleaning and all.''

Actually, Leda looked more than tired—she looked frail and ill—but Kendra didn't comment on this directly, planning to ask Gregory later about his mother's health. And more. Maybe he wouldn't take kindly to her interference, but if neither she nor Gregory could find a maid soon, she meant to argue that she saw nothing wrong with the three of them dining in the kitchen to save time and trouble.

Gregory, it turned out, wouldn't be joining them for breakfast. His custom was to rise late, around ten, unless he had a case in court. After washing the dishes and setting the kitchen straight, Kendra left Leda to tend to her son's late breakfast and drove into Tremaine's Wold.

The village's main street consisted of a combination post office/general store, a small garage with two gas pumps in front, a family-type café and a grocery store. A small Catholic church stood on a rise behind the garage. There was a bar on one of the three side streets and on another was a barbershop. There were no other visible businesses.

Kendra parked next to a motorcycle and climbed the two steps into the general store. A quick glance took in fishing tackle, pots and pans, children's toys, greeting cards, spools of thread, garden and hardware supplies and a pay phone.

Since she didn't like to ask for change without buying something, she wandered through the store, finally settling on a colorful apron for Leda. As she paid for the apron at the counter, she heard raised voices in the rear of the store and turned to look at a young leather-clad couple who were obviously angry with each other.

"Nothing good ever comes from them hoodlums on motorcycles," the graying clerk muttered as she counted out change for Kendra. Intent on the quarreling pair, she didn't really notice Kendra until she handed her the money. Then she blinked, obviously taken aback.

"You're a Tremaine!" she cried.

"Yes, I'm Collis's sister," Kendra said, making an attempt to be friendly. "From New York."

"You're the little girl," the woman said. "The one the old man's second wife took away when she left." She leaned across the counter and lowered her voice. "Better if you stayed away."

Without giving Kendra a chance to respond, she sidled around the counter and started for the couple at the back of the store, calling, "There'll be no fighting or name-calling in this place—you hear?"

Unsure whether the clerk had warned her she wasn't welcome in Tremaine's Wold or was telling her to be careful, Kendra shrugged and walked to the pay phone, which was near the post-office window.

After being shunted from one department to another at the University of Michigan in Ann Arbor, Kendra was finally connected to someone who'd heard of Dewolfe Rainwalker.

"No, Professor Rainwalker is not in residence," a woman's voice told her after Kendra said she was trying to reach him. "I can't tell you where he is, because we don't know."

"The last I saw him was in April, in New York City," Kendra said uncertainly, wondering whether she spoke the truth or not.

"We haven't heard from him since April," the woman said. "And, since he didn't return for a scheduled speech at a department-sponsored dinner the first week in May, we're somewhat concerned. If you should run across him, please ask him to contact the university."

"Yes, I will. One more thing—I do want to be certain we're speaking of the same person. Is Dewolfe Rainwalker a tall, broad-shouldered man with black hair and eyes? A man who sometimes wears an Indian headband?"

"You've described him perfectly."

Kendra thanked her and hung up. As she turned away from the phone, she found herself facing a tall, broad-shouldered man with black hair and eyes, a man who was not wearing a headband.

"You!" she cried. "You eavesdropped on my phone call."

He nodded, thumbs hooked in the pockets of his jeans, apparently at ease as he watched her.

"Then you know they're worried about you in Ann Arbor. They want you to—"

"I'm not Dewolfe," he said, taking her arm and pulling her with him to a more secluded spot in the store. "I'm Hartzell. Wolfe and Hart Rainwalker. We're twins. Identical twins."

Kendra glared at him angrily, uncertain whether to believe his new story or not.

Hart sighed. "You're put out with me and convinced I'm a chronic liar. I can offer some proof other than my driver's license. I've visited Wolfe at the university more than once. Go ahead, call them back. They'll tell you Wolfe does have a twin.''

Kendra took a deep breath and let it out slowly. "Okay, I'll accept the twin story. But why didn't you tell me the truth to begin with?"

"Because the only thing I knew about you was that you were a Tremaine. I don't trust Tremaines. And that's all I'm saying until we can talk privately."

"But where is—"

He help up his hand, stopping her. "I told you—not here. It's too public."

Reluctantly, she realized he was right. In silence, she trailed him out the door. A red-haired woman in her early twenties sat hunched on the lower step of the store, sobbing, her hands over her face. A small backpack lay beside her feet. Recognizing her as the one who'd been fighting with the man inside the store, Kendra glanced around. The motorcycle had vanished and there was no sign of the man.

Letting Hart go on ahead, she paused beside the woman. "My name's Kendra," she said. "Anything I can do to help you?"

The woman peered up at her from reddened eyes. "That son-of-a-bitch Lonnie rode off without me," she complained bitterly. "I don't have any money—what am I going to do?"

Feeling sympathetic, Kendra sat on the step beside her. Tremaine's Wold was not the best place in the world to be stranded. As far as she knew, there was no way out of the village except by private car. Or motorcycle.

"Maybe he'll come back for you," she said consolingly.

"Not him! 'Good riddance to bad rubbish,' he yelled at me." The redhead kicked at her backpack. "So here I am stuck in Hicksville at the end of nowhere, a place where they don't trust outsiders like me. I hate men!"

Kendra's impulse was to help her. But how? She discarded a couple of ideas before it finally dawned on her what she could do. "Would you consider a live-in job as a maid?" she asked.

The woman, wiping her eyes with paper tissues, gaped at Kendra. "You serious? You don't know zip about me."

Kendra shrugged. "You don't know anything about me, either. We're both taking a chance. I'm staying at a place near here, and we desperately need a maid. Would you be interested?"

The woman thrust out her hand. "I'm Patrice Mendell," she said. "Thanks for the offer. I never tried being a maid before but I guess I can learn. Right now I don't seem to have much choice."

"You may not be making the right choice." Hart's voice startled both women. "The estate's isolated, you can't swim in the lake and you take your life in your hands if you leave the house at night."

Patrice sprang to her feet, and Kendra rose, too. "Who're you to be telling me what to do?" Patrice demanded belligerently.

"His name's Hart," Kendra said. "He's the grounds keeper." By now she knew he was no more a real grounds keeper than Patrice was really a maid. His true reason for being at the estate obviously had something to do with his twin. As soon as she got him alone she would make him tell her exactly why he was there. But that was none of Patrice's affair.

Turning her back on Hart, Patrice said, "I'll take the maid job, Kendra. At least till I get some money. I can't promise how long I'll stay on, okay?"

Kendra assured her it was fine, wondering if she hadn't been a bit hasty. The opportunity to help the stranded Patrice and acquire a much-needed maid at the same time had seemed heaven-sent. And Gregory *had* said if she could find anyone she should hire her.

There was the matter of Patrice having no references, but then Gregory hadn't asked Hart for any. What was the harm of giving Patrice a chance? Leda certainly needed help desperately.

"I'm sort of surprised you're willing to take a chance on me," Patrice said, her fingers twisting the intertwined double hearts dangling from a gold chain around her neck.

Before Kendra could reply, Hart said, "*You're* the one who's taking a chance, Patrice. The Tremaines might not be the greatest people in the world to work for."

Patrice shot Hart an appraising look. "You're working for them, aren't you? Anwyay, I don't see where it's any of your business what I do." Turning to Kendra, she added, "Men bring nothing but trouble, but I still keep getting mixed up with them—that's the story of my life." She picked up her backpack. "I'm ready to go anytime you are."

From the cab of his battered pickup, Hart watched Kendra drive away with Patrice. He didn't like the idea of another young woman at the estate one bit. How could he be expected to keep on eye on them both? Kendra might scoff at his mythological monster, but she had more sense—at least, he hoped she did—than to defy Morel's order to stay in at night.

Patrice, though, was another story. She might be streetwise, but her veneer of toughness, plus her current mistrust of men, could make it impossible for him to convince her that she was in danger. No matter how certain he was that terror stalked the Tremaine grounds at night, would she believe him? He doubted she would.

He already knew in his heart that his twin was dead; he was sure he'd felt Wolfe's death at the time it happened. Though there was no way to prove it, since his vision of the kingfisher, he was all but convinced his brother had been killed on the estate grounds. And he believed whoever or whatever had murdered Wolfe was still there. Watching.

Waiting for his next victim.

CHAPTER THREE

Muttering to himself, Hart stopped his pickup at the village garage for gas. Seeing the motorcycle parked outside the general store had upset him, even though he knew it wasn't his brother's. Then, after the bike's owner had roared off in a rage, Kendra had befriended the rejected Patrice by offering her a job at the mansion.

Why wouldn't Kendra listen to him? Why couldn't she understand the danger he was convinced was hidden beneath the innocent-looking waters of Lynx Lake? Didn't she understand she was offering Patrice peril as well as a job?

Furthermore, he was convinced that many of the villagers—maybe all of them—dreaded the Tremaine estate. Some, at least, must have seen his twin. And yet not a one would admit to either. Where strangers were concerned, they were as closemouthed a bunch as his relatives on the reservation.

"Something I can do for you?" a stocky blond teenager asked.

"Yeah, fill 'er up," Hart said. He swung himself from the truck and sauntered over to lean against one of the pumps, determined to keep trying. "I just watched a guy on one of those big bikes go by like a bat out of hell," he said. "You get many up here?"

"Naw," the blond kid said. "Just now 'n' then."

"My twin brother drives one like that. Told me he stopped for gas here last month."

The kid glanced at Hart, taking a good look at him for the first time. He blinked, his gaze sliding quickly away.

Sure he'd seen recognition in the teenager's eyes, Hart spoke before the kid had a chance to deny anything. "Yeah, we *do* look alike, don't we? Only I don't wear a beaded headband."

"Might've seen him." The admission was reluctant.

While not exactly a confirmation Wolfe had been here, it was the most he'd gotten from anyone in Tremaine's Wold so far. Hart didn't dare admit he was searching for his brother, in case word got back to Gregory Morel. He wanted to extract whatever information he could from the kid, but further questions about when Wolfe had been at the garage elicited even vaguer replies. Finally he changed tack.

"I'm the new grounds keeper at the Tremaine place. Whoever was there before me left some things he might want back. Know where he lives now?"

"Uh, not in town."

"Where, then?"

"Back of beyond, you ask me." The kid screwed the cap on tightly, hung the gas hose on the pump and peered at the numbers.

"Lots of beyond in the mountains," Hart persisted. "What direction?"

"Can't say exactly. That'll be—"

"Who *can* say?" He took a step forward and stared into the boy's blue eyes, seeing the pupils dilate in alarm.

"Uh, maybe old Matty down by the creek." He pointed toward a tar-paper shack just past the small bridge coming into town. "I seen 'em talkin' a couple times. Hell, I never even heard the guy's name. That'll be ten-fifty for the gas, mister."

As he drove away, Hart asked himself, not for the first time, where Wolfe's motorcycle might be hidden. He'd searched the estate grounds and outbuildings without success. The boathouse had been locked, but a look through the one high window showed only a small sailboat and an outboard motor inside. Since he doubted that the bike had been dumped in the lake, that left the house itself to check out.

Hart pictured his twin brother as he'd last seen him, three months ago, the two of them cross-country skiing over the snow-covered hills of Michigan's Upper Peninsula. Though Wolfe often went home to the Chippewa reservation on Keweenaw Point, Hart rarely did. He was a biochemist at Stanford, and California was a long way from the Upper Peninsula—or so he told himself.

The truth was that Wolfe was closer to his roots than Hart wanted to be.

On their last skiing trip, Wolfe had been certain he was about to uncover some esoteric mythic nugget linking a Celtic myth with a Chippewa myth. His eyes, so dark a brown they looked black, had flashed with enthusiasm as he'd rambled on.

"There's a persistent rumor about an old Welsh family estate in the Adirondacks where something strange goes on in June—Midsummer Eve, to be exact. No one admits to knowing exactly what happens or where this place may be, but I damn well mean to find out. If there's anything to it, I'll make what I learn the highlight of the book I'm writing on the similarities between Celtic and Native American mythology."

"Publish or perish, hey?" Hart had said.

His brother grinned at him. "You know it, bro."

Wolfe wore a tattered deerskin vest over his ski sweater, and his shoulder-length black hair was held back with what he called his Chippewa talisman, a thunderbird beaded band, one of a kind, made by their Aunt Mary. He had the same eyes, the same hair as Hart's. The same tan skin, prominent nose and six-two height. An identical strong, well-tuned body. The only way most people could tell them apart was when they were stripped to the waist and the wide crescent-shaped scar on Wolfe's chest was visible.

If it hadn't been for Hart's savage leap onto the assailant's back and his twisting grip on the would-be killer's arm, the knife that slashed the scar would have buried itself in Wolfe's heart. The irony was that the man's quarrel was with Hart. He'd mistaken one twin for the other.

Hart had kept the knife, one with a distinctive deerhorn handle. Yes, he had the knife, but where was his brother? Where was Wolfe?

The last letter—a note, really—from him was postmarked Tremaine's Wold. "Looks like that weird rumor about the Tremaines may have some basis," Wolfe had written, cautious with his words as usual. "My next report's going to lift your hair, bro."

There'd been no next letter. Four days later Hart had roused from sleep abruptly, convinced his twin was in terrible danger. He'd flown east from California as quickly as he could, targeting Tremaine's Wold as his destination because of Wolfe's letter.

So here he was, following his brother's trail, even though he no longer thought Wolfe was alive—this morning's vision of the kingfisher confirming what he already believed. The twinship link between them was broken; it had vanished before Hart boarded the eastbound jet, leaving him more alone than he'd ever been in his life.

He might be too late to save Wolfe, but it was never too late to exact vengeance.

Kendra reluctantly postponed her confrontation with Hart in order to introduce Patrice to Gregory.

"You challenged me to find household help, and I did," Kendra told him. "It's a relief to me, because I was worried about your mother. She doesn't look well and she shouldn't be working so hard."

Gregory asked very few questions of Patrice, no more than he'd asked of Hart, almost as though he didn't care what kind of people worked at the estate.

"You understand it's not safe to walk around the grounds at night," he warned Patrice, going on to explain about the herbicide in the lake.

"Whatever you say," Patrice agreed.

When they left Gregory's office, Leda was hovering in the entry, obviously curious about Patrice.

"I don't like outsiders in my kitchen," she muttered after the introduction.

"Patrice won't bother you while you're cooking," Kendra said firmly, "but she'll help with the serving and do the cleanup so you won't have that to worry about."

"I'm not the world's greatest cook," Patrice put in. "I sure won't interfere, Mrs. Morel."

Leda eyed her, noting, Kendra was sure, Patrice's tight black leather pants and jacket. If she had any doubts, she didn't voice them, saying only, "There's no use to try to keep the whole house spick-and-span—it's too big. Just clean the rooms we use."

"Which ones are they?" Patrice asked.

Leda told her, adding, "You won't have cause to go into the vaults. We don't store food or anything else you'll need down there."

Patrice raised her eyebrows. "The vaults? Sounds like some kind of dungeon."

"That's what we call the basement," Kendra said quickly. "If you're through, Leda, I'll show Patrice through the downstairs, then take her up to her room. Which one would you suggest?"

Leda pondered for a moment or two. "I don't see any point in putting her up on the third floor alone in the old servants' quarters when it would be easier all the way round to use one of the guest rooms on the second floor. The blue room in your wing, Kendra, is in good condition—we had it done over for Collis's wife."

Kendra was taken aback. "His wife? I didn't know my brother had ever married."

Leda shook her head sadly. "Lydia didn't last long, poor thing. Died one year to the day after the wedding—two Junes ago, it was."

On the night of June 23? Kendra almost asked, but she bit the question back.

"What happened to her?" Patrice asked.

Leda shot her a quelling, mind-your-own-business look and answered with dismissing finality, "She was killed in an accident."

As Collis had been. But now, with Patrice standing by, was not the time to probe for details. "Tell me which room is the blue one," she said to Leda.

"Two doors down from yours, on the opposite side of the hall. Patrice will have to make up her own bed."

During their rapid tour of the kitchen area, Patrice noticed something Kendra had not. "You sure must keep a lot of food around," she said. "Besides this freezer in the pantry, there's that great big one in the storeroom. And a refrigerator."

Since she knew nothing whatsoever about the housekeeping arrangements, Kendra could only shrug and move on to the dining room. Patrice, awed by the mansion, kept chattering away.

As they climbed the stairs, she said. "Jeez, it's like living in a castle. All those towers. Servants' quarters. Vaults." She slanted a sideways look. "You sure there aren't any dungeons?"

"Not to my knowledge." Which, Kendra had to admit, was imperfect. Still, though she'd never been in the basement, the idea of a dungeon down there was pretty farfetched.

"Well, I'm glad I don't have to clean the whole damn place—I'd never get finished." Patrice stared down at the entry chandelier. "You know, staying here for a while might be kind of fun, even if I do have to work my butt off. I mean, it's isolated and all, but it's different. And that guy—Hart?—he's a real hunk."

Kendra was surprised to find herself less than amused. "I thought you were off men."

"Sort of, but it won't last. It never does." Patrice fingered the hearts on her gold chain. "Like—I don't do drugs, but I'm seriously addicted to men."

Kendra couldn't help but wonder if Patrice would appeal to Hart. There was no denying the redhead was, in macho lingo, stacked. But what difference did it make if he was attracted to Patrice? She had no claim on Hart. There was certainly nothing between them. Nothing at all. If anything, he annoyed her.

"I guess no one cares if I work in jeans and a T-shirt?" Patrice asked. "That's all I have in my backpack."

Since she was taller and slimmer, Kendra feared nothing she owned would fit short, buxom Patrice, but she decided to take a look at her clothes and see. The pack was small; Patrice must be carrying next to nothing.

"Jeans are okay with me. If you need toothpaste and such, let me know." Kendra opened the door to the blue room. As she stood aside to let Patrice enter, she glanced around the room, concluding she wouldn't care to sleep here.

The many shades of blue blended well, creating a harmonious whole, but it gave Kendra the uncomfortable sensation of being underwater.

Apparently Patrice had no such qualms. "I love it!" she exclaimed. "Everything matches. It's like being in some fancy hotel." She flung open a closet door and gasped. "My God, it's stuffed with clothes! Must be from that woman who died." She lifted a blue dress from the rod and held it in front of her. "Not a bad fit. Would anyone care if I borrowed a few of these?"

"I shouldn't think so, but I'll ask Leda." Though she tried not to be repelled by Patrice's avid appropriation of a dead woman's clothes, Kendra couldn't watch as Patrice pulled one garment after another from the closet. "I'll leave you to get settled, then," she said, wondering if she'd been too hasty in bringing Patrice here to work. Maybe it would have been better to have offered to drive her to a town farther down the mountain and given her bus fare to get home.

"Yeah, okay." Intent on the clothes, Patrice spoke absently. Her "Oh, and thanks for everything" didn't reach Kendra until she was halfway down the hall.

She was almost at the head of the stairs when someone knocked on the front door. The heavy sound of the cast-iron merman hitting against the striker plate reverberated through the entry. Having a feeling that Gregory wouldn't answer the summons, Kendra hurried down the stairs, hoping to spare Leda a trip from the kitchen.

She was too late. Leda reached the door first and opened it. Kendra was just in time to catch her when the old woman staggered backward, half falling.

"Is she sick?" Hart asked as he stepped through the open door and tried to help Kendra hold up Leda.

"Get him away from me," the old woman quavered. "Don't let him touch me."

Hart retreated. Pushing away from Kendra, Leda supported herself by leaning against the door. She stared long and hard at Hart.

"Who is he?" she asked Kendra, her words barely audible.

"I'm the new grounds keeper," Hart said before Kendra could answer. "My name's Hart. I'm sorry if I startled you, ma'am."

"I thought you were—" Leda paused. "Never mind. The new grounds keeper, you say?"

Hart nodded. "Hired yesterday by Mr. Morel. I came to see him about where to order supplies, but maybe I should have knocked at the back door instead."

"It doesn't matter." Leda was rapidly recovering her composure. "I'll tell Gregory you're here." She waved away Kendra's offered support. "Don't fuss over me. I'm quite all right."

She watched Leda disappear inside Gregory's office, wondering what had brought on the old woman's attack. Did she have some underlying illness or did her sudden near-collapse have something to do with the sight of Hart?

Kendra turned to him. "You still owe me that explanation you avoided in the store."

"I'm leaving in a few minutes to buy supplies to repair the wall," Hart told her. "Meet me at four in the woods where I built the fire this morning."

She hadn't gotten around to asking him why he'd risen at dawn and built that fire. One more question for him to answer later today.

"I'll be there," she said.

Hart was leaning against a pine trunk, watching the lake, when she arrived at four. She felt an annoying leap of her pulse when she first caught sight of him, and she shook her head. This was not a man to get involved with.

He nodded, acknowledging her presence, but kept his intent gaze on the lake. She turned to look, seeing nothing but the ripple of blue water in the light breeze. Branches on the lake's little island, stimulated by the same breeze, were the only things moving.

"Am I missing something?" she asked.

"No," he told her. "All we can see is the surface of the water. What lies beneath is hidden. Keep in mind when you listen to me that the mythic lake I speak of would look equally innocent on the surface."

"Mythic lake? I came to hear why you've been lying to me, not to listen to more stories about lake monsters and such."

His gaze fastened on her, his eyes so dark that she could almost believe they were fathomless and if she fell into them she'd be lost.

"In your opinion," he said, "you and I inhabit the same world, a world accessible to the five senses. You're wrong. Reality in your world is what is seen, heard, touched, tasted and smelled. I was raised to accept that the intangible is also part of the world. Some of my people still believe this, some don't. My grandfather did. He showed my brother and me ways to cope with the intangibles. Myths are a part of his teachings, so I begin with a myth that is also a truth." He gestured. "Sit down beside me and listen."

Bemused by his words, she obeyed. Though she knew she was being fanciful, it seemed to her that the shadows between the trees crept closer to them. Or was there but one gray shadow? Kendra glanced quickly around. They were alone.

"In the days my grandfather told of," Hart said, "the animals could speak. Manabozho is the Chippewa trickster-hero, human in a sense, but actually a demigod who can change his shape when necessary. The manitous are spirits." Sitting cross-legged beside her, his gaze once more fixed on the lake, he began the tale, his voice low, almost sing-song.

"Wolf came to live with his brother Manabozho. Because he killed meat only for Manabozho and refused them any, the other animals grew jealous and asked evil manitous to kill Wolf. They agreed. And so it was that White Deer treacherously led Wolf to a lake covered with snow that hid a hole in the ice. Wolf fell through the ice into the depths below and was captured, killed and eaten by Mishibezo, the evil water monster.

"Manabozho searched for his brother, found the tracks and the hole in the ice and realized what had happened. He called on Thunderbird to send summer, and in four days the ice melted.

"Kingfisher, sitting on a nearby cliff, noticed meat scraps floating in the water, dived for them and ate what he found. Seeing him fly past with meat in his beak, Manabozho recognized what Kingfisher carried as part of Wolf. He asked Kingfisher what he knew about the meat and Kingfisher said he'd seen Mishibezo's cave deep under the water where the monster laired with what remained of Wolf.

"Manabozho was grateful enough to give Kingfisher a necklace of shells—which is why the bird has a white band around his neck yet today—but he was also angry because Kingfisher had been eating parts of Wolf, and so he grabbed for him, meaning to twist his neck but only getting hold of a tuft of feathers that he pulled upright—the crest Kingfisher still wears.

"Waiting for Mishibezo to come up from the water to sun himself, Manabozho turned himself into a stump. Evil manitous suspected what the stump really was, forcing Manabozho to battle them. He wounded them, and they fled to the underwater cave to warn Mishibezo. Disguising himself as Medicine-Toad-Lady, Manabozho followed, singing how he could cure the injured manitous, tricking them into letting him inside the cave.

"He fought Mishibezo and the evil manitous, killing the manitous and recovering all that was left of Wolf—his pelt—from the monster's lair. Mishibezo escaped and flooded the world to punish Mana-bozho." Hart paused and spread his hands. "But that's another story."

Kendra, mesmerized by Hart's recounting of the myth, blinked, coming out of the spell he'd cast. Taking a deep breath, she let it out slowly as his grisly tale circled in her mind. The similarities—the brothers, the monster in the lake—were obvious.

"You think your brother is dead, don't you?" she asked at last.

"I know he is. And I know where he died." Hart nodded toward the lake.

Kendra shook her head, denying what he'd said. "You can't be sure Dewolfe is dead."

"We're twins. I *know*. I came here because this was where I last heard from him. This morning Kingfisher confirmed what I already knew and showed me where Wolfe had died by flying over the lake."

Watching grief twist his face, she understood that Hart truly believed his brother was dead. According to the woman at the University of Michigan, Dewolfe's whereabouts *were* unknown. There was no doubt he was missing.

"But even if your brother is dead," she said, "you've no proof he died here. A bird flying over the lake is not exactly concrete evidence."

He ignored her words. "I know he was trying to interview the Tremaine family for his book or at least those Tremaines who lived in this Adirondack mansion. I wasn't aware until I met you that he'd also contacted another Tremaine—you—in New York City."

Sifting brown pine needles through her fingers as she talked, Kendra told Hart about her meeting with Dewolfe. "I really didn't tell him much of anything," she finished. "How could I when I know so little about my father and his family?"

"What reason did your mother give for slipping away from here with you in the middle of the night?"

Kendra concealed a shiver, recalling terrifying fragments of that night. Or was she remembering shards of the nightmares that had plagued her afterward? She'd never been sure.

"I was just eight years old," she said slowly, "so my memory of our flight is vague. All my mother told me was that I'd be safer in the city. She died less than a year later, and my mother's sister raised me. When I questioned Aunt Meg, she always said that my mother refused to talk to her about why she left her husband and the mansion so abruptly. Before she died, Meg told me she'd promised my mother to do her best to keep me from ever coming back here."

"You should have listened."

Kendra frowned. "How could I? When my half brother died a month ago, he left the estate to me."

Hart raised his eyebrows. "Surely you don't plan to make your home here."

Kendra glanced around her. She loved the woods and the mountain air, but something about the estate made her uneasy. She wouldn't want to live here permanently. "No, I intend to return to the city before September. I'm a school counselor in Queens."

"You could have stayed in the city and still inherited the estate. Even negotiated a sale of the property from there, if you wished."

"I couldn't. Collis's will had a codicil. Unless I remain here until after Midsummer Night—the twenty-fourth of June, or actually the eve of the twenty-third—Cousin Gregory is authorized to hold the estate in trust for me for thirty years, during which time I'd be unable to sell it."

Hart leaned forward. "I take it Gregory Morel was your brother's lawyer, as well as a cousin?"

"His lawyer, yes, but the relationship is more complicated. As well as being a distant cousin through our father's side, Gregory was also Collis's uncle on his mother's side."

"Do you have any idea why your brother added that codicil?"

"No. Except—" She hesitated. "I don't know that there's any connection but my mother fled from here with me on Midsummer Eve." The coincidence had bothered her before, but she'd tried to dismiss it. Now she wondered if it really was a coincidence. Was there some hidden reason her brother had chosen that date?

"I don't like it," Hart muttered, rising and pulling her to her feet. His hands came to rest on her shoulders as he looked at her. "I don't want anything to happen to you," he said urgently, a light she hadn't seen before glowing in his dark eyes.

Breathless, her heart beating rapidly, Kendra tried to lighten the moment by saying, "I thought you didn't trust any Tremaine."

He half smiled. "Let's hope my one exception isn't a fatal mistake." Slowly, almost reluctantly, he lowered his head until their lips met.

Hart hadn't intended to kiss her. Once he realized he couldn't stop himself, he meant to make the kiss brief and casual, a seal of friendship. He failed. Once he tasted her, he wanted more. Needed more.

Kendra leaned into Hart's kiss, responding without thinking to the warm and ardent message of his lips, aware she'd been waiting for this to happen from the moment he'd come out of the trees and walked toward her the day before. Though she'd believed he was Dewolfe then, she knew she hadn't felt the same attraction to his brother at their one meeting.

Yet at the same time, she realized she mustn't allow herself to be overcome by chemistry. Even if she suspected there was more than that between her and Hart. There were too many undercurrents, things she didn't understand. Regretfully, she pulled away, only to be disappointed when he let her go without protest.

"I ought to get back to mending the wall," he said after a moment.

"And I have things to do." But she didn't turn to go, and neither did he.

"I think Mrs. Morel saw Wolfe," he said abruptly. "And I believe she knows he's dead. That's why my appearance startled her so much."

Much as Kendra wanted to deny his words, she couldn't help but recall thinking that Leda looked like she'd seen a ghost. "I don't know," she said cautiously, "but I'm going to try to find out."

"Don't be too curious."

She raised her eyebrows. "Don't you want to discover the truth?"

"Yes, and I will. But I don't want you hurt. You live in a Bluebeard's castle—if you open the wrong door, you may walk into a trap. Asking questions about Dewolfe could be dangerous."

"Leda dangerous?" She shot him an incredulous look.

"Who knows? How many deaths have there been here during the eighteen years she and her son Gregory have lived here?"

"Three. My father, my half brother's wife and Collis. I was told my father had a fatal heart attack."

"Your brother and his wife, too?"

"They died in separate accidents."

"On the road? Or on the estate?"

Kendra blinked. "I assumed they were auto accidents, but I didn't ask."

"You left out Wolfe's death," he said. "I doubt that was an accident."

She stared from him to the gray shadow slipping between the trees behind him. "There it is!" she cried, pointing. "That gray dog I saw yesterday. A stray must have gotten onto the grounds."

Hart whirled, scanning the woods. "I don't see anything."

"He's gone now. I swear he can vanish like smoke in the wind."

Hart turned to face her, but his gaze rested beyond her and, she sensed, beyond the estate itself. "Like smoke," he echoed.

She nodded but she didn't believe he noticed.

"Wolfe's thunderbird talisman failed him in the end." Hart spoke so softly she strained to hear him.

"The beaded headband he wore?"

Hart nodded, not looking at her, wrapped in his own thoughts. "Patrice didn't strike me as one to obey rules," he said finally. "Try to make her understand these grounds really aren't safe at night, that they're damned dangerous."

Why was he suddenly worried about Patrice? "Gregory warned her already," she said tersely. "I'll remind her."

"Wolfe mentioned Midsummer Eve to me last February. Now your brother's will binds you here until after that date. Why? Look back, Kendra. Ask your-self what happens here on Midsummer's Night. Try to get in touch with the child you once were and see what that child remembers about the eight years she lived here."

She shook her head, ashamed to admit her fear of remembering. "Nothing comes to me but odds and ends about Collis teasing me. He was seven years older than I and must have considered me a nuisance. I used to feel sorry for him because he limped."

"It puzzles me that your father never came after you and your mother. Since she went to her sister, it would have been easy to trace the two of you. And then your mother died and still your father made no effort to re-claim you."

Kendra had often wondered why he hadn't. "Nei-ther my mother nor my aunt ever communicated with him," she said. "He didn't call or write. Or send money. I decided while I was still a child that he must have been glad to see us go. Nothing has changed my mind."

"You thought he was glad to be rid of you? Or glad that you were out of danger?"

"The first." Despite all the years that had passed, a a tinge of bitterness mixed with sadness crept into her voice. "You're right, if my father had wanted me, he could easily have found me."

He touched her cheek lightly and briefly with the tips of his fingers. "Consider the second option, Kendra. He might have wanted to keep you safe."

Not giving her a chance to answer, he turned and strode away. She watched him until the trees hid him, then she turned and looked at Lynx Lake. Taking a deep breath, she began to walk toward the water, now bloodred from the lowering sun.

Hart's mention of the June date troubled her more than she'd admitted to him, making her uneasy and apprehensive. All this emphasis on the same eve couldn't be the coincidence she'd hoped it was.

Still, it's merely a date, she told herself. Just as the lake ahead of me is merely a lake. There are no mythical monsters lurking in caverns beneath its waters. Dewolfe may be dead, but I can't believe he was lured into the lake to be killed and devoured by something evil.

Evil and good are opposites, and both are abstract notions, she reasoned. Depending on the customs of the land and the people of that land, the words differ in usage and meaning. But pure evil doesn't exist. Monsters don't exist. Anywhere. Not here in the United States and not in the Wales of my ancestors, either.

As she reached the shoreline, she heard the distant clang of metal on stone—Hart working on repairs to the wall—and realized how alone she was.

And perfectly safe, she assured herself, gazing at the small island—a wooded islet, really—in the center of the lake. She caught her breath at the sight of a bird perched on the top branch of one of the trees, silhouetted darkly against the sky. Almost before she had time to wonder if it was a kingfisher, with a raven's mournful croak the bird spread black wings and launched itself into the air.

Of course the bird wasn't a kingfisher. No matter what Hart believed, whatever happened to Dewolfe couldn't be a reenactment of a Chippewa myth. But she wasn't cheered, recalling Poe's raven, a symbol of death. *"Once upon a midnight dreary..."* The poet's words echoed somberly in her mind.

Kendra shuddered and dug her fingernails into her palms as a long-buried memory flashed unexpectedly before her....

Midnight. The big clock in the hall striking twelve times, striking terror farther into her heart with each deep note and she, a child of seven, huddled in her bed, waiting, fearing what even now flopped hideously from one step to the next, climbing up, up, up from the vaults, making its way to the stairs leading to the floor where her bedroom was.

It knew where she was, knew she waited helpless and alone, and it was coming for her. There was no escape....

Something splashed in the water in front of her, the sound bringing her back to the here and now. To the lake. Kendra gasped, staring at the crimson water, seeing ripples spreading. Stifling a scream, she whirled and fled toward the house.

CHAPTER FOUR

By morning Kendra had convinced herself she'd panicked over a few ripples in the lake. As she dressed, she asked what she'd actually run from. A fish rising to snap at an insect? A frog jumping into the water? A turtle diving after surfacing? She blamed Hart for hypnotizing her with his mythic Chippewa tales, but she was also at fault for taking his words too much to heart.

Despite what he'd said about intangibles, she was far better off continuing to trust in her own five senses to test the world's reality rather than allowing herself to be spooked by her imagination.

But she couldn't deny he was right about one thing—Leda must have seen Dewolfe at some time. Nothing else would account for her extreme reaction when she opened the door to Hart yesterday. Apparently Gregory had never seen Dewolfe, though. Kendra had witnessed his first meeting with Hart, and Gregory hadn't exhibited the slightest sign of recognition.

Since she'd never seen Leda so much as venture out of the house, much less leave the estate, the fact she'd recognized Dewolfe suggested he'd been not only on the grounds but in or near the house.

In New York, Dewolfe had said that Collis's lawyer wouldn't let him through the gates. Which probably meant Gregory had spoken to him on the phone but hadn't met him face-to-face. Yet Dewolfe *had* gotten through the gates. Or had he? He might have entered the grounds by climbing over the crumbling section of the wall, the break that Hart was currently repairing.

Kendra had planned to discuss the matter with Leda before breakfast but was frustrated by Patrice's presence in the kitchen. Later, as Kendra was finishing breakfast alone in the dining room, Gregory joined her, much to her surprise.

"You must have a case in court this morning," she said after greeting him.

He frowned briefly, then smiled. "I see my mother has laid bare all my secrets. No, no court case. While it's true I do sleep late some mornings, this isn't one of them." He lifted a cut-glass bell from the walnut server and rang it.

The tinkle had scarcely died away before Patrice appeared in the archway of the hall leading to the kitchen. Under her white apron she wore a blue dress that Kendra recognized from the dead woman's closet.

"Patrice, isn't it?" Gregory asked. At her nod, he told her what he wanted for breakfast, and she returned to the kitchen. "Rather attractive young woman, isn't she?" he said to Kendra. "I suppose that means she won't be with us long. It seems I barely grow accustomed to a maid before she leaves."

"I don't know how long she'll stay, but you really need several maids and a cook for this big place, Gregory. That is, if the estate can afford to hire more help. Your mother shouldn't have to work."

He sighed. "I know and you know she shouldn't, but Mother refuses to listen to anyone, myself included. She's done the cooking here ever since we came, and she's reluctant to give up *her* kitchen. There's no need to pinch pennies—it's simply difficult to find anyone who wants to work in this isolated spot, as I believe I've mentioned.''

"I'm sure you're right. But I can't help worrying about your mother's health.''

"As I do. Unfortunately, she's as single-minded about what she wants to do as any Morel, and my family has long had a corner on stubbornness. Morels never give up. My mother is equally tenacious. I hate to think what that makes me.'' His smile gave him a momentarily boyish look.

He poured coffee into a delicate bone china cup and took a sip before announcing, "I've cleared my calendar—today is yours.''

"Mine?''

"If you wish we can tour the house and the grounds while we discuss the problems concerning the estate. Or we can talk in my office, if you prefer.''

As she wondered what the problems might be, Kendra realized Gregory was offering her the perfect opportunity to ask him questions about other matters. "I'd like to walk around the grounds while we talk,'' she said.

The day was cool and overcast, with a hint of dampness in the brisk breeze. Kendra, hands thrust into her jacket pockets as they strolled along a piney path, breathed deeply. "Everything in the mountains smells so fresh and clean,'' she said.

"I'm glad you're enjoying your stay here.'' Gregory snapped off a twig and began removing its needles one by one. "I assume you plan to sell the estate once you've met the requirement for immediate inheritance—that is to say, on June 24.''

Kendra bit her lip. For many years this had been his home, his and Leda's. In effect, if she sold she'd be turning them out. "It's impossible for me to live here," she said.

"I understand."

"And keeping a mansion as a summer vacation home is clearly impractical. The upkeep alone..." Her words trailed off.

"I assumed from the start you'd sell, and so I've gone ahead with my own plans." She thought she heard a faint echo of amusement in Gregory's voice and wondered why.

"I've purchased a home near Albany," he continued, "but Mother and I will be happy to stay on here and look after things until it's sold."

"How kind of you! I'd hate to think what might happen if the house were left empty. Especially since the people in Tremaine's Wold seem to dislike the place so much. Why, do you think?"

Gregory shrugged. "I believe there've been bad feelings between the villagers and the Tremaines for generations. Who knows what starts such senseless feuds."

The sound of a mallet striking stone somewhere off to the left distracted Kendra. No doubt Hart was mending the wall. Gregory seemed to have the same thought.

"I'll be glad when the wall's intact once more," he said. "Last month Mother complained of being bothered by a trespasser, the first we've had in years. They're always strangers—the locals have more sense."

Kendra glanced at him, striving to keep her voice calm. "Did you see the trespasser?"

"No, I wasn't at home when the man appeared. Our former grounds keeper was still here at the time and apparently he took care of the problem for Mother."

Deciding it was safe to push a little, she asked, "What did the trespasser want?"

"The usual, I assume—food, a place to sleep. Or else he was one of that strange breed who believe their curiosity deserves satisfying no matter whose privacy is invaded."

Kendra said as casually as she could, "You make me wonder if he might have been the man who sought me out in the city last month because he was curious about the Tremaine family. He claimed to be an anthropologist."

"What did you tell him?"

"I know so little about my own family, there was nothing to tell."

"I would have supposed your mother must have mentioned a few things."

"She refused to talk about the Tremaines or the estate to either me or my aunt. And my father—" Kendra sighed. "He didn't care about me."

Gregory rested his arm comfortingly across her shoulders. "I think he did care. He often spoke of you, always with fondness and regret."

Kendra didn't know whether to believe him or not. "Then why didn't he ever contact me?"

"My dear, he didn't tell anyone why." His voice was soothing, gentle. "Perhaps he believed you'd been turned against him. It certainly wasn't because he feared you'd ask for money. Not after he tried in vain to convince your aunt to accept financial help to raise you."

Kendra was dumbfounded. "Aunt Meg never told me!" she cried. "I wish I'd known. I didn't even hear my father was dead until weeks after his funeral."

"Now you've come home at last," Gregory said.

Made uneasy by the note of triumph she fancied thrummed in his words, she bent to pick a blue jay's feather from among the brown needles, thus escaping his arm. Why should he be happy to have her here? she wondered as she ran the feather through her fingers.

"You don't happen to recall this anthropologist's name, do you?" he asked.

"It's slipped my mind," she said, unwilling to reveal all she knew since she wasn't entirely certain she could trust Gregory. Or anyone else.

Uncomfortable with lying, Kendra switched the subject. "You've never told me exactly how and where my half brother died."

His glance assessed her. "I didn't want to risk distressing you. Collis's accident was here on the grounds. I won't go into details except to say we were forced to specify a closed coffin."

Kendra winced, closing her eyes briefly. What little she knew of Collis was a child's memory of being cruelly teased, but he *had* been her brother, and Gregory's words disturbed and pained her.

He drew her to him, his arms enclosing her loosely, and murmured, "I'm sorry if I've hurt you."

Kendra looked into his silver-gray eyes, surprising a fleeting glimpse of desire. Until this moment Gregory had given no clue to his feelings about her. Startled, she stepped back, and he released her immediately.

"You're far more attractive than I expected," he said huskily.

Deciding the best approach was to ignore his comment, she resumed walking toward the silvery water of the lake gleaming through the trees. That water no longer seemed peaceful to her. "Collis wasn't drowned, was he?" she asked abruptly.

Gregory shook his head.

"Was he near the lake?" she persisted. "On the island, perhaps?"

"Collis tended to avoid the lake after Lydia—his wife—had her fatal boating accident there. He was not near the water nor was he on the island. Why do you ask?"

She could hardly recite Hart's Chippewa myth, but nothing else came to her except something Dewolfe had told her. "The villagers are frightened of the lake," she said lamely.

Gregory raised his eyebrows. "A few of them might be superstitious enough to believe in haunted lakes, but surely you're not so credulous."

Was she? She thought not. And yet . . . "My brother's wife died in a boating accident?" she asked, echoing his words. "How did it happen?"

They came out of the trees, and Gregory stopped, staring at the lake as he spoke. "Lydia loved to sail, but she scorned lifejackets. She took the boat out alone one summer evening with a thunderstorm brewing. If any of us had known what she was up to we would have prevented such folly. The storm struck. Lydia was a good swimmer, but the wind kicked up giant waves and she never reached shore." Sadness shadowed his face. "She was a lovely woman. Collis was never the same afterward—he seemed to court death."

"Court death how?"

"Neither my mother nor I were with him when he was killed, but it was clear to me his accident was caused by his reckless disregard for his own safety." He swung about, turning his back to the lake. "Enough morbidity. Come, we'll inspect the repairs to the wall."

Kendra, aware there was one more possible death she hadn't mentioned to him, gave a last look at the placid, serene surface of the lake before following Gregory. A shudder rippled through her. If Dewolfe Rainwalker had died on the grounds, as Hart believed, did those innocent-seeming waters conceal his body?

Hart, working steadily since sunrise, had easily demolished the sagging, broken wall only to discover that fitting the stones back together was not as simple as he'd expected. Thought had to be given as to how each stone would fit with its neighbors before it could be mortared into place. A science or an art? He wasn't sure. Perhaps, like medicine, something of each.

When he was younger and had imagined science would provide the answer to all his questions, he'd chosen biochemistry as his field. Wolfe had gone another way, choosing to believe the answers were to be discovered in the cultures and mythologies of the past.

Hart sighed and leaned against the nearly rebuilt wall for a momentary rest, the stones cool against his bare back. They'd been wrong. Not completely wrong, for both his way and Wolfe's provided clues. But he'd come to realize that no man ever had all his questions answered while he lived.

While working, he'd sensed his brother's presence so clearly, it seemed that if he looked up, Wolfe would be there, grinning at him. Remembering Kendra's description of the gray shadow she'd mistaken for a dog,

Hart swept his gaze through the woods around him, hoping for a glimpse of whatever it was she'd seen, but he searched in vain.

"I'm here, bro," he said softly, "even though I've come too late."

The sudden squawk of a jay, the woods' sentinel, warned him someone was coming. He pushed away from the wall, alert and watchful, relaxing when he heard voices he recognized—Gregory Morel, coming to check out the expertise of his new grounds keeper, with Kendra accompanying him. Moments later he glimpsed them through the trees.

Kendra wore a red jacket, a bright contrast to her unusual buttercup-yellow hair. He liked her looks and the way she walked, light on her feet, as though springing upward with each step. He smiled wryly, aware that wasn't all he liked about her. In fact, *like* was far too weak a word for what he felt. Remembering her response to his kiss the day before, he decided the attraction wasn't one-sided. Still, he couldn't forget she was a Tremaine.

Morel was an unknown as yet. Though Hart distrusted him, he hadn't uncovered enough evidence to either condemn or absolve the lawyer.

Morel nodded to him and immediately inspected the wall. Kendra paused beside him, saying, "I should think you'd be freezing with no shirt on."

He grinned at her. "Thanks for worrying about me, but I'm fine."

"You're coming along, Hart," Gregory Morel said. "What you've done looks good and solid. The sooner the wall's completely intact again, the better."

"I understand." Hart spoke the truth. He knew as well as Morel did that the estate grounds had something to hide. Something fearful and deadly.

He watched Morel lay a proprietary hand on Kendra's arm. "Come along, my dear. We mustn't keep our workman from his labor."

Hart bristled. Not so much at the words as at the way Morel was touching her and she was letting him. When they walked away, he shook his head, annoyed by his reaction. He had no claim on Kendra. Even if he did, there'd been no real reason to get upset. Yet he was.

Cool it, he warned himself. You can't wall off a woman like you can estate grounds, and you know it. You've never wanted to before—what's with you all of a sudden, Rainwalker? Protect her from danger, if necessary, yes, but keep focused on why you're here. You can't afford to get distracted.

He turned and lifted one of the stones, fitting it carefully into place. If he worked straight through, he'd be finished with all but the replacement of the cement top before dark. There'd be time to drive to Matty's shack by the bridge leading into town. With luck he'd find the old man home and learn the name and present whereabouts of the previous grounds keeper. He needed information and he needed it fast.

For the remainder of the week, Gregory kept Kendra busy going over estate account books and then sorting through old papers of her father's, discarding what had no bearing on the family or the estate. She found nothing at all pertaining to her mother or to her. On Saturday, Leda, at her son's request, brought Kendra to the room that had been her father's.

"Everything's just as it was when he died," Leda confided. "Collis couldn't bear to touch any of his father's belongings. Just as I hung on to Lydia's far too long because I was fond of her. But the keeping of a loved one's belongings won't bring back the dead. It's past time to go through and get rid of useless things."

The task was less painful than Kendra had supposed, far less heartbreaking than sorting through her aunt's belongings after she died. No doubt because she'd loved her aunt, while her father was no more than a vague memory. She set aside very little—a gold pocket watch with a glowing amber cairngorm on the fob, a snapshot of a tall, blond man, her father, standing next to a brown-haired young woman Kendra recognized as her mother, and a beautifully crafted statuette of a merman.

Later she asked Leda if she knew where the little statue came from.

"My daughter Beth gave that to Randall when they married," Leda said.

Randall Tremaine. Her father. Kendra wondered if he'd loved Beth Morel, his first wife, more than he had her own mother. She'd long suspected Collis, Beth's son, had been his favorite child, while she, the daughter of his second wife, was a mere afterthought. It also occurred to her that no one had ever mentioned what had caused Beth's death.

"The statue is a Morel family heirloom," Leda went on. "Did you know I'm also a Morel by blood? Yes, Gregory's father and I were distant cousins."

Kendra immediately stopped running her fingers over the iridescent scales covering the merman's tail and offered the statue to Leda. "I wouldn't feel right keeping this," she insisted. "If it's been in your family for generations, the statue belongs to the Morels, not to the Tremaines.''

"You're sure?'' Leda eyed the merman longingly but made no move to take him.

"Definitely.'' She closed Leda's fingers around the man-fish. "Do you know what the statue's made of? I couldn't tell.''

Leda fondled the merman lovingly. "I was told the upper part is bone and the lower a substance so rare there's no name for it.'' She sighed, her face bleak. "Our legacy,'' she whispered.

Kendra didn't have the slightest idea what she meant, but the look of despair in Leda's eyes kept her from asking.

On Sunday morning, Patrice announced to Kendra and Leda that she was riding with Hart to the nearest town down the mountain, about forty miles away.

"I need some underwear and stuff,'' she said. Looking at Leda, she added, "I really appreciate you letting me have the pick of those clothes left in the closet, but somehow I just can't wear another woman's panties—you know what I mean?''

Leda nodded. "You've worked hard—you deserve a day off.''

"Yeah, hard is right. It's kind of different. I never did this kind of thing before.''

Kendra couldn't deny that Patrice deserved time away from the house, but she wondered where and when she'd made these plans with Hart. He hadn't come to the house, so that meant Patrice had met him somewhere on the grounds. Unless she'd gone to his apartment. But, of course, he wouldn't be there during the day. Only at night.

Kendra eyed Patrice speculatively, recalling her self-proclaimed "addiction to men." Patrice had been warned it was dangerous to leave the house after dark, but would that stop her? Kendra doubted it.

Patrice smiled at her slyly, almost as though she read her thoughts. "Maybe you'd like to come with us," she said, toying with the double hearts on the golden chain.

"Thanks, but I'm too busy." Which was true enough. She still had odds and ends of Collis's to sort through.

She immediately marched upstairs, entered Collis's room and determinedly opened his closet. But her heart wasn't in the task. She found herself listening for the telltale clang of the gates that would mean that Hart's pickup, with Patrice as passenger, had driven through and was gone. Once she heard the clang, she paused with the box she'd taken off the closet shelf still in her hands.

Hart hadn't asked *her* to go. He obviously preferred Patrice's company to hers. Not that it mattered. What he did and with whom was no concern of hers.

She'd thought, though, that she and Hart were partners joined together in trying to discover the truth about his brother's disappearance. But she hadn't tried to talk to him in private for the last four days, and he hadn't made the slightest effort to get in touch with her.

Once she'd become convinced he was not Dewolfe but his twin brother, she'd believed all that Hart had told her. Maybe not the myths exactly, but everything else. Had she been too hasty? Actually, she was guilty of a being partner in a conspiracy—Hart was working here under a false name. She knew it but hadn't told Gregory. What if Hart had kept hidden from her the real reason for his presence here? What if he was using her in the same way he was using Gregory?

Disturbed, she sat on Collis's bed, the wooden box on her lap. Her mind on Hart, she lifted the lid of the box, hardly aware of what she was doing. Inside was a slim leather-bound book which she removed. Absently opening it, expecting nothing, to her surprise she saw familiar handwriting. Her mother's!

"Merry Christmas to Collis," her mother had written, adding her signature underneath.

Below that, someone—Collis, no doubt—had scrawled, "She wants me to write in this. I wasn't going to at first because I hate her. I changed my mind. Not about hating her but about writing—this'll be my hate book."

Taken aback, Kendra turned the page and read on.

If it wouldn't make my father feel bad I'd tell Tola to kill my stepmother. And he'd do it, too. Tola almost always does what I tell him.

I was going to write Kendra's name in this hate book, but I guess I don't really hate her on account of she's part Tremaine. But it's fun to scare her. She believes all the weird stuff I make up to tell her. She'd probably wet her pants if I ever really did call Tola.

Only I can't, because I promised my father I wouldn't. Tola's our secret, his and mine. I think Tola likes me better than he does my dad. Maybe it's because I'm part Morel and dad isn't. I think Tola *knows* about me.

Kendra flipped through the rest of the pages, but Collis hadn't written any more. Upset and confused by what she'd read—who was Tola?—she rose from the bed still holding the diary, forgetting the wooden box on her lap. As it thunked onto the floor, the bottom seemed to jar loose.

After she knelt to pick up the box, she saw she'd been mistaken—the box was still intact. Apparently there'd been a false bottom. And under that false bottom—

Kendra gasped, rejecting what she saw. Impossible! She'd told herself she believed Hart, but until this moment she hadn't really come to terms with the truth. Now she had no choice.

Reaching down with reluctant fingers, she lifted the beaded headband and ran it through her fingers, staring in horror at the blue thunderbird design on a field of red and white. She'd last seen this one-of-a-kind band holding back Dewolfe's dark hair. Later, Hart had told her his brother was never without it.

Here was Dewolfe's headband, but where was *he?*

CHAPTER FIVE

After lunch, Kendra retreated to her room. She wound the music box and, as it played, she stood by the window, turning the beaded headband over and over in her fingers. There was no doubt in her mind it was Dewolfe's, and she longed to see it safely in Hart's hands.

He and Patrice had been gone for over four hours— were they never coming back? The notes of *Swan Lake* tinkled ever more slowly and, though the music box was behind her, Kendra knew the little ballerina was twirling round and round on the top of the box, forever following the same predestined path.

Going in circles, like I am, Kendra told herself.

Since she'd found the band hidden in a box in Collis's closet, it must mean that her brother had put it there. Therefore, Collis must have been involved with Dewolfe either before or after he died. Or both. Was he the only person who knew exactly what had happened to Dewolfe? Unfortunately, Collis was no longer around to answer questions.

Kendra, eager to share her discovery with Hart, fumed at his continuing absence. Why had he chosen today to drive down the mountain? And what was taking him so long? Forty miles, even on the narrow, twisty road shouldn't take more than an hour each way.

At last she gave up her vigil by the window and went downstairs to see if Leda needed help in preparing the evening meal. She found her sitting at the kitchen table sipping a cup of herb tea.

"We're having cold sliced ham," Leda said, "with a bean salad, brown bread and what's left of last night's cake. I don't cook fancy meals on Sunday. If Patrice isn't back by the time everything's ready, you might carry the platters into the dining room for me."

"She and Hart seem to be taking their time to return," Kendra said.

Leda shot her a shrewd glance. "Does it matter?"

"Why, no. Not at all." Kendra turned away from the old woman's too-knowing gaze and pretended interest in an old and ornate iron trivet hanging on the wall near the stove. "What an odd design," she said, unable to decide whether the figure was man or fish. "I've never seen another like it."

"That trivet came from Wales, so your father said. He told me it represented an ancient sea god called Lyr. It's my fancy that the merman statue you returned to me is also Lyr."

A Celtic god? Kendra wondered. She noticed that next to the trivet hung a large brass key. "What door does this key open?" she asked.

"The door to the vaults. We keep it locked. You won't be needing the key since there's nothing to see down there."

"I quite agree," Kendra said fervently. To her relief, Gregory hadn't suggested they tour the vaults. She had no desire to explore whatever lay beneath the house. In fact, it gave her a chill even to think about it.

"When I was small," she told Leda, "my brother used to frighten me by saying something horrible lived in the vaults and was going to gobble me up some night. He scared me so much I still shudder at the idea of going down there.'' She thought of mentioning the name Tola to Leda but changed her mind, instead asking, ''Did Collis ever talk about me to you?''

Leda shook her head. ''Never mentioned your name, not to me.''

In his will, Collis had left her, the sister he couldn't quite hate, the estate. Of course, she *was* the last of the Tremaines—that might have been the reason. She'd ask Gregory. Since Gregory was her brother's lawyer, Collis must have discussed his will with him.

As if summoned by her thinking of him, Gregory walked into the kitchen. ''Shall we attempt the attics this afternoon?'' he asked Kendra. ''I believe you've seen the rest of the house.''

Except for the vaults, she thought, and she wasn't about to mention them. ''What's in the attics?'' she asked.

''Discards from every generation of Tremaines who've lived in the house. Some things they squirreled away may be valuable, but I fear junk far outweighs possible treasures. Actually, the attics should have been cleared long ago. I hope while you're here that you'll be able to finish going through what's stored up there.''

''I'll be glad to help,'' she told him.

The attics, on the fourth floor, were separated into two large rooms reached by two separate doors. Though the first two stories of the house featured gleaming hardwood paneling and flooring, pine floors and painted walls had been considered sufficient for the servants' quarters and attics.

On the third floor, they walked along a narrow corridor past the bleak emptiness of servants' rooms to the door to the north attic. Gregory, carrying a battery-operated lantern, opened the door, and Kendra looked up a curving staircase that was thick with dust. As they climbed, she noted there was no railing. Dim light filtered through small windows, giving poor illumination. There was no electricity.

Kendra paused at the top of the stairs, glancing around the shadowed room cluttered with trunks, wooden boxes and old furniture. "It would take months to sort through all this," she said in dismay. "Is the south attic the same?"

"I'm afraid so," he said.

"Isn't it a fire hazard?"

He shrugged. "Perhaps. But the destruction of Lynx House won't come about by fire."

"Because the house is built of stone?"

"Not exactly. Shall we begin?"

Seeing Gregory didn't intend to say any more about the possible destruction of the house, Kendra returned her attention to the jumble before her. Sorting through it would offer her the chance to learn more about her family, but she balked at facing the cleanup job alone.

"We can make a start today," she said, "but I assume you'll be too busy to help me during the week." After he nodded, she added, "Then I'll need Patrice and maybe Hart to carry the discards down all those stairs."

"Certainly." Gregory gazed at the littered floor. "Where do you suggest we begin?"

After a moment's thought, Kendra made her decision. "With the trunks. Once we clean one out, we can use that trunk as storage for whatever we decide to keep."

Gregory cleared a space in front of the nearest trunk, an unwieldy black affair, wooden with brass fittings, then removed a dust cover from an old rosewood chair with no seat. He spread the sheet on the floor for them to kneel on, pried open the trunk's latch and opened the lid, setting the lantern on a cloth-covered table nearby. The trunk was packed to the brim and the strong scent of mothballs plus the dust in the air made Kendra sneeze.

Kneeling side by side, they began removing the contents, mostly woolen baby clothes and blankets, moth-eaten despite the supposedly preventative naphtha. Examining the tiny garments, she saw they were beyond salvaging and stacked them all into a "don't save" pile. Eventually she put aside a china-headed doll and a set of McGuffy's readers, creating a "save" pile. Then she lifted a small wooden ship with *Tola* lettered on its hull.

She drew in her breath, startled not only by the name, but by the ship itself. It resembled a Viking longboat, but without the traditional dragon's head at the prow. Kendra stared at the monstrous head that made up the prow—neither man nor beast, but somewhere in between.

She glanced at Gregory who was examining a collapsible brass telescope. "What *is* this?" she demanded, holding up the boat.

He stared at the boat for a moment, then his silvery gaze shifted to her. "Probably a child's toy, but beautifully made." He took the ship from her and laid it on the save pile.

"Does the name on it mean anything?" she persisted.

He shrugged.

"I've heard the name Tola before," she said, determined not to let the matter drop.

Again his strange silvery eyes rested on her face. "Where?"

"I'm not clear as to when I first heard it," she temporized.

"Other than this boat, do you connect the name with Lynx House?"

"I'm not sure." Which was certainly true—she wasn't sure of anything.

Gregory was giving nothing away. If he knew who Tola was, he obviously didn't intend to tell her. Though the attic was overly warm, Kendra felt a chill. How far could she trust Gregory?

"Sorry, I can't help you," he told her, leaning into the trunk again.

She watched him take out the last item, a small velvet-covered box. When he opened it, she craned her neck to see what was inside.

"It's a miniature painting," he said, removing an oval frame that held a young girl's portrait. "I think she looks very much like you. Note the topaz lavaliere she's wearing. I do believe that exact piece of jewelry was among my sister Beth's things when mother and I packed them away after she died. Obviously the jewel came from the Tremaines, from your father. Perhaps as a wedding gift when he married Beth. I'll make certain to return the topaz to you."

"Please, no. That's not necessary. A gift is a gift."

"I insist." He smiled. "The topaz will be my gift to you."

Before she could find a tactful way to tell him she didn't want any gifts from him, he put one hand at the nape of her neck, bent his head and kissed her. His lips were warm and gentle and she didn't find the kiss unpleasant. But she felt nothing—no thrill, no urge to respond. After a moment she pulled away and rose.

He got to his feet. "Now you'll think I had ulterior motives in luring you to the attic—and maybe I did. You must know I'm attracted to you."

What was she supposed to say when the truth was she wasn't in the least attracted to him? "I consider you a friend and advisor" was all she could come up with.

He raised rueful eyebrows. "In other words, thanks, but no thanks."

There was no possible reply to that. "I think we should call it a day," she said. Nodding at the miniature he still held, she asked, "That ought to go on the save pile."

"I'd like to keep it, if you don't mind."

Though made uncomfortable by the probability he wanted the miniature because he fancied that the girl in the portrait resembled her, Kendra merely said, "Whatever you wish."

Supper was an informal meal, buffet-style, enabling Leda to eat with the two of them. "That girl's not back yet," she remarked as she sat down at the table with her plate. "Nor the young man."

Gregory shrugged. "There's plenty of time for them to return before dark. I don't know about Patrice, but I think Hart has enough smarts to pay attention to warnings. He's done a good job on that wall repair, by the way, Mother. I don't think we'll have any more trespassers."

Leda's gaze darted from him to Kendra and back. "Don't forget we're into June," she muttered.

June. Was she referring to Midsummer Eve? But what did that have to do with the wall having been repaired? Gregory nodded, apparently comprehending what his mother meant.

After a short silence, Kendra said, "I was asking your mother if Collis ever talked about me."

Gregory glanced at her. "Not often. Except when we drew up the will. He knew your father wanted the estate to remain in Tremaine hands. Actually, there was an agreement when your father left the estate to Collis that, if Collis should die without issue, the estate would go to you. It was only fair, since when your father died you were left nothing."

"I didn't expect anything."

"Perhaps not, but attorneys view with caution wills giving no inheritance to a legitimate heir. Of such wills are lawsuits made."

"I would never have done that." Indignation laced her words.

"In any case, the estate is now yours. Or will be in another—" he glanced at the calendar on his watch "—ten days. I believe there'll be a full moon on Midsummer Eve."

As Kendra wondered what a full moon had to do with her inheritance, she heard Leda make an indeterminate sound—of pain?—and turned to look at her. Though she made no move to eat, the old woman's gaze remained on her plate.

"Are you all right?" Kendra asked.

"As right as can be expected," Leda snapped. "Don't fuss over me."

"All right. But I intend to wash the supper dishes and clean the kitchen."

Leda didn't argue.

After Kendra finished her tasks, she went out through the back door. The sun was down; it was clearly evening, though still light. Neither the sweet scent of the roses from the nearby garden nor the sleepy chirps of roosting birds soothed her restlessness. It was almost dusk. Where was Hart?

She paced tensely under the rose arbor where thorny branches intertwined above and around her, and she noted after a time that the light had faded enough to make it difficult to determine the exact colors of the blossoms. Surely Hart had more sense than to delay his return until after dark. Or was he planning to stay away all night and come back in the morning? Stay with Patrice.

She whirled abruptly, intending to march into the house, and then held, listening, hearing what she'd been waiting for—the creak of the gates opening. Both relieved and provoked—unless he came to the house before going to his apartment, he'd returned too late for her to show him the headband before morning—she hurried inside and was sitting at the kitchen table leafing through a magazine when Patrice came in the back door.

Setting her packages on the counter, she grinned at Kendra. "Waiting up?" she asked.

"I was afraid you wouldn't make it before dark."

Patrice rolled her eyes. "Just exactly what's going to get me out there at night—the big bad wolf?"

"Gregory says there *are* wild animals roaming the grounds."

"Yeah, I know what he says. That doesn't mean I got to believe him."

"Why else would he warn you stay in at night?"

Patrice's smile was sly. "To keep the help from frat-ernizing after hours, what else?"

Kendra stared at her. "Don't forget he warned *me,* as well."

"So? Maybe he doesn't want you out there hunk-hunting, either."

Kendra ignored the remark. "You don't really mean to go out after dark, do you?" she asked.

"That'd be telling." Patrice picked her packages from the counter and crossed to the back stairs. "Don't worry, I can take care of myself." At the stairs, she paused and turned to face Kendra. "Why so con-cerned about what I do at night? You got the hots for Hart yourself?"

Doing her best to ignore her flare of anger, Kendra said, "Please take Gregory's warning to heart. I *know* it's not safe outside at night, even though I'm not sure why."

Giving her one last disbelieving look, Patrice flounced up the stairs.

Angry and troubled, Kendra wished she *wasn't* so convinced it would be dangerous to leave the house at night. She hated to wait until morning to show Hart the headband. Why didn't Gregory have a communica-tion link between the house and the grounds keeper's apartment? He'd said the estate didn't have to pinch pennies. But there was none. If she wanted Hart to know about the headband, she'd have to go to his apartment in person. Safe or not, she was tempted.

Tola. The word echoed in her mind as the grotesque head on the toy boat flashed before her eyes. She hugged herself, suddenly chilled to the bone.

After reading those pages in Collis's diary, she was sure Tola existed. Not only that, but she had a nag-

ging feeling that she'd actually heard the name somewhere before reading it in Collis's diary, even if she
couldn't recall where or when.

Giving up all notion of leaving the house, she decided to look in the library for old books pertaining to
the house or her family. After a search turned up
nothing useful, she pulled out a lavishly illustrated
volume of Irish and Welsh tales. If she couldn't find
anything about the Tremaines, at least she could read
up on Celtic mythology.

When she got to her room with the book, she flicked
on the light and noticed with disturbed surprise a
brown velvet jewel box on her bed. Immediately sus-
pecting what was inside, she lifted the box, opened it
and drew in her breath. The miniature had been too
small to show the golden glow of the multifaceted
topaz set into the lavaliere. She'd never before seen
such a dazzling gem. Though tempted to take the lavaliere from the box and hold it to her throat, she shook
her head.

Tremaine heirloom or not, the topaz had to go back
to Gregory; she'd return it in the morning. She closed
the lid and set the box on the dresser, at the same time
noticing a paper half-hidden under the dresser scarf.
Frowning, she eased the paper free and unfolded it,
reading the printed words with increasing shock.

*"Death waits for you here. Leave while there's still
time."*

There was no signature.

Kendra stared numbly at the words of warning.
Who'd written the note? Who'd crept surreptitiously
into her room to place it on her dresser? Obviously
Gregory had been here—the jewel box was proof
enough—but did he also leave the note? She shook her

head. Not Gregory. He'd realize she'd know he'd been in her room. Who, then?

Leda? She had the opportunity, but why would she write these frightening words?

Patrice? She'd have had time to write the note and put it here, but why would she insist there was danger ahead for Kendra? Unless Patrice wanted to get rid of her by scaring her away. But for what reason?

Hart? It wasn't impossible for him to have left the note, especially if he'd used Patrice as his messenger, but Kendra thought it was unlikely. He'd already openly urged her to leave the estate—why write an anonymous note?

Yet one of those four was guilty. Did they truly believe what they'd written, or was the warning a ruse to frighten her into leaving? Why?

If she left before June 24 she'd forfeit control of the estate for thirty years, and mother and son would be assured of staying on. Leda and Gregory definitely had a motive.

Unnerved, Kendra walked to the window and stared into the gathering darkness, still clutching the note in her hand. *Death waits for you here.* Chilling words. How could she ignore them? Suddenly realizing how vulnerable she was standing in front of the window with the light on, she hurried to flick off the switch, then returned to gaze into the night. The crescent moon hadn't yet risen, and the stars cast little light. A pale glimmer showed through the trees from Hart's apartment over the garage.

If she had the courage to brave the darkness, she wouldn't need to wait for morning—she could bring the headband to him now and ease her fears by sharing them with Hart. But the note had made her even more apprehensive about venturing into the night.

A dark memory struggled to the surface, a long-buried memory from her childhood, from the eight years she'd spent in this house before her mother spirited her away.

It was night and she was a little girl, standing by this same window and seeing the flicker of flames in the distance. By the lake? She hadn't been sure. Then, as now, the window had been open at the top and little Kendra could hear faint voices chanting, repeating a word over and over. *Tola,* she thought they said. *Tola, Tola.*

The word meant nothing to her and yet she was terrified. Sensing a formless terror in the night, she'd scurried back to bed and pulled the covers over her head, waiting in panic to be plucked from her cocoon by the unknown horror that she had been sure searched only for her.

She was no longer a child, but she still feared the night. Not so much in the city, dangerous as it could be at times, because there were lights in the city, and there were people. Bad things could happen there—muggings, rapes—but frightful though they were, they were known perils and she could try her best to avoid them.

Here on the Tremaine estate, she didn't know what lurked in the dark and she wasn't about to step outside at night. For how could anyone take preventative measures against the unknown? Even if she named the unknown, called it Tola, she was no farther ahead. She was still not safe.

She was about to turn away from the window when she caught a glimpse of something white moving below, heading away from the house. For a moment she froze, holding her breath. Then it occurred to her that what she saw could well be Patrice, heedless of any danger, sneaking off to Hart's apartment as she'd more or less boasted she meant to do.

Had he invited Patrice? Kendra shook her head. If Hart was sincere in his insistence that something dangerous roamed the grounds at night, it wasn't likely he'd urge Patrice to visit him at night, even if he was interested in her. This rendezvous could well be entirely Patrice's idea.

Kendra couldn't decide whether she was more frightened for Patrice's safety than she was angry at her. Angry at Hart, too, for that matter. If Patrice did reach his apartment, what would he do? But she knew. He'd never allow her to venture back into the dark, so he'd keep her there until dawn.

She jerked the curtains closed, whirled away from the window and turned on the light. Determined not to dwell on what might happen between the two of them, she sat on the bed, propped herself up on pillows and opened the book she'd brought from downstairs, leafing through it listlessly. As she focused briefly on an illustration of four children changing into swans, the name Lir, a powerful ancient king, sprang out at her. Had he been a sea god, too, like the creature on the old trivet?

The tale began long, long ago, before the time of mortal heroes, when the *Tuatha De Danann,* those of magic, ruled Ireland. Before long, Kendra was caught up in the tragic tale of a jealous stepmother who set a spell on Lir's children by his first wife, turning them into swans. Though the wicked stepmother was transformed into a raven as punishment, her spell could not be broken, and the children remained swans, regaining human form only when they died.

The story troubled Kendra, as did other illustrations in the book, mostly of creatures not quite human but not quite animal, either, like the selkies. These were neither seals nor men, but resembled one or the other as they wished. Selkies mated with mortal women, producing children who could change at will into seal pups and swim away with their selkie fathers, leaving the deserted wives and mothers behind to die of grief.

Tales, all of them—myths, not true stories—and yet, reminded of the monstrous head on the boat in the attic, Kendra was haunted by a feeling she'd stumbled upon a secret, a mystery she ought to be able to unravel. . . .

She was jerked from her reverie by the faint sound of voices coming, she thought, through her partly open window. Springing to her feet, she clicked off the light and hurried to the window, arriving in time to catch a glimpse of white again, this time very close to the back of the house. Patrice?

Without pausing to think, Kendra threw open her door and raced down the back stairs. When she reached the kitchen, the back door was already open. Patrice stood just inside, facing Hart who was framed in the opening.

"This is really dumb," Patrice snapped. "Nothing, but absolutely nothing happened to me on my way over to your place. Why did you insist on dragging me right back here? I mean, I could've stayed there till morning if you were so scared of boogeymen wandering around at night."

"Don't try it again." Hart spoke harshly. "I've got enough to worry about without you slinking around in the dark." His gaze shifted, and he saw Kendra.

"You'd better come inside," she said to him. "If the night's not safe for Patrice, then you're in danger, too."

Patrice whirled around to face her. "What're you doing, spying on me?"

"Damn it, you've caused enough trouble for one night," Hart told Patrice as he eased inside the kitchen. "Shut up and go to bed or you'll have the Morels on your neck."

Patrice glared at him, opened her mouth to reply, changed her mind and marched across the kitchen. She stomped up the stairs without looking back.

Hart smiled wryly. "I'd apologize if I had anything to apologize for."

Kendra had made up her mind to ignore the entire episode and be very calm, very cool and very collected. Instead, to her distress, she heard herself say tartly, "Something must have given her the idea you'd have the welcome mat out."

He shrugged, not answering.

Her annoyance with him increasing, she said crossly, "And it certainly took you long enough to drive down the mountain and back."

"It was my day off." His voice was even, matter-of-fact.

Kendra pressed her lips together to prevent herself from going on in this vein. Why, she sounded positively jealous! And she wasn't, not at all.

Taking a deep breath, she let the air out slowly. "I don't mean to suggest you've done anything wrong," she said carefully. "I guess I'm upset because of what happened while you were gone." She glanced around and lowered her voice. "I meant to wait until morning to talk to you but, since you're here—" She paused, wondering if the kitchen was the best place for a confidential conversation. Besides, she needed to give him the headband. "You'd better come up to my bedroom," she said.

He smiled slightly. "Anytime."

She ignored his comment, turning away. He followed her up the back stairs, along the hall and into her bedroom, closing the door behind him. She opened the closet, reached into the pocket of her robe and removed the headband.

While she was doing this, Hart had evidently seen the note she'd discarded on the dresser, because when she turned around he was reading the paper.

"Who in hell sent you this?" he demanded.

"Never mind about the note for the moment— look!" She held out the headband on the palms of her hands.

Hart drew in his breath as he took the headband from her, staring down at it for long moments. When he glanced up again, anger glinted in the depths of his eyes. "Where?" he asked.

She told him about the box she'd found.

Hart listened, his expression growing more and more perplexed. "But why would your brother hide this?" he asked when she finished. "Wolfe's body is missing. His motorcycle is missing. If your brother had destroyed the headband, there'd be nothing except the letter Wolfe wrote me, plus my intuition, to tie his disappearance to the Tremaine estate."

He raised the band and slipped it onto his head.

Kendra shivered, feeling as though, by donning the headband, he'd somehow evoked his brother's presence here in her bedroom. "No," she protested. "Don't. It makes me—"

A loud clanging, similar to the one she'd thought she'd heard in a dream, interrupted her. The sound rose from the bowels of the house, an alarming and insistent demand.

"What the hell is that?" Hart demanded.

"Tola." Her whisper was involuntary.

"Who's Tola?" Hart asked.

Kendra shook her head. "I don't know why I said that. I don't even know who Tola is. But I think I do know where the noise is coming from." Her voice quavered. "I'm afraid it's coming from down in the vaults."

CHAPTER SIX

"What vaults?" Hart asked, listening for a renewal of the clanging. The noise was not repeated.

"That's what we call the cellar," she told him.

"Below ground, you mean?"

After she nodded, he said, "I'm going down and take a look."

"No! No, you can't do that." She looked so frightened he yearned to comfort her.

But he feared if he put his arms around her there'd soon be more than comfort on his mind, and neither of them could afford to be distracted right now.

"Why can't I go into the cellar?" he demanded.

"The door's locked, and anyway I don't know what's down there. It might be dangerous."

He closed the door and faced her. "Do you mean something dangerous is locked in the cellar? Tola?"

"No. I mean, I don't know." Kendra bit her lip. "When I was little my brother used to tease me by saying something was going to come after me out of the vaults, and I guess I never really got over being afraid of what's down there. Leda says nothing is except the furnace, that they don't use the cellar for storage."

"I wonder why it's locked, then. Do you know where the key's kept?"

"On a hook in the kitchen." Her voice was unhappy. "But I don't really think you ought to investigate. I mean, Tola does exist, even if I don't know who he is. Collis wrote about him in a diary he started when he was young. The diary was in the box with the headband. He wrote about calling Tola to come and kill my mother. He makes Tola sound dangerous.''

"Tola is a person, then?''

She stared at him. "What else could he be?''

Hart reached up to touch Wolfe's headband, running his fingers across the beaded thunderbird. "It might be Tola is the Tremaines' name for Mishibezo. I have to find out, starting with your vaults.''

Kendra hugged herself. "I'll go with you.''

"No need.''

"I insist. I'm frightened, but some of my fear comes from my childhood, a time when I was too young to understand what I was afraid of. I need to confront that childhood fear and conquer it.''

Since he could hardly keep her from entering a part of her own house, he didn't protest.

Hart half expected to encounter one of the Morels as they made their way to the kitchen, but neither mother nor son appeared. In the kitchen, Kendra pointed to the brass key. He retrieved it and fit the key into the old-fashioned lock of the cellar door. It turned smoothly, indicating the door was locked and unlocked with some regularity. Was that why neither Gregory nor Mrs. Morel had responded to the fearful clanging? Because they knew what caused it?

Hart opened the door, hearing Kendra, behind him, draw in her breath as they gazed down into darkness. He smelled the dankness of mold and another scent he couldn't identify, an alien scent that made his hackles rise. What in hell was down there?

He glanced at Kendra, saying, "Why don't you wait in the kitchen?"

She shook her head.

Stubborn. At the same time, Hart admired her courage in attempting to face her fear. He flicked the switch at the top of the stairs and a light went on somewhere below, providing dim illumination, probably from a bare bulb on a cord dangling from the ceiling. From where he stood, he could see nothing alarming, so he started cautiously down the steps.

The house could stand a few modern improvements, he thought—for starters, rewiring, floodlights outside and an intercom system that included the apartment over the garage. As they descended the stone stairs, an ancient dinosaur of a furnace came into view, and he added a new heating system to his list.

Hart paused at the foot of the stairs and looked around warily. A single overhead bulb of meager wattage left the corners of the vast room in shadow, but, except for the furnace, its oil tank and boiler and a rack of tools apparently left over from when the furnace used coal, the cellar appeared empty. Morel's mother hadn't lied when she said nothing was stored here.

To make certain he didn't miss anything, Hart paced around the room with Kendra close beside him. Except for spiderwebs, the corners of the cellar were as bare as the rest of the room and there were no doors in the stone walls.

"Did you expect to find your brother down here?" she asked.

"Not really. Though I'm glad I had the chance to be sure." He lifted his head to sniff the air but found no trace now of the unidentifiable odor.

He'd left until last an examination of the metal insert on the cellar floor near the furnace. To his surprise he found a reinforced steel trapdoor bolted shut. Even in the dim light, it was obvious the door was new, as was the steel frame it fitted into. He crouched to study the two massive bolts that closed it fast.

Kendra, crouching beside him, said, "I don't think I've ever seen such huge bolts. And I'm no expert on vaults—I mean cellars—but why would anyone put a trapdoor in a cellar floor?"

He shook his head, mystified, and reached for one of the bolts. "We'll find out."

"No!" She grabbed his hand. "Don't open that." Her eyes were dark with fear and her voice trembled. "Collis used to threaten that he'd let him out."

"Let who out?"

"Tola. Please don't, Hart."

"The trapdoor's new," he said patiently, hoping to calm her. "Put in no more than a few months ago."

"But this steel door could have replaced an older one." She tightened her grip on his hand. "Let it be."

Much as he wanted to see what lay underneath the trapdoor, he knew she very likely was right about it being a replacement. Remembering the loud clanging that had brought them down here to begin with, he decided she might well be right about the danger, too.

The furnace went on, throbbing throatily as it heated the boiler water. There was some gurgling from the water as it traveled up the pipes to the radiators, but no sound remotely resembling the clang they'd heard.

He doubted someone had been down here beating the metal sides of the furnace or the steel of the trapdoor with one of the old coal or clinker shovels—what would be the point?

It also seemed unlikely, though not impossible, the clanging could have been from something hitting against that steel door from the other side. If so, it wasn't his brother. He'd sense Wolfe's presence if his brother lived. What might be hidden behind that door?

Tola, she kept saying. What *was* Tola? His skin crawled with unease as he stared at the dull gleam of the steel.

"That's why they keep the door to the vaults locked," Kendra whispered. "So no one can come down here and let it out."

"Let what out?"

"I don't know. Oh, Hart, I'm so scared."

Seeing shudders course through her, Hart rose, pulled her up and held her close. "You're safe," he murmured, hoping he was right. "Safe with me."

Sooner or later he'd have to make certain his brother's body wasn't entombed beneath that door, but tonight wasn't the time, not while he was unarmed. And certainly not with Kendra, already frightened, beside him.

Keeping an arm around her, he helped her up the stairs. As they neared the top, the door swung open and he reflexively thrust Kendra behind him, leaving both hands free.

Leda, wearing a dressing robe over her nightgown, peered down at him. Her gaze traveled over him, fixing on the headband he wore. Her mouth opened to scream but only a thin thread of a cry emerged.

"You," she whispered, clutching the doorframe. "This time it *is* you. You've come through the caverns, come back to haunt me." She sagged forward and would have fallen down the stone steps if he hadn't caught her.

Hart carried the unconscious Leda into the kitchen with Kendra at his heels. Her fright momentarily forgotten in her concern over Leda, Kendra shut the cellar door, locked it and, without thinking what she was doing, put the brass key in her pocket.

"You'd better carry Leda up to her room," she told Hart, leading the way to the back stairs.

After Hart eased the old woman onto her bed, Kendra gestured for him to leave the room, believing it was best Leda didn't see him when she came to. She leaned over the bed and grasped a frail, thin-skinned hand.

"Leda," she said urgently. "Leda, this is Kendra. Everything's all right. You're safe in your room."

The old woman's eyelids fluttered and opened. She stared dazedly up at Kendra. "Why, it's the bride," she mumbled. "Tola's bride."

Her words made no sense to Kendra, though she felt a frisson of fear trickle along her spine at the name Tola.

"I'm Kendra," she repeated. "You fainted. How do you feel?"

Leda pulled her hand free, ignoring what Kendra had said. "He came from the vaults," she mumbled. "I saw him with his headband. He's dead but he came from the vaults. Who'll come next?"

The door, left ajar, opened, and Patrice looked in. "I heard people talking," she said. "What's going on?"

Not wanting to discuss what had happened with Patrice, Kendra simply said, "Leda fainted."

Patrice, wearing a long T-shirt as a nightgown, came over to the bed. Leaning down, she asked, "You okay, Mrs. Morel?"

Leda focused on her with effort, then reached with her hand. "Patrice," she whispered. "Stay with me."

Patrice looked at Kendra, raising her eyebrows questioningly.

It was reassuring that Leda recognized Patrice. And since it was clear that for some reason Leda preferred Patrice's presence to hers, Kendra decided it made sense to have Patrice, rather than her, stay with the old woman for the rest of the night. "Would you mind?" she asked Patrice.

"Not a bit. She reminds me of my old granny. The bed's a double, I'll just crawl in with her." Patrice looked down at Leda. "That okay with you, Mrs. Morel?"

Leda nodded, her eyes drooping shut, her hand still gripping Patrice's.

"Call me if she seems worse," Kendra said.

"Yeah, I'll do that."

When she left Leda's room, Kendra expected to find Hart waiting in the hall, but he was nowhere to be seen. She tensed. Surely he hadn't been foolish enough to try to return to his apartment. Not at night.

She found him in her room, staring from her window into the darkness. "Moon's up," he said without turning around. "Waxing. Ought to be full in about ten days."

"Yes," she said as she closed her door. "On Midsummer Eve."

"Yeah, I figured that. I waited in your room because we need to talk." He left the window and crossed to her.

She tensed, willing herself not to reach out to him. Much as she needed the comfort of his arms, once he held her close, she'd find herself wanting more than comfort.

"I want you to pack," Hart said. "Now. After sunrise, when it's safe, drive like hell down the mountain and never come back here. Unless inheriting the estate is more important to you than your life."

She was tempted to do exactly what he said. But, of course, she couldn't. Not with Leda's health so precarious. Who would take care of her? Patrice might well decide to leave once she had some money saved up. And there were other considerations, too.

"Leda's far from well," she said to Hart.

"Her son lives here. She's his responsibility. And don't forget you'll eventually inherit the estate even if you do leave in the morning."

"Thirty years from now, yes. But that's no longer my only reason—or even my main reason—for staying. If I run away like my mother did, I'll have to live with my own cowardice for the rest of my life. Actually, I'm in no more danger that anyone else here—why should I desert the rest of you?"

Hart held up a crumpled piece of paper. "Whoever sent you this note thinks you're in considerable danger."

"Are *you* leaving?" she asked.

He shook his head. "You know I can't. Not until I know how Wolfe died and who was responsible."

After a moment she said, "Leda saw the headband and thought you were Dewolfe, returned from the dead."

"I gathered that. 'Through the caverns,' whatever she meant by that. And where was Morel while we were all running around the house tonight?"

"Maybe he's a sound sleeper. His room *is* in the other wing, you know."

"Nobody could sleep through that clanging. Go back to the city, Kendra. Don't stay here."

"I'll admit I was afraid down in the vaults, so afraid I became a child again, scared of Collis's made-up monster. I intend to overcome my old fears."

"You said yourself Tola existed. Tola the lake monster. Why do you say your half brother's monster was make-believe?"

"Do you expect me to accept that my father and Collis knew about and protected a monster and that Leda and Gregory are now doing the same?" She shook her head. "That's just not reasonable, Hart."

"It might explain why your mother slipped away with you so secretly."

"Don't you think I've wondered all my life why she did? I've come to the conclusion she probably had more than one reason, which had to do with her relationship with my father."

"I can see I'm getting nowhere." He started to turn away, and she grasped his arm.

"You can't leave the house," she said urgently. "It's not safe to go out into the darkness."

He put a hand on her shoulder. "So you do believe in monsters when it comes right down to it?"

She tried to ignore the warmth spreading through her from his casual touch. "I think danger lurks outside at night. Why else would Gregory warn us? Maybe it *is* Tola, whatever he is. But I can't accept a—a Mishibezo. A monster. I wasn't raised on Chippewa myths as you were. But something stalks the night—you *must* stay here."

He smiled slightly, glancing around her bedroom, then meeting her gaze. "Here? That's an invitation I can't refuse."

She started to say "here" didn't necessarily mean her bedroom but the glow in his dark eyes stopped her words, fueling her inner warmth into heat, making her realize that's exactly what she had meant.

His hand on her shoulder urged her closer, closer until she was in his arms. Is this wise? she asked herself as he bent his head to kiss her. But already she was breathless, her heart was racing and, after their lips met, reason fled.

Her worries, fears and caution vanished, routed by the passion evoked by the intensity of his kiss. Her imperative need to respond left no room for any other emotion. His lips, his hands, his body told her how much he wanted her. His need enveloped her, heating her, enticing her to offer him the gift of her own desire, a desire rapidly escalating out of control.

She wanted to run her fingers over his bare chest, to feel the satin smoothness of his skin overlaying the hard muscles underneath. She longed to feel the exquisite sensation of pressing close to him, flesh to flesh. She yearned to touch him everywhere, with no barriers between them.

The thrill of his lips on her throat seduced a moan from her, the heated rasp of his breath increased her craving for more and more and more of his caresses.

"I've wanted to hold you from the moment we met in the woods," he whispered. "Didn't you feel it, the spark between us?"

With her mind on hold, she couldn't think, couldn't remember. But if there had been a spark, it was a full-fledged forest fire now. No other man had ever aroused her so quickly and so potently. She slid her hands under his shirt, sighing when she touched his skin.

He responded by unbuttoning her dress, easing it from her shoulders and cupping her breasts through the silk camisole she wore beneath.

"Do you have any idea how much I want you?" he asked hoarsely.

"Yes," she whispered.

He groaned and kissed her, hard and deeply, stirring desires she didn't know she possessed, making her weak with wanting. Nothing existed for her except Hart, nothing mattered but his lovemaking.

His lips left hers and he gathered her to him, pressing her head against his chest. "Do you want me? Now? Tonight?" His voice was heavy with need.

The tiny voice that had asked, *Is this wise?* returned to war with her desire to go on making love with him. "I—I don't know," she admitted regretfully, pulling away from him. She didn't want to leave his embrace, but she felt somehow that the Tremaine house wasn't the right place for them to come together. Neither the house nor anyplace within the estate walls.

He released her. Feeling somewhat embarrassed by her disheveled appearance, she turned her back while she put the top of her dress in order. When she faced him again, smoothing her hair, he was smiling wryly.

"Maybe I shouldn't have asked," he said.

She flushed, aware how eagerly she'd responded to him. Too eagerly?

His smile faded. "But something felt wrong. Not you, never you. You couldn't feel more right to me."

She was about to share her thoughts about the house with him when a sharp rap at the door startled them both.

"Who's there?" she asked.

"Gregory. Are you all right?"

Before she could respond, to her dismay Hart opened the door. Gregory, fully dressed, stood in the hall.

"Ms. Tremaine is recovering, Mr. Morel," Hart said. "I thought it best to stay with her until she felt better. It was quite a shock for her—first being frightened by noises in the vaults and then upset by your mother's near accident. Mrs. Morel almost fell down the stairs to the vaults, you know."

Gregory stared from Hart to Kendra. "I've been to see my mother," he said. "You should have roused me sooner."

"I mentioned that to Ms. Tremaine," Hart said, "but your mother seemed better so she decided to wait until morning to talk to you. In case you're wondering why I'm in the house—I brought Patrice back. Apparently she didn't take your warning to heart about wandering around the grounds at night."

"I'll have a serious talk with her," Gregory said. "But really, Kendra, you should have come to me if you were frightened by strange noises."

"No doubt she would have," Hart said, "if I hadn't happened to be handy. I accompanied Ms. Tremaine down to the vaults. We found a steel trapdoor set into the floor but nothing to account for the clanging noise."

"I thought it a rather odd place for a trapdoor. A new trapdoor," Kendra added. At first she'd been somewhat annoyed that Hart hadn't given her a chance to speak, but now she understood that he was feeding Gregory a diluted version of the truth, hoping to extract information from him.

Gregory sighed. "Shall we adjourn to the kitchen while we continue this little chat? Since Hart obviously must remain in the house until dawn, perhaps we might all have coffee and a bite to eat."

Remembering the awful brew he'd made in his apartment, Kendra refused to allow Hart to help her fix the coffee. Using the cold cuts leftover from supper, she made sandwiches and sliced the remainder of the cake, placing everything on the kitchen table. Gregory might prefer the dining room, but she was determined they'd eat here.

"I'd hoped to spare you this," Gregory began as he stirred sugar into his coffee. "Yes, the steel door *is* new. I had it put in to prevent anyone from suffering your brother's fate."

In chorus, Kendra and Hart said, "Brother?"

Gregory shot Hart a stern glance. "I was speaking to Kendra. Strictly speaking, this is none of your affair, being family business, but because you've been down in the vaults, I'll make an exception. Collis Tremaine died in a collapse of the tunnel between the caverns and the islet in Lynx Lake."

"Caverns?" Kendra asked. "Tunnel? I didn't know any such things existed on the estate."

"They've been here since God knows when. Before the house was built, I'm sure. Your father, Kendra, was injured in a rockfall in the tunnel, bringing on his fatal heart attack. After that happened, Collis was determined to personally shore up the tunnel walls, though I repeatedly warned him of the danger of further rockfalls. He refused to listen." Gregory spread his hands. "What could I do? Belatedly, I'll admit, I had the steel door installed to replace the rotting old wooden one. 'Strong enough to hold back an elephant,' the workman had said, though, of course, it didn't need to be.'' He smiled slightly. ''I'm aware of no elephants in the Adirondacks.''

His smile faded. ''Even the steel door wouldn't have saved Collis—he was determined to go on with his dangerous work, come what may. I've come to feel nothing could have saved him. But at least with the steel door in place, now no one can accidentally fall into the caverns.''

Kendra gazed at him, trying to assimilate what he'd told them. Apparently both her father and Collis had died in a tunnel under the house, which seemed odd. ''What's on the little island?'' she asked. ''Why would anyone want to go through a tunnel to get there?''

Gregory shrugged. ''The islet has nothing in particular to recommend it. Perhaps I wasn't clear—the tunnel is a natural formation, like the caverns. Nobody built it to reach the islet from the house. For some reason old Ezekial situated the house to take advantage of this natural phenomenon. Your father, who sometimes visited the island, occasionally used the tunnel rather than sailing across the lake in his boat.''

''Ms. Tremaine was impressed by the size of the bolts closing off the trapdoor,'' Hart said.

''The bolts were the choice of the workman who installed the door,'' Gregory said. ''He seemed fixated on elephants. As to the noise you heard—rocks still fall from time to time under the house. We often hear the sound quite clearly.'' He smiled at Kendra. ''I regret not mentioning this earlier, thus preventing your unnecessary fright, but as I said, I'd hoped to spare you the unpleasant details of your brother's accident.''

Kendra could think of no appropriate reply. As she searched for something to say, Hart spoke again.

"I gave your mother quite a scare coming up from the vaults," he said to Gregory. "Ms. Tremaine was behind me, so I was the only one Mrs. Morel saw. In the dim light she must have believed I was a stranger. Luckily I was able to catch her when she fainted."

"Mother seemed somewhat confused, mumbling about that headband you have on. Apparently, like me, she hadn't seen you wear it before. I gather she thought you were a ghost for some reason. She does tend to be superstitious."

Gregory had a reasonable explanation for everything, Kendra thought. Except for the huge bolts on the trapdoor—those still bothered her. Since anyone wishing to open it could simply shoot back the bolts, no matter how large, why bolt the door at all? Unless you wanted to prevent someone from entering the house from the other side. Or some*thing*.

She was about to mention this when Hart said, "I noticed a sailboat in the locked boathouse. Any chance of me taking it out on the lake sometime?"

Gregory frowned. "Don't go in or on the lake under any circumstances. As I've already explained, I don't want anyone poisoned. Besides, the boat isn't usable. We salvaged it after Collis's wife Lydia drowned, but the hull's badly damaged." He looked from one to the other of them, his expression sorrowful. "To tell you the truth, we haven't been a lucky family."

"Judging from what you've told me, you've been extraordinarily unlucky," Hart said bluntly.

Gregory put his hand over Kendra's. "She'll change things. A new owner, like a new broom, sweeps clean."

Hart frowned but remained silent, staring at Gregory's hand covering hers.

"After Midsummer Eve, that is," Gregory added.

Kendra pulled her hand free and reached to pour herself more coffee, doing her best to ignore the prickle of apprehension that raised gooseflesh on her arms. *Midsummer Eve*. She was beginning to dread hearing those words.

June 23 was but ten—no, nine—days away. And that would be the eve. Seeing that her hand was trembling, Kendra set down her cup and clenched her hands together in her lap, more and more certain Collis had chosen that particular date for some reason she didn't understand. Collis, the half brother who'd enjoyed tormenting her while she'd lived here.

What would happen on Midsummer Eve?

I I S A W I L D E R N E S S R A N C H

for one summer, and I had decided I could handle it
to my...Word, what did Leda mean when she meant to be
very nearly the right it she would sell the estate.

CHAPTER SEVEN

Though tired from lack of sleep, Kendra rose at eight, expecting to help Patrice with breakfast. When she reached the kitchen, to her surprise Leda stood by the stove frying bacon.

"You ought to be in bed," Kendra scolded her.

"I'll have you know I'm quite recovered," Leda said stiffly. "I've never been one to baby myself. And Patrice is all the help I need, thank you."

"I'm sorry you were so startled last night. I—"

"I don't choose to discuss what happened last night." Leda turned her back on Kendra.

Dismissed, Kendra ate a meager breakfast, then spent the rest of the morning in the south attic, sorting through old Tremaine belongings while trying to keep herself from dwelling on what had happened between her and Hart in her bedroom.

It seemed as though she were being threatened from the outside by some mysterious menace here on the estate and at the same time from within herself. She'd always been in control of any relationship with a man—but not with Hart. When he kissed her, she forgot everything except him and she found it frightening to lose herself in a way she never had in the past.

Instead of asking herself, as she customarily did, *Do I want to get involved with this man?* and considering the answer carefully before coming to a decision, she'd forgotten caution and all but thrown herself into Hart's arms. Worse, she might be even more reckless at her next opportunity. He enraged, fascinated and excited her.

Though she knew she ought to be concerning herself with the strange events, both past and present, occurring on the estate, all she could think of was Hart.

Near noon Patrice appeared at the top of the attic stairs with a box of trash bags.

"Mr. Morel told me to come up and help you," she said.

Nothing in her voice or manner showed any residual resentment from the previous night. Since Kendra was more than perfectly willing to let bygones be bygones, she made no reference to anything that had happened except Leda's collapse.

"Thanks for staying with Leda last night," she said.

"Oh, I didn't mind." Patrice gave her a twisted smile. "I've slept with worse. She's unbelievably modest, though. When I tried to help her change into her nightgown, you know what? She wouldn't let me touch her. Not only that, but she made me turn my back so I couldn't watch her change."

"Do you think she's well enough to be downstairs working?"

Patrice shrugged. "If she thinks she is, we can't stop her, that's for sure. At least her mind's clearer than it was last night. She claimed she saw a ghost coming out of the cellar."

Kendra gave her a selective explanation. "What she actually saw was Hart and me. I suppose she didn't expect to see anyone, and the shock was so great she fainted."

"You and Hart were down in that cellar?"

"Before he could leave last night, he and I heard a noise down there, so we investigated."

"And?"

"We didn't find anything. Gregory says rocks sometimes fall in the caverns under the house and that's probably what we heard."

"Caverns under the house? Hey, that's real spooky."

"Unusual, anyway."

Patrice's voice took on a sarcastic tone. "I suppose something weird like trolls live in the caves, nasty little trolls that only come out when its dark, and that's why old Greg laid into me for leaving the house last night." She shot Kendra a defiant look. "He can't stop me from doing what I want to do. And neither can you. I don't appreciate being cooped up. It's like serving time behind bars.

"I may as well tell you loud and clear—as soon as I earn a few bucks to rub together, I'm outta here. I mean, you did me a favor, sort of, but this kind of deal isn't what I'm used to, you know, not by a long shot. Hey, I want some action—not stagnation."

"I understand," Kendra said. She wasn't exactly happy staying here herself—except for Hart. "Let me know when you're ready to go, and I'll give you a ride to the nearest town where you can catch a bus or train."

"That's Yokelsville, or whatever its name is, where Hart and I went Sunday. I thought he'd be fun. Man, oh man, was I wrong. In fact, he makes me wonder which way he swings." She stopped stuffing rejects in the plastic bag she held and gazed narrowly at Kendra. "Or maybe he just prefers the heiress to the help."

Kendra, aware she'd flushed, turned away from Patrice. "Speaking of Hart," she said coolly, "when you bring that trash bag outside, would you please ask him to come up here and carry down some of the heavier junk?''

"No problem." Patrice said jauntily. Glancing at her, Kendra watched Patrice fingering her double-heart necklace, the smug expression on her face saying, *Aha! Caught you.*

Maybe if she suspects there's something between Hart and me, Kendra thought, she'll leave him alone. And maybe not. But surely Patrice ought to have enough sense not to try to visit his apartment at night again.

They worked in silence until finally Patrice said, "You know, on account of the freezer, I thought for sure there was something hidden in the cellar. Are you sure you and Hart didn't find anything down there?''

"Nothing but the furnace. What do you mean 'on account of the freezer'?''

"Maybe you noticed there's two? A small freezer in the pantry and that great big one in the storeroom off the kitchen.''

"Yes, I saw them both. Leda said two freezers were needed to keep extra food in case they were snowed-in during the winter.''

"Yeah, I was handed that line, too. But did you ever happen to open the big one and look inside?''

Kendra shook her head.

"If you take a peek under the black plastic across the top, the freezer's full of raw meat. Sides of beef and things like that, not cut up or wrapped or anything. I swear there's enough to stock a butcher shop. Or feed all the animals in a zoo. What's it for, do you think?''

Against her will, Hart's story of the monster under the lake filled Kendra's mind. Mishibezo. She shook her head. Not only was Mishibezo a myth, but she couldn't imagine Gregory or Leda storing meat to feed a monster, even if monsters did exist.

But what about Tola? Who and where was he?

"I couldn't figure it out, either," Patrice went on. "I'd say old Greg's not the type to get off by butchering his own meat, so what's the reason? I put two and two together—all that meat and the locked cellar—and figured there must be some kind of wild animal caged up down there—sort of gave me the chills, you know? But then you said there's no animal or even a cage in the cellar, so I guess I was way off base."

One more inexplicable item to add to her growing list, Kendra told herself. But perhaps the meat in the freezer could be explained if she asked either Leda or Gregory, which she intended to do. And, come to think of it, though Gregory had denied any knowledge of Tola, she'd never mentioned the name to Leda.

As if reading her mind, Patrice said, "I'll bet if you ask Greg he'd just feed you a lot of crap about that freezer full of meat. I never did like lawyers—they won't tell anyone the straight truth about anything." She crammed a final tattered baby blanket into the trash bag and cinched it closed. "Full. I'll haul it outside."

At the top of stairs with the bag, Patrice turned back to look at Kendra. "You didn't happen to notice that blond hunk pumping gas, did you?"

Kendra blinked. "In the village, you mean?"

"Yeah. That's what Lonnie—he was the biker who left me—got so upset about, 'cause he thought I was coming on to him." Patrice shrugged. "What if I was? It wasn't, like, serious, you know? But I might just look the guy up before I leave here. It all depends."

On what? Kendra wondered as she watched Patrice bump the plastic bag down the attic stairs. On how long she stays? On whether she can interest Hart?

When she returned, Patrice said, "Hart's stacking wood in the shed by the back door. He says he'll be along as soon as he's done. I wouldn't mind owning that fantastic headband he's wearing." She gave Kendra a speculative stare, opened her mouth, then closed it again, shaking her head.

"What?" Kendra asked.

"I'm not supposed to tell anyone."

After her several years of counseling teenagers, Kendra recognized game-playing when she saw it. Since she'd learned very quickly not to play the role intended for her, she merely shrugged, knelt beside another one of the trunks and began emptying the contents.

After a moment or two, she held up a dented pewter teething ring. "I wonder how many Tremaine babies chewed on this?" she said, setting it aside.

Apparently reminded by the pewter ring, Patrice said, "I've been meaning to tell you I think your brother's wife was pregnant when she drowned, 'cause I found some maternity clothes in her closet."

Kendra sighed. "A double tragedy. How sad." No wonder, she thought, that Greg believed Collis courted death. Her brother had suffered two losses.

They worked in silence until Patrice asked, "This boat with 'Tola' on it—that's not to be thrown out, is it?"

"No, the boat's on the save pile. All of those things can go back in that empty trunk."

"He bought one, you know."

Her back to Patrice, Kendra smiled slightly, realizing the game had been resumed. She murmured a disinterested "Oh?"

"Hart did. He bought a boat. A canoe."

Kendra whirled around. "A canoe!"

Patrice's smile was triumphant. "Yeah. One of those little lightweight ones. I asked him if he was going on the lake with it, but he wouldn't say yes or no. He left the canoe at some old guy's shack by the bridge instead of bringing it through the gates, so I'd lay odds he plans to paddle across to that island and doesn't want Greg to know he's got a boat. You going to tell him?"

Wondering exactly what Hart did mean to use the canoe for, Kendra answered absently, "Tell Gregory? No."

"I figured you wouldn't. You've got something going with Hart, haven't you? That's why he won't give me the time of day. Come on, admit it."

She could either tell the truth or inform Patrice it was none of her business. Neither alternative appealed to Kendra. While she didn't want Patrice to know, she also didn't like to snap at her. The sound of footsteps on the attic stairs saved her from having to make a decision.

Certain it was Hart, she gazed toward the top of the stair, unable to even pretend to be working, breathlessly waiting for him to appear, behaving like one of those moonstruck teenagers she'd counseled at school.

Snap out of it, she urged herself. You may as well print Take Me, I'm Yours across your forehead as be this obvious.

Gregory, not Hart, appeared in the doorway. "Something came up unexpectedly and I must drive to

Albany," he told Kendra. "I hope to return tomorrow but I might be gone until the end of the week. You will keep an eye on Mother, won't you?"

"Yes, of course. Both Patrice and I will."

"Yeah, sure," Patrice chimed in. "I can sleep in her room again if you want."

"Thank you, Patrice, but I don't think that will be necessary." His eye fell on the *Tola* boat that Patrice was about to place in the trunk. He held out his hand. "May I have that?" When she gave the boat to him, he glanced at Kendra and said, "I believe I'd like to put this on my desk."

"Why don't you?" she asked, realizing with a sinking heart that the events of the past night, coupled with her lack of sleep, had made her completely forget her vow to return the topaz lavaliere to Gregory as soon as possible. Now she'd have to wait until he came home.

As he descended the stairs, Patrice said in a low voice, "You know, if he weren't so tight-assed he'd be kind of cute."

Her words made Kendra smile. Gregory was good-looking enough, but *cute* wasn't a word she'd apply to him.

"If I was staying on here, I might make a play for old Greg," Patrice continued. "It'd take a while to loosen him up, but I bet I could. Only then he'd probably bore me to tears. If staying on here didn't drive me bats first. I think I'll try Blondie over at the garage instead. He's already hot to trot."

Her eyes widened and she gasped, covering her mouth with her hand. "Jeez, Hart, how'd you get up here without making any noise? You scared me to death."

Kendra stared at Hart, who stood at the top of the stairs. She hadn't heard him on the steps, either.

"We of the blood have our secrets," he said loftily. "That's how I know that guy at the garage is too young for you, Patrice."

She glared at him. "I'm a better judge of what's too young than you are, blood or no blood."

He shrugged. "Mrs. Morel needs some help mopping the kitchen floor—she doesn't look up to the job."

Patrice let her gaze drift from Hart to Kendra and back before saying, with a sly smile, "Are you sure you two ought to be left without a chaperone?" She turned and clattered down the stairs, leaving an uncomfortable silence behind her.

"What can I do for you?" Hart asked finally. Then he grinned. "Bad choice of words. I'd better rephrase that. Or shall I let it stand?" When she didn't immediately reply, he said, "I can tell you what I'd like to do."

Kendra relaxed, suddenly at ease with him—or as much at ease as she could be with her acute awareness of him. "No, don't tell me. This isn't the right time or place for anything but sorting through and tossing out."

Hart glanced around the cluttered attic. "A firetrap," he muttered, echoing her earlier words. "Why do people hang on to possessions they no longer want or use?"

"Since they do, and my ancestors were no exception, it's up to us to get rid of this clutter." She spoke briskly, hiding her need to touch him. "But Gregory claims the house won't be destroyed by fire, whatever that means."

"What *will* destroy a fortress like this one?"

"He shied away from discussing it."

Hart wore jeans and a denim jacket with the same casual assurance she felt he'd bring to a shirt and tie. Though he was obviously physically strong, he projected an inner strength that made her feel that here was a man she could count on, a man who'd never a friend let down.

But it was something more that drew her to him, intangible filaments so strong she could barely resist their pull. She knew without a doubt she belonged in his arms. Not here, though. When she'd said this was not the right time or place, she'd meant making love in this house wouldn't be right for them. Not in Lynx House. Never here.

"I see you're still wearing the headband," she said.

He nodded. "Wolfe knows I have it. I can feel he does."

Kendra blinked, peering intently at a corner of the attic. As Hart spoke, she thought she'd seen a gray shadow slip into that corner. Nothing moved now. In fact, the dim light made her uncertain she'd seen anything. She should have brought Gregory's lantern up with her.

"We'd better get started," she said. "You can begin by disposing of that broken chair." She watched him pick up the chair and carry it toward the stairs. Without realizing she meant to say anything, she blurted, "Why did you buy a canoe?"

He set down the chair, turned and offered her a wry smile. "I figured Patrice couldn't keep her mouth shut. Does Morel know?"

Kendra shook her head. "You haven't told me why yet."

"Because I might need to investigate the island and I sure as hell don't intend to swim across Lynx Lake when I wouldn't so much as wade in that water. Even before I asked, I knew Morel would find an excuse not to let me use the sailboat, and there's no other boat on the estate. So when I had the chance, I bought a canoe."

"Don't use it on the lake."

"How can I say I won't when I don't know when or if I might have to?"

"But you believe in a lake monster, so why would you risk paddling a flimsy canoe across Lynx Lake? The canoe's not much safer—if any—than swimming."

"While you *don't* believe in a monster. So why are you so worried about me going canoeing?"

"Maybe there's no monster," she said, "but something's wrong on this estate. We don't know who Tola is, for one thing. Maybe he lives on the island. I don't want you taking unnecessary risks."

"I value my neck, never doubt that, but I'll do whatever I have to do to track down Wolfe's killer." He picked up the chair and, holding it, frowned. "Do you really believe this Tola you keep talking about lives on the island?"

She shrugged. "Maybe it's being in this attic that made me start thinking about how in the old days people sometimes used to lock deformed or deranged relatives in attics to hide them from anyone's knowledge. Couldn't there be a little cabin, hidden in the pines on the island? It could account for Gregory's refusal to let anyone take a boat onto the lake."

"But not for his warning that the grounds are dangerous at night. If you're right and if Tola can and does leave the island—why only at night? And why is he so dangerous?'' Leaving her to think that over, Hart descended the attic steps with the chair.

When he returned for another load, Kendra had a question of her own. "You left the canoe at someone's cabin. Whose? I wasn't aware you knew anyone around here."

"Didn't I mention Matty Cusick? I thought I'd told you about him. Matty and I met a few days ago. He's an old trapper—retired now, he claims—who knew Pete Yettman, the former Tremaine estate grounds keeper."

"You might have said something of the sort."

"I plan to question Yettman about my brother, but Cusick says his cabin is off the road, 'out beyond.' I'll have to hike in." His troubled gaze rested on her. "I don't like leaving you alone on the estate—how about coming with me?"

"When?"

"This weekend, on my day off."

"I'd love to get away from here for a few hours." It was true. He didn't need to know how her heart had leapt at the chance to spend those same hours with him.

"Rain or shine," he cautioned.

She smiled. "I haven't yet melted in city rain and I doubt that Adirondack rain is any wetter. I'll be there, no matter what."

"Good. By the way, I've decided to stay in the house tonight. Downstairs, to resist temptation."

Kendra ignored the bit about temptation. "Did Gregory ask you to stand guard duty while he's gone?"

Hart shook his head. "Strictly my own idea. It might be best if you didn't mention my presence to Mrs. Morel. I wouldn't want to upset her."

"I tried to discuss what happened last night with her. She refused. But you've been in and out of the house today with the headband on—she must have seen you."

"I don't know who or what she thinks I am—she turns her head away from me. I wish I could find out what she knows about Wolfe's death. Even if she'd talk to me, though, if I explain to her the real reason I'm here, I'd blow my cover and lose my job. I can't risk that."

That evening, Kendra went to bed early. Whether because she was exhausted or because she felt secure with Hart in the house, or both, she fell asleep immediately, slipping into a dream....

The moon rose, full and gleaming, its silver rays caressing her awake. Or was it the deep boom of the gong summoning her to her destiny that had roused her?

She eased from her bed and glided barefoot in her gossamer white gown beneath an arbor of roses, their sweet scent perfuming the air. A thin ribbon of moonlight paved her way to where the flames of the Solstice balefire danced in the night, celebrating the midseason and beckoning the bride. Beckoning her.

For she was the bride, the Chosen One. Her groom did not yet await her, he would not appear, he would not come to claim her until she had undergone the rites of purification.

Many brides had he taken. Most had failed him. She would not fail. And yet her feet seemed reluctant to carry her to him—why did her steps lag until she scarcely moved?

Hurry, the notes of the gong urged. Hurry.

The stump of a pine tree blocked her path. The kingfisher perched on the stump cried, "Go back, go back! Death lies ahead."

She could not. Her destiny awaited her at the balefire. Ignoring the kingfisher's warning, she skirted the stump and drifted toward the flames. Closer now, she saw others had gathered around the fire burning near the verge of the lake, circling the fire counterclockwise.

Pausing, she watched their shuffling dance, knowing that, though she saw them clearly, they could not see her. Two she recognized. Dewolfe. Collis. And the woman next to Collis must be Lydia, her brother's wife, Lydia, who cradled an infant no larger than a tiny baby doll. The others, pale wraiths, were women and girls. The brides who'd failed, the lost brides.

Dewolfe turned his head toward her as if sensing her presence. "Mishibezo," he whispered.

The lost brides moaned, "Tola, Tola," as they faded into nothingness one by one. Collis and Lydia, holding hands, vanished next. Then Dewolfe's body shifted and flowed, becoming a shadow but not quite disappearing.

Once more the gong sounded, a summoning from deep under the dark water. She turned toward the lake. Purification awaited her in its waters. As her unwilling feet carried her inexorably toward the lake, the shadow that had been Dewolfe blocked her path.

A faint and far-off voice called her name. The shadow vanished, the fire winked out and the moon hid behind the clouds, leaving her alone in the night. Something splashed in the lake, so close to her that droplets of water wet her lips. She sensed a darkness far

*blacker than the night, an alien darkness she could find
no name for.*

*Her heart drummed a rapid tattoo of fear. Tola was
coming for her, coming for her alone, just as she'd always feared when she was a child. She couldn't turn
away—his call was too powerful. She could only walk
deeper and deeper into the water. Toward where he
waited for her. She was beyond help. She was doomed. . . .*

CHAPTER EIGHT

Someone called her name. Struggling free of the frightening web of her nightmare, Kendra opened her eyes. By the pale light of the moon shining through the open curtains, she saw a dark figure bending over her. She gasped and shrank away.

"It's Hart," he said. "I came in because I heard you moaning and thrashing around. Bad dream?"

Kendra sat up. Bad dream? Yes! Gathering her wits, she said, "You heard me? I thought you were sleeping downstairs."

"Next door, actually, since you're the one I'm worried about. Move over."

She obeyed, scooting to the far side of the bed before it occurred to her what she was doing. She had no chance to protest—Hart eased onto the bed next to her, propping himself up against the headboard.

"Unusual, maybe, for the palace guard to crawl into bed with the princess of the castle," he said, "but this way I know you're safe."

"From everything except the guard," she murmured.

"From the guard, as well. I promise. At least, as long as we're on Tremaine property. I realize now it would be wrong. For many reasons. You know that's true."

Knowing it was true was difficult to keep in mind when he was sharing her bed. To distract herself from her urge to snuggle up to him, she said, "I had a terrible nightmare."

"Tell me about it. Grandfather, for different reasons than Freud, insisted dreams should never be ignored."

Before she began, Kendra propped herself up as Hart had done. Relating her dark dream, she found she was also reliving her terror. By the time she finished, she was trembling.

Hart clasped her hand in his. She wanted more, wanted the comfort of his arms around her, but she also knew what would happen if he held her, so she tried to content herself with gripping his hand.

"What meaning does the dream hold for you?" he asked.

"You're a shrink as well as a biochemist?" she said, taken aback.

"Grandfather taught Wolfe and me that dreams can be visions. In dreams we sometimes see what lies ahead, and if what we see is bad, we can try to alter our path to avoid disaster."

She sighed. "I'll look for meaning, but I warn you, I'm not a mystic. Let's see—the kingfisher, the stump and the name Mishibezo came from your Chippewa story. As for Tola and the brides, well, Leda rambled on about 'Tola's bride' while she was recovering from her faint."

"Did you ask her what she meant?"

"She won't talk about that night. I'll ask her about Tola when I think she might answer. As for the fire—"

"Balefire, you called it."

"Yes, but I don't know why. The word's not familiar to me."

"Wolfe once mentioned that the ancient pagans lit bonfires as part of their celebration of the change of seasons. He called them balefires. Around the balefire in your vision dream you saw the dead dancing widdershins—another of Wolfe's words meaning against the sun. In other words, counterclockwise."

Kendra shivered, clutching his hand tightly. She hadn't thought of it during the dream, but her brother, his wife and their unborn child were certainly dead as Dewolfe probably was.

"Ask yourself what their deaths have in common," Hart added.

"They died here. On the estate."

"I think there's more. What connects them to the lost brides, as you called them, of Tola?"

"Oh, Hart, I don't know," she said with mixed frustration and apprehension. "I haven't the slightest clue who Tola is."

"Or *what* Tola is."

"It was a dream!" she cried, wanting to thrust all memory of it away. "A bad dream. You can't expect to make any sense from nightmare visions."

"Listen to me." His voice was urgent. "You saw yourself as Tola's bride, a bride being led reluctantly to the balefire by the lake where the dead circling the fire warned you of your fate. Correct?"

None of it had seemed that clear in her dream, but the truth in his words settled heavily into her heart. "Leda called me Tola's bride," she whispered.

"And the fate of all of Tola's brides is death. If you dreamed a true vision you must alter your path or that might be your destiny."

She jerked her hand free. "What you're saying makes no sense! For one thing, I'm not planning to be anyone's bride in the near future."

"The kingfisher warned you to go back. He was telling you to leave the estate before Midsummer Eve, the date when pagans celebrated the solstice. And my brother's warning—"

"No, I won't listen. I don't want to hear any more about death or warnings or pagan celebrations." What she really wanted was to be in his arms with the fires of desire stirring in them both, the sweet heat banishing her chill of fear.

As if attuned with her hidden wish, Hart drew her close, holding her tightly against him. "I want to keep you with me like this, keep you safe," he murmured.

She raised her face and his lips covered hers, gentle at first, then with increasing urgency, sending a heated yearning circulating through her. His hand caressed the side of her breast, slipping down over the curve of her hip, making her long to have him touch her everywhere.

She wanted him, needed him in every way a woman needs a man. From the hint of desperation in his kisses, she knew his need was as intense as hers.

"You have no idea how much I want you," he murmured into her ear. "When I hold you like this my good intentions haven't a chance."

His masculine scent surrounded her—enticing, compelling and pure Hart. She ran her fingers gently over his face, trying to convey the tenderness she felt for him. He caught her hand and pressed her palm to his lips, touching it with his tongue. Desire uncoiled deep inside her, its tendrils expanding, growing.

When his hand found her breast, she moaned, arching against him.

Suddenly he tensed, drawing away. "Did you hear a noise?" he whispered.

She'd heard nothing and said so, reaching for him. He held her for a long, warm moment before releasing her. After kissing her on the forehead, he sprang from her bed.

"I thought I heard a clang," he said. "Maybe it was only an interior warning bell to remind me that whether I like it or not, the watchword is *wait*. Not here and not now."

She knew he was right. Something deep inside her whispered the same thing. Making love with Hart anywhere on the Tremaine estate would be wrong. But how she longed to pay no attention to her inner warning.

"Having you near enough to touch is too much of a temptation," he told her. "The closer I am to you, the faster my willpower leaches away. I'll fetch my sleeping bag from the next room and sack out on your bedroom floor for the rest of the night."

Once he'd settled in, Kendra, certain she'd never be able to go back to sleep, closed her eyes and drifted off almost immediately. When she woke in the morning, he was gone, having left his sleeping bag rolled up in her closet. On the following three nights, he slept in the room next to hers.

By the time Gregory returned home on Friday morning, Kendra, with Patrice and Hart's help, had cleared most of the south attic of the accumulated throwaways of generations of Tremaines, leaving only keepsakes.

In the afternoon, Patrice, who'd grown increasingly sullen, rode into Tremaine's Wold with Kendra to shop in the general store for Leda. She made her purchases quickly.

"I'm just going to put these packages in the car," she told Kendra. "Okay?" She was out of the store before Kendra, intent on her own list, could nod.

As before, the woman behind the counter took her money grudgingly, obviously unhappy about Kendra being there. She found it a relief to get back outside. When she reached the car, Patrice's packages were piled inside, but there was no sign of Patrice.

Kendra glanced along the street and caught sight of her—there was no mistaking that bright red hair—at the garage, leaning against a gas pump talking to a young blond man. Getting into her car, Kendra drove toward the garage, thinking she may as well fill her gas tank since she had to stop there for Patrice, anyway.

When she pulled up beside the pumps, she saw Hart hadn't been far off the mark—the blonde, despite his man's body, didn't look a day over sixteen.

"Yeah, we got a tow truck here at the station," he was saying to Patrice.

"Joey, you've got *everything*," Patrice purred.

Overwhelmed by Patrice's attention, he could hardly manage to pump the gas for Kendra.

"So, ciao for now, Joey," Patrice told him when he brought Kendra's change. "See you later."

"Yeah, later," Joey said eagerly.

They drove away from the village in silence. When they crossed the bridge over the creek, Patrice pointed to a tar-paper shack below them, on the creek bank. "That's where Hart left the canoe," she said.

"At Matty Cusick's. Yes, he told me."

"So, okay, lovers have no secrets from each other."

Kendra kept her mouth shut. Whether she and Hart were lovers or not was none of Patrice's business.

"What'd you think of Joey?" Patrice asked. "Isn't he a hunk?"

Kendra shrugged, determined not to be provoked into revealing how she felt about any possible involvement between Patrice and Joey. It was none of her affair.

"Yeah, he's young," Patrice admitted, "but if you looked close at those tight jeans he was wearing you could plainly see he's not *too* young. It's kind of fun to teach a guy his age, you know?"

Thinking of her high school students, Kendra couldn't imagine being romantically interested in any of the boys she counseled. But then, she wasn't Patrice.

"I mean *I'm* only twenty-five," Patrice added. "Jeez, Louise, that's not exactly ancient."

Kendra smiled at her. "It's younger than I am, at any rate."

She'd already tentatively eliminated Patrice from the list of those who might have put the warning note in her room. This trip to the village had convinced her Patrice hadn't written it.

She may be devious, Kendra told herself, but only to satisfy her own needs. She's not the anonymous-note type.

Who then? Hart's repeated attempts to convince her to leave argued against him. Why would he leave an unsigned note when he was already overtly pleading his case?

That left Leda and Gregory.

Which reminded her—she must return the lavaliere to Gregory without any more delay.

Back at the house, Kendra found Gregory in his study. Though he invited her to come in when she tapped at his door, it was obvious from the papers strewn across his desk that she was interrupting.

"I'm working on a quite difficult case," he said. "I'd rather it hadn't come along at this particular time but—" he spread his hands "—I can't expect clients to arrange to have their problems at my convenience."

"I'm returning the topaz." Not finding a clear spot to set the jewelry case on his desk, she tried to hand it to him.

"No, no," he protested, "the Tremaine topaz is entirely yours. Independent of the Midsummer Night provision in your brother's will. I know your father would have wanted you to have the topaz, and as executor of the estate, I insist that you keep it."

"But I—"

"No arguments, my dear. Besides, I haven't the time to hear them." He waved her away. "We can discuss the matter in the future if you're troubled over the legality of your ownership of the topaz, but for now you must do as I say."

Kendra eyed his frown and his obvious eagerness to return to his work. If she persisted, she'd only annoy him. "Later, then," she said, refusing to give up entirely.

"Yes, of course." He spoke absently, his gaze already on the paper in front of him.

As she closed the door behind her, the jewel case still in her hand, she reflected that this was certainly not the right time to ask him why the large freezer was full of uncut meat or if he'd left the warning note in her room.

But she could ask Leda.

Patrice was alone in the kitchen. "I persuaded Mrs. Morel to go up and rest for an hour or so," she said. "I told her I'd fix Spaghetti à la Patrice tonight and dessert would be hot-fudge sundaes."

"That sounds good to me. Is Leda all right, do you think?"

"If you want my opinion, she looks worse than she did when I came here, but she's a stubborn old lady and I guess she's made up her mind she's not going to die in bed. Who can blame her? When my time comes, I hope it's fast." Patrice shivered, one hand coming up to twist the gold hearts. "Jeez, what a downer. This gloomy old place makes a person morbid real fast."

Kendra couldn't help but agree.

"The gloom's even creeping into my dreams," Patrice went on. "They're getting weirder and weirder. Like, I'm outside in the moonlight and something's calling me to come to the lake. I don't want to go, I'm scared and yet I can't resist the calling. I got to answer, got to wade into that damn lake." She paused and shook her head. "I wake up scared as hell, you know?"

Kendra almost admitted she knew only too well but instead said, "That's more like a nightmare than a dream. Do you ever see what's calling you?"

Patrice shivered. "I don't want to *ever* see that!" Feeling a responsive frisson shudder along her own spine, Kendra decided it was time to change the subject. "Would you like some help with the meal?" she asked.

"No, thanks. Like Mrs. Morel, I'd rather cook by myself."

Kendra wandered outside, telling herself she meant to take a walk in the pleasant warmth of the late afternoon. Though the nights were still cool, summer had eased into the Adirondacks and the days provided perfect June weather. Wanting no reminder of her bad dream, she avoided the rose arbor and the lake, turning Patrice's similar dream over in her mind as she strolled along. Much too close to hers for coincidence. What did it mean?

When Kendra found her pace picking up as she heard the sound of wood being chopped somewhere beyond the garage, she frowned.

You know perfectly well who's wielding that ax, she chided herself. Admit it—he was your goal from the moment you stepped outside.

She saw Hart, stripped to the waist, ax in hand, before he was aware of her presence. Half-hidden by lilac bushes run rank, the smell of pine resin thick about her, she watched him split short lengths of a pine trunk into four pieces and toss the wood onto a growing pile.

He wore Wolfe's headband, the thunderbird image bright blue against the white-and-red beaded background. Sweat sleeked his skin, his muscles rippled as the ax rose and fell and, behind him, from the shadowy spaces between the pines, something watched him.

"Hart!" she called in warning. But even as he straightened to look at her, whatever she'd imagined she'd seen was gone.

She hurried to him. "The gray shadow," she said. "I thought I saw it again. Watching you. But I don't now."

He nodded. "I felt him. I have before. Though when I look, I see nothing."

"What do you mean—him?"

"My brother. Or rather his spirit. Unquiet, unable to rest. Or to travel the Spirit Path to what lies beyond the stars, as Grandfather believed. What remains of

Wolfe is trapped here unless I can find a way to set him free. Trapped here like the wraiths of the brides you saw in your dream.''

His words, spoken somberly, raised gooseflesh on her arms.

"That's enough!" she cried. "First Patrice, now you. Death. Graves. Spirits." She flung up her arms. "Look at the beautiful day, feel the sun's warmth, smell the clean scent of the pines. Celebrate being alive!''

Hart stared at the ax embedded in the cutting block, his gaze shifted to the lengths of logs still waiting to be cut, then he turned his back on them, facing her. "You're right."

From an overhead branch a cardinal, scarlet against the pine's green, whistled its approval, and Hart laughed. "Even the birds are on your side." Pulling her into his arms, he looked deeply into her eyes. "We *are* alive, you and I. And I mean to keep us that way.''

His mouth covered hers in a probing kiss, and she opened to him, tasting his wild flavor, savoring the scent of his skin and the contrast of his hard body against her softer one. She was about to lose herself in her rush of desire when the squawk of a jay startled her.

Hart immediately released her, took two strides and jerked the ax from the block.

"What's wrong?" she whispered, alarmed.

"Nothing," he said softly. "Someone's coming, that's all. I don't think they're close enough to have seen anything." He raised the ax and brought it down, splitting the half log resting on the block.

"Someone" could only mean Leda, Gregory or Patrice. She had every right to be here with Hart if she wished, but somehow she had the urge to hide what was between them.

"So if you want to sample Spaghetti à la Patrice," she said in a normal tone, as though continuing a conversation, "stop by the kitchen before dusk for a plateful."

"Sounds like an irresistible offer," he said. "I'll be there. Thanks."

She waved and turned away, her gaze seeking movement among the trees as she began to walk back to the house. She saw no one, and the jay's raucous cries grew more and more distant, as though the "someone" had changed course and angled toward the lake.

Later, she and Patrice persuaded Leda to sit at the dining room table and be served.

"I cooked and I'll serve," Patrice announced. "You take the evening off, Mrs. Morel."

Leda, protesting, complied. But she ate little. When Gregory noticed and chided her gently, Leda pretended to eat while doing nothing more than shifting the spaghetti around on her plate.

"Don't you like it?" Kendra asked. "I'd be happy to get you something else from the kitchen."

"No, no, the spaghetti is very tasty. Stop fussing." Leda put a small forkful into her mouth. After swallowing it, she added, "It's just that I haven't had much appetite lately."

"You'll improve after next week," Gregory said.

Leda's glance at her son was apprehensive, and Kendra wondered why. Next week? What was next week? Then she remembered—Midsummer Eve. It would be a relief to have the day behind instead of before her. Did Leda feel the same?

"You won't be gone again next week like you were this past week, will you?" Leda asked her son.

"I may have to appear in court. But I'll be back for Midsummmer Eve, you can count on that." He smiled at Kendra. "I wouldn't miss it for the world."

Gregory disappeared into his study after the meal. Kendra assisted with the clearing up, though Leda refused to allow her to help with washing or drying the dishes, saying, "Patrice and I will manage just fine."

Not wanting to be alone in her room until she had to be, Kendra decided to read in the library. Unfortunately, she couldn't find a book that appealed to her. She hadn't particularly missed watching TV for the last few weeks, but now she wished there was a set in the house so she could distract herself for a few hours.

She finally decided to go to bed. But before she climbed the stairs, she stood in the foyer gazing up at the fearsome hybrids carved on the banister posts and thinking that surely old Ezekial hadn't ordered the man who fashioned the staircase to decorate the posts with such gruesome creatures. Or had he? Judging from the ancient, not-very-well-executed oil portrait of him in the dining room, her ancestor, his golden hair half-covered by a sort of tam-o'-shanter, had been a rather sullen young man.

She had no other clue to his temperament or any idea if he'd mellowed with time or grown irascible.

"Why so pensive?" Gregory asked.

Since she hadn't heard him come out of his study, she started. Calming herself, she said, "Are there any old family records you're aware of? I didn't find any in the library, and there weren't journals or photograph albums in the south attic trunks."

Gregory shook his head. "The Tremaines were a secretive family. If any of them kept journals or diaries, someone must have disposed of them. As for photographs, a few have survived. I found them tucked away in drawers, where, no doubt, they'd been forgotten, but I've never run across a picture album."

"I'd like to see what photographs you do have."

"Certainly. Come into the library with me."

Gregory waved her to a seat and, taking out a key ring, unlocked the door of a massive mahogany cabinet on the west wall. He half turned, holding up the key ring. "I'm reminded, my dear, that the key to the vaults, a key commonly kept in the kitchen, seems to be missing. I believe you might have been the last to use it. You or Hart. And he denies all knowledge of its whereabouts."

Kendra frowned. "I think I did take the key from the door after relocking it, but I can't recall exactly where I put the key afterward. I'll do my best to find it."

"When you do, I'd appreciate it if you'd put it back in its place. Fortunately, I have a duplicate, but there are only the two keys."

"I'm sorry to be so thoughtless."

Gregory waved a dismissive hand. "I'm sure my mother's collapse that night drove every other consideration from your mind. And rightly so." Turning back to the cabinet, he opened the door, revealing drawers and small, apparently locked, cupboards within. From a drawer he removed a manila envelope.

"You're much better organized than I am," Kendra observed.

"Success or failure sometimes depends on knowing exactly where everything is."

She didn't argue, though she doubted she'd ever manage to know where everything she owned was at any given time.

He brought the envelope to where she was perched on a red velvet love seat and sat down beside her. He made no move to touch her, and she chided herself for wishing she'd chosen a chair instead.

"This is your father," he said, pulling a photo from the envelope.

She gazed at a picture of the same blond young man who was standing with her mother in the earlier snapshot she'd found in her father's room. This time she fancied she saw a resemblance to Ezekial's portrait, even the same droop to the mouth. "He looks like Ezekial."

"All the Tremaines resemble one another to some degree. You favor your mother but you have the Tremaine hair. Even I bear a faint resemblance to Ezekial, though of course I have the Morel eyes, as your brother did. Ezekial lived into his late nineties, and when he died the family split into two branches—yours and mine."

Her interest caught, Kendra asked, "Why?"

"There are no records to give us reasons. The Morels always believed the Tremaines hadn't acted in good faith, somehow persuading Ezekial to leave all he possessed—including this estate—to the Tremaine side."

"You mean, the Morels were cut off without a cent?"

"Something like that, as I understand it. It was something of a coup for the Morels when your father fell in love with my sister the first time he saw her. As well as being something of a beauty, Beth was was a most virtuous young woman. If he wanted her—and he did—he had no choice but to marry her. A fitting fate for one of Ezekial's direct descendents to marry a Morel, I've always thought."

Kendra didn't quite follow what he meant, but let it pass. "Are there any pictures of your sister?"

He shook his head. "Your father destroyed them all—even their wedding picture. After you were taken from Lynx House by your mother, he invited my mother and me to come here to live so we could help take care of young Collis. After we did, your father violated our privacy by clandestinely searching our belongings for pictures of the Morels. He burned every last one. My mother never got over it."

"What a strange thing for him to do."

"I fear he saw himself as lord of the manor, an absolute ruler." Gregory pulled out another picture. "Here's one of Collis and you, apparently taken by the lake. As I said, these photos survived because they'd been in obscure places, either forgotten by or hidden from your father."

Collis, instead of looking at the camera, was gazing at the water, pointing with one finger. Kendra decided she must have been about five, and from the expression on her little girl's face, Collis had just told her something frightening. Though her father's picture still rested in Kendra's lap, she quickly handed the photo of Collis and herself back to Gregory, upset at being reminded of her unhappy relationship with her half brother.

There were three more photos, one of her mother holding her, which she asked to keep, another of her father and a teenage Collis, and the third of the lake, showing two blurred and indistinguishable figures on the island, one of whom seemed to be waving.

"Who are they?" she asked.

He shrugged. "Impossible to tell, but I believe the one waving is Collis." Something—was it amusement?—in his voice made her glance at him, and she surprised a secretive smile that faded quickly.

"Could the other one be Tola?" she asked.

Gregory blinked. "Tola? Whatever gave you such a strange idea?"

"Who *is* Tola?" she persisted.

He reinserted all but the two pictures she'd kept into the envelope, set it aside and turned to face her. "I can't tell you now. Not until after you've inherited the estate."

"But that's ridiculous! What possible difference can it make if I know now or on June 24?"

"I'm sorry, it's not my decision but your father's. He instructed me that if the estate fell into your hands, then you were to be told the Tremaine secret. But not until then. I intend to abide by his wishes."

"Tola's the secret?"

He smiled at her. "Exactly." He leaned closer. "You're a most attractive woman, Kendra. Even prettier than your mother."

Before she understood what he meant to do, he captured her hand, raising it palm upward to his lips. Though she hadn't been unduly disturbed when he'd kissed her a week ago, she found the feel of his mouth on her palm repulsive and was unable to hide her distaste.

He dropped her hand and rose. Staring down at her, he muttered, "You may look like your mother but you've turned out to be your father's daughter, after all, haven't you?"

Upset, wanting to escape, Kendra didn't stay to watch him lock the pictures away but fled up the stairs to her room, Gregory's remark about her father echoing unpleasantly in her head. In what way did he mean she was like her father? She didn't wish to be, not at all.

Did Gregory think she was playing lady-of-the-manor just because she hadn't welcomed his coming on to her? If her unexpected reaction to his kiss on her palm hadn't taken her by surprise, she might have managed to conceal her distaste. But she was just as glad he understood how she felt. Why had her reaction been so extreme? Was it because she remembered the erotic touch of Hart's lips on her palm?

What disturbed her the most, though, was Gregory's refusal to tell her about Tola while tacitly admitting that Tola did exist.

Too unsettled to change into her nightgown, she paced her darkened room, pausing now and then to glance into the night, which was lit by a gibbous moon. A breeze ruffled the branches of the trees, making them dance in the moonlight, but she couldn't appreciate the night's beauty. She left the window to sit on her bed, only to rise and begin pacing restlessly once more.

How was she ever to relax enough to sleep tonight? Perhaps she could if she knew Hart was in the next room in his sleeping bag. But Gregory was home, and so there was no reason for Hart to stand guard in the house.

Returning to the window, she looked for the light from Hart's apartment, saw it and sighed. Close enough, but he might as well be as far away as the moon, separated as they were by the danger of being outside at night.

About to give up and try to get some sleep, Kendra held, gripping the frame of the window, her attention caught by a flicker of white drifting across the lawn away from the house. A human figure.

Someone was braving the peril of the dark. Who?

CHAPTER NINE

Kendra shook her head as, from her bedroom window, she watched the moonlit figure flit across the lawn. It must be Patrice. How could she be so reckless? Was she trying her luck with Hart again, despite his rejection?

Doubt caught at Kendra. Would he reject Patrice this time? Would he—?

Her conjecture ceased abruptly when she realized Patrice wasn't cutting across to the garage but hurrying toward the gates. The locked gates, because there'd been no telltale creak of them opening. How did Patrice expect to get out?

Suddenly Kendra gasped in shock, gripping the window frame as an insistent call shuddered through her, a call more felt than heard. An urgent summons. She must go into the night. Now.

Terrified, Kendra fought the summons, remembering her dreadful dream.

Clutching desperately at the window's wooden frame to prevent herself from leaving her room, she noticed that Patrice had halted and was turning away from the gates. "No," she whispered, recalling with horror that Patrice's nightmare had been almost the same as hers.

When Patrice began to walk slowly toward the lake, Kendra could almost feel her reluctance. A dry sob caught in her throat as she stood helplessly watching, frozen in place, wanting to fling up the lower sash and call a warning, but aware that if she loosened her death grip on the window frame, she'd be compelled by the summoning to go into the night herself.

Horror trickled along her spine. What was that dark shape she saw moving out of the shadows between the pines? Was it waiting for Patrice? Though she couldn't see it clearly, Kendra could tell the thing stood on two feet, looming larger than any man.

Oh God, it was reaching for Patrice. Embracing her. At the same time as Kendra heard a strangled scream, the summons thrumming through her ended as suddenly as it had begun. She sagged against the window, the cool glass pressing against her forehead.

Patrice and the thing in the night disappeared from her view into the trees. Beyond the pines, Kendra knew, the lake waited. Forcing herself to move, she shoved the window up and shouted Patrice's name over and over.

Her bedroom door burst open and she whirled, her heart in her throat.

"What's wrong?" Hart demanded. "Are you all right?"

She ran to him, grabbed his hand and pulled him to the open window. "Out there," she gasped. "Patrice. And—and something . . ."

Hart stared into the moonlit night. Nothing moved except tree branches, teased by the wind. There was no sound—no owl hooted; even the frogs were silent. Beside him, Kendra gripped his hand, holding to it as though she meant never to let go.

"I saw Patrice," she whispered. "Darkness summoned her and she—she obeyed. It took her into the pines. To the lake."

"What do you mean by darkness? What took her?"

"I don't know. It was huge and it walked on two feet."

"Like a bear?"

She stared at him. "I thought you said the bears around here didn't attack people."

"They don't usually. Where was Patrice?"

"At first she seemed to be heading for the gates but then she stopped..."

He listened to Kendra's story of what she'd seen, chilled when she added, "I know it called her, because it called to me as well. The summoning stopped after—" her voice quavered "—after it took Patrice."

His arms closed around her, holding her close. She clung to him desperately. "I couldn't warn her," she said brokenly and began to sob.

Hart soothed her as best he could. When her sobbing finally eased, he held her away from him and said, "I'd better take a look."

Kendra clutched at him. "No! Don't go out there. It'll get you, too."

He tried to loosen her grasp, but she clung to him tenaciously, shivering. "You can't save Patrice—it's too late. Don't go, don't go."

Holding her against him, he stroked her back as he tried to reason with her. "We don't know that it's too late. If it was a bear, there's still a chance she might have survived." He believed it *was* too late for Patrice and he didn't for one moment think what she'd encountered was a bear, but he wanted to calm Kendra down.

"Now," he said, his voice low and soothing, "think. Are you sure you saw Patrice?"

Her convulsive trembling eased. "Who else could it have been?" She spoke against his chest, her words muffled.

"I don't know. What you're telling me, though, was you didn't actually recognize Patrice, right?"

"Not exactly." She pulled away from him, mopping her face with a tissue. "Let's look in her room."

"Why don't you do that while I—"

"No! Come with me."

He wasn't surprised to discover Patrice missing from her room, but both he and Kendra were startled to find all Patrice's belongings gone. They were returning to Kendra's room when Gregory appeared in the corridor.

"Here again, Hart?" Gregory said with raised eyebrows.

"I heard Ms. Tremaine screaming, so I came to see what was wrong," Hart said. "Patrice seems to be missing."

"Missing?" Gregory smiled thinly. "Hardly missing. If you mean she's left my employ and Lynx House, yes, that's true."

"But—when?" Kendra asked.

"Soon after you retired," Gregory said to her, "Patrice came to the study and informed me she'd packed her things and intended to leave immediately. I tried to dissuade her but she was adamant. I had no recourse but to pay her what she was owed, cautioning her that she must wait until morning. She refused." Gregory spread his hands. "Dangerous though it was to venture out, I felt the least I could do was see her safely through the gates, which I did."

"*You* saw her through the gates?" Kendra asked.

"Yes, my dear, I did."

Hart tried to decide if he might have missed hearing the gates open and close. He'd dozed off, so it was possible.

"But I saw someone outside," Kendra said. "Alone."

"I assure you my mother is sound asleep in her bed," Gregory said. "The rest of us are present and accounted for. Are you quite certain it was a person you saw? Will-o'-the-wisps are common on the estate. You may be familiar with the phenomenon I'm referring to—ignis fatuus, a phosphorescence that appears to flit here and there. The moving light is often mistaken for a living being."

Hart, watching Kendra, sensed her confusion. He knew she must be wondering whether or not she actually had seen someone.

"I don't know what to think," she said at last.

"Stop worrying about Patrice," Gregory told her. "I'm sure such a resourceful young woman must have arranged beforehand to be met by someone. As for you, Hart, I heard Kendra's calls, too, and it seems to me you reached her room in record speed, considering the distance between your apartment and the house."

Hart saw Kendra's eyes widen and knew she'd just now realized how quickly he'd gotten to her. Addressing Gregory Morel, he said, "I take your warning about the grounds being dangerous after dark seriously. Very seriously. Because of that I might well have broken an Olympic record getting here."

Gregory frowned. "I suggest from now on you allow me to take care of matters within the house. The next time you rush into the night may be your last."

Hart nodded. He didn't intend to tell Morel the truth. Without being seen, he'd entered the house by the back door at dusk, made his way up the back stairs with his sleeping bag and settled into the room next to Kendra's. He was taking no chances with her safety, whether Morel was in the house or not.

"You can sleep on the couch in the library until morning," Gregory went on, "but I don't expect to find you you here again at night. Is that clear?"

"Perfectly clear," Hart said.

"I'll just see you downstairs, then." Gregory turned to Kendra. "Goodnight, my dear."

"Goodnight," Kendra said, walking slowly away.

Glancing over her shoulder to make certain Gregory was out of sight, she opened the door of the room next to hers. By the light of the moon shining in through the uncurtained window, she spotted Hart's sleeping bag. The idea that he'd been standing guard, after all, warmed her. Not wanting to take the chance that Gregory might find the bag, she rolled it up, returned to her room and stashed it in her closet.

Once she was ready for bed, she hesitated to turn off her bedside lamp, uncertain that she wanted to be alone in the dark. Gregory must be telling the truth about Patrice—why would he lie? Will-o'-the-wisp? She supposed it was possible. And the monstrous darkness that rose and walked on two feet might, as Hart had suggested, have been a bear.

And yet what about the summoning? Her fearful struggle against it was still vivid, still frightening. She had definitely not imagined *that*.

Knowing she couldn't possibly sleep, she wrapped herself in a quilt and sat uneasily in the rocker, wishing she'd stood up to Gregory and demanded Hart remain with her. Finally she rose and padded down the stairs to the library. If she found Gregory standing guard there to make sure Hart stayed put, she'd simply spend the rest of the night with both of them for company.

The library was in darkness except for a sliver of moonlight slitting through the break in the draperies. She located the couch and found it empty. A moment later, strong arms encircled her from behind. She bit back the scream rising in her throat when Hart spoke her name.

"I didn't mean to frighten you," he said softly, turning her into his embrace. She wrapped her arms around him, holding him close.

"I don't want to be alone," she whispered.

His lips touched her temple, trailing along her cheek to her mouth. She opened to his kiss and, as he deepened it, passion warmed her, dissolving the shreds of fear clinging to her. Before her mind jumbled into a haze of desire, an awareness flashed into life.

Hart was the only man she could ever love. Would ever love.

He held her hard against him, letting her know how much he wanted her. His kiss promised even as it demanded, and she yearned to be a part of him, to make him a part of her. But she couldn't dismiss the warning voice that whispered, *Not here.*

Difficult as it was, she forced herself to pull back. "We can't," she murmured regretfully.

"I know, damn it," he said hoarsely.

Taking her hand, he led her to the couch where he swung an afghan around her. Settling beside her on the couch, his arm about her, he said, "Lean against me and try to get some sleep."

She closed her eyes.

* * *

The next thing she knew she was blinking in the grayness of predawn, roused by Hart whispering in her ear.

"Go up and get dressed," he said. "We'll take a look outside before Morel has a chance to hide anything that doesn't back up his story."

When she rejoined him after pulling on a warm jogging suit, they crept into the kitchen and slipped through the back door.

"Show me where you saw this supposed will-o'-the-wisp," Hart said.

Kendra obeyed, walking toward the gates to the point where she'd seen Patrice—or whatever it was she *had* seen—turn and walk toward the lake. Hart followed her as she repeated what she'd seen Patrice do. Finally she stopped.

"It came out of the trees and was waiting here," Kendra told him, her voice quivering as she relived her terror. "When Patrice came close, it reached out and—and took her." Glancing down, she gasped.

Hart bent and picked up entwined golden hearts. After he rose, his dark gaze held hers and she released a long, shuddering breath.

He knelt and examined the pine needles, though she could see nothing of interest there. He got to his feet and walked in an ever-increasing circle around the spot where she stood, at last pausing under the pines and staring at the ground. She hurried to him.

He was looking at a spot where pine needles were scuffed aside to reveal the ground beneath. Several indentations showed. Was it a footprint?

"A bear?" she asked.

Hart shook his head. "No animal I know of leaves a print like this. It's something like a large human footprint—if a human had webs between his toes and claws at the ends of them."

Kendra bit her lip. "Gregory said he saw Patrice out through the gates last night," she said. "But we found her gold hearts here, not near the gate. And I saw—something."

"He's either lying or there's an explanation we haven't yet uncovered. I lean toward the lying, but then I haven't trusted him from the beginning."

"Tola," she whispered, gazing at the pines hiding the lake from her view.

He grasped her hand. "Listen," he said, "I don't think Gregory Morel trusts me any more than I do him. Don't tell him or his mother you're going with me tomorrow. Take your own car and pretend you're going for a drive down the mountain. I'll be waiting for you along the way. And keep my sleeping bag in your closet. I'm damned if I'm leaving you alone tonight or any other night. Go on in before you're missed. I'll look for more footprints."

Neither Gregory nor Leda were downstairs when Kendra returned to the house and went to her room. Uneasy in her mind—what had she seen? how could Gregory be telling the truth?—she showered and redressed. Descending the stairs, she vowed to get some straight answers from both the Morels.

Finding Leda in the kitchen, she took one look at the frail old woman, noting her abnormal paleness, and her determination faltered.

"Do you know where Patrice is?" Leda asked.

Kendra told her what Gregory had said about Patrice leaving.

"She was a nice enough girl," Leda said. "And a fair worker. But this is no place for young people." She glanced at Kendra. "No place for you."

"I don't think it's the best place for you, either," Kendra said. "There's too much work to be done, for one thing. At your age you ought to be able to take it easy. Maybe when you and Gregory move to Albany—"

"Albany? Who said we were moving to Albany?"

"I thought that's what you intended to do once the estate was sold."

"I'm too old to think of changing," Leda snapped.

Deciding the possibility of moving was a sore point between Leda and her son, Kendra dropped the subject.

Later, when they were washing the breakfast dishes, Kendra decided that she had to ignore Leda's obvious ill health and ask questions or she'd never learn the truth.

"I don't mean to upset you," she said, "but the night you fainted you said something that's been bothering me ever since. You called me 'Tola's bride.' Why? What does it mean?"

Leda's busy hands stilled in the dishwater. Without looking at Kendra, she said, "I must have been rambling, out of my head."

"Who *is* Tola?" Kendra persisted.

"Don't ask me that. I can't tell you."

Apprehension tensed Kendra. "But there *is* such a person as Tola?"

"Tola does exist, yes." Leda turned, and Kendra saw with surprise that her eyes were full of tears. "They should have told you," she said brokenly. "Your father. Your brother."

Kendra's need to know overrode her reluctance to distress Leda. "What should they have told me?"

Shaking her head, Leda said, "It's too late. Leave it be. Don't interfere in matters you know nothing of."

"But—"

"I won't put up with your questioning me. It's more than I can bear. This isn't a court, and I'm not on the witness stand. I will say one more thing and then the subject is closed. Your mother should never have taken you away from this house. Once she did, however, you should never have returned." With that, Leda dried her hands and hurried up the back stairs, leaving Kendra to finish the dishes by herself.

Since Gregory was nowhere to be found, Kendra decided to distract herself by starting to sort through what had been stored in the north attic, but one look at the clutter dissuaded her. The large room was even more crammed than the south attic had been, with stacks of old magazines besides. To think of plunging into the mess alone was daunting, and she would be alone because Patrice was no longer here to help.

Where was Patrice? Was she safely beyond the gates of the Tremaine estate as Gregory insisted? Kendra clenched her hands together. She couldn't bear to consider the alternative but she had to know the truth.

If Patrice had actually left the estate, Joey must have been the one she planned to meet, Kendra told herself. I'll drive into the village and see if I can find him.

Joey wasn't at the garage.

"He asked for today off," a bull-chested, fiftyish man told Kendra, his glance sliding over her. "Didn't see his pickup by his house, neither, so I reckon he ain't in town." He narrowed his eyes. "Molly told me another Tremaine showed up at the old place—that's gotta be you, right?"

"I'm Kendra Tremaine," she admitted.

"Yeah, you got the Tremaine look. What d'you want with Joey?"

Ignoring his suddenly belligerent tone, she said, "I think he drove a young woman named Patrice down the mountain last night. When Patrice left, she dropped her gold necklace and I'd like to see that she gets it back. I thought Joey might know where she was going."

"Patrice. She's the redhead the biker left behind, right? Been working for you, I hear. So she's gone?"

"Yes. Last night. She was talking to Joey yesterday afternoon."

"I heard. That don't mean he took her anywhere. 'S matter of fact, he had the tow truck out last night. Ain't likely he'd use that to take a girl somewheres. The truck's back, so Joey must've come back, but he ain't around now."

Exasperation shredded the last of Kendra's patience, allowing tartness to sharpen her voice. "They made a date and it could have been for last night. When you see Joey, please ask him to contact me."

"I suppose I could do that," he said grudgingly.

As she started to thank him, he held up a hand. "You're sure this Patrice left the grounds?"

Kendra stared at him. "Why do you ask?"

He shrugged. "Pretty close to St. John's Day, ain't it?" Evidently noticing her puzzled look, he added, "Used to call it Midsummer Day till Father Reynolds—" he gestured toward the old wood-framed

Catholic church on the rise behind the garage "—chewed the hell out of us. He's a good man, Father is, and we respect him. St. John, too. But there's some things—" He broke off and scowled at her. "It stays Midsummer Day to the Tremaines, don't it? And Midsummer Eve, too." Turning his back, he walked into the garage and shut the door behind him.

Kendra drove home, considerably shaken. After parking her car under the porte cochere, she walked to the front of the house and stared at the pines, trying to convince herself that if Joey wasn't in Tremaine's Wold it was possible he *had* picked up Patrice last night after Gregory had let her through the gates. Maybe Joey had given her a ride down the mountain.

"There you are," Gregory said from behind her. "I was wondering where you were."

Turning, she saw he carried a single white rose. "For you," he said. "Though you deserve an entire bouquet of roses."

Kendra took the rose and was inhaling its sweet essence when it occurred to her that brides carried bouquets of white roses. Her enjoyment of the rose's perfume vanished.

"Why do I deserve a bouquet?" she challenged.

"Why, for the remarkable job you did in cleaning up the south attic, of course." Was it her imagination or were his words ever so slightly flavored with amusement?

She no longer knew what to believe.

"You're not having second thoughts, are you?" Gregory asked as silence stretched between them.

"About what?"

"Staying at Lynx House until Midsummer Day."

She saw her chance. "I intend to stay. But I'm troubled by what I saw last night. I may not have seen Patrice, but I did see something frightening, something that walked on two legs but couldn't have been a man."

"A bear, perhaps."

"Not . . . Tola?"

"Come, come, Kendra. I don't intend to break my promise to your father, so it's no use to keep probing. You'll learn everything there is to know about Tola when the time comes. Everything."

His words didn't reassure her. Reminded of what Hart had asked her to do, she said, "I really feel the need to get away for a few hours." God knows it was the truth. "I believe I'll take a long drive tomorrow. That's permissible under the terms of the will, I imagine, as long as I return by dusk."

"My dear, I hope you don't consider me your jailer!"

She gave him a level look. "Should I?"

He sighed. "I wish you would believe everything I do is for your own good."

Kendra gazed at his troubled face, feeling more confused than ever. Perhaps she had wronged him. What was it she suspected him of? Lying about Patrice? Concealing some dark secret? She had no proof he was guilty of either. Except for finding the entwined gold hearts. Should she mention that? She decided to consult with Hart first.

"I'm upset about Patrice leaving so unexpectedly," she said. "And without telling me." But was that true? Patrice had repeatedly warned that she was "outta here" as soon as she earned a little money.

"We're all upset. Especially my mother."

"I'm worried about Leda," Kendra said. "I think you should make a doctor's appointment for her. She needs a thorough medical checkup."

"I've discussed that very thing with her. She's seen a doctor in the past and she's agreed to an appointment with him but not until after Midsummer Day."

"Everything seems to hinge on that day."

He smiled. "It does, doesn't it? I have a court case on Monday morning and can only hope it won't carry over until the next day, forcing me to remain in Albany overnight. I've never before missed being home on Midsummer Eve. We Morels are traditionalists. Of course, so are—or were—the Tremaines. You're the last of the direct line, my dear."

"Yes, but not, I'm afraid, much of a traditionalist." She glanced at the white rose she held. Stepping closer to Gregory, she tucked the stem into his shirt pocket, smiled and walked away.

Though she wasn't aware of him entering the house, when Kendra retired to her bedroom that night, Hart stepped out of her closet with his sleeping bag and spread it by the windows.

"I'm not much for skulking in closets," he said, "but I had to make sure Morel wasn't doing a room-to-room check to make certain I wasn't in the house." He sat cross-legged on the bag. "I'm staying here. Patrice's disappearance makes next door too far away."

"Disappearance?" she echoed. "Then you don't believe Gregory?"

Hart shook his head. "Not after finding those double hearts and seeing that footprint."

"Did you discover anything else? Any other trace of Patrice?"

He shook his head, watching her hug herself as though chilled by his response, and he had to fight the urge to go to her. It was going to be difficult enough to try to sleep in her room, knowing she lay in bed only a few feet away.

If he touched her, he might not have the willpower to let her go. He couldn't afford to be distracted, not with the presence of evil so thick around him he could all but taste it. What a hell of a time to have Grandfather's prediction come true.

"In a man's life," Grandfather had said, "women come and women go, some more important than others, but none necessary. Not until the appearance of the one woman whose spirit speaks to your spirit. If a man allows that woman to go, he will never be whole."

"But how can we tell a woman like that from any other?" Hart had asked.

Grandfather smiled. "If she comes into your life, you'll know."

"If?" Hart asked.

"The world is large, and life is short." Grandfather's voice had been sad. "You may never have the chance to meet her."

His brother's life was cut short—before he had the chance. As for him . . . Hart sighed. Grandfather had been right. He'd known moments after meeting Kendra that she was his spirit woman. He'd also sensed her response to him and promised himself he wouldn't let her get away. But how the hell could a man pursue the woman he knew was meant for him when both of them were surrounded by deadly danger?

Kendra turned off the bedroom light, walked to the windows and sat down on his sleeping bag, not touching him but within arm's reach. "I drove into the village today to talk to Joey," she said, and went on to tell him what had happened.

"So the garage man either doesn't believe or wouldn't admit that Joey might have met Patrice last night," she finished. "Maybe with a tow truck, of all things."

"Joey couldn't have met her," Hart said. "Patrice never left the grounds. But she might have intended to meet Joey. Probably did intend to. The tow-truck hoist would provide a way for her to get over the gates instead of having to go through them."

"I don't want to believe you're right," she whispered.

The moonlight streaming through the open curtains enhanced Kendra's loveliness while revealing her haunted expression. He longed to comfort her, to hold her close and never let her go. But she wasn't safe in his arms. She wouldn't be safe until he got her away from here.

"Don't stop to meet me tomorrow," he said. "Drive on. Drive back to the city and stay there, stay where you'll be safe. Don't ever return to this damn estate."

"I will if you'll go with me and promise not to come back, either."

"You know why I can't make that promise."

She gazed at him steadily. "Then don't ask me to go and leave you behind."

"Mishibezo isn't a myth," he warned.

She tried to repress a shiver, but he noticed her slight involuntary shudder. "It lives partly on the island and partly in the lake." Her voice, not quite steady, sounded as though she were quoting. "My brother told me that when I was seven. I believed him then."

"Believe him now," Hart advised.

"But monsters don't exist!"

"Two months ago I might have agreed with you. I grew up and grew away from what I was taught as a child. Since then I've learned that Grandfather, as usual, spoke the truth. Evil is real. There is evil out there in the night, evil in a monstrous form. Evil that killed my brother. Evil I must destroy."

She leaned toward him. "If you believe the evil is Mishibezo, are you Manabozho? Didn't it take Manabozho's special powers to vanquish Mishibezo?"

"I have no supernatural powers. But as a Chippewa warrior I mean to avenge my brother."

"Yet you expect me to sit quietly in my safe apartment in the city while you take all the risks?"

"If you were safe I'd be a damn sight less distracted," he muttered.

"Did you ever stop to think that *I* might feel the need to discover what happened to Dewolfe?" she asked. "If he was killed on Tremaine property and his death concealed, then, since I'm a Tremaine, I intend to uncover the truth. You say you're a Chippewa warrior? I say I'm a woman descended from Celtic warrior stock. We face this together, Hart."

In his heart he applauded her courage, knowing their spirits were truly linked. His mind, though, kept right on trying to figure out a way to keep her on the sidelines, away from danger.

Kendra meant every word she said while fervently wishing she felt as brave as she sounded. She'd never in her life, even in the city, confronted real danger. If she couldn't quite bring herself to believe in monsters, she did know something was dangerously wrong here on Tremaine land, her land. Was it Tola? What in

God's name was he? She couldn't turn her back and pretend everything was normal.

If Gregory was guilty—and she had to accept that he might be—he must be made to pay. If the wrongness involved more than Gregory or someone other than Gregory—Tola?—she'd do her best to find a way to conquer whatever it might be. Alongside Hart. Never mind that she was scared half to death before she'd even started.

CHAPTER TEN

When Kendra woke early Sunday morning, Hart was already gone from her room. She dressed for hiking, ate a hurried breakfast, got in her car and drove down the mountain. She'd gone only a mile or two when she saw Hart standing beside his pickup on the shoulder. He showed her where to pull her car off the road onto a barely visible track, and she parked it behind trees that concealed the car from passing motorists.

Sliding into his pickup, she leaned against the seat and smiled as he pulled back onto the mountain road. "I feel like a kid skipping school."

"Did you ever?"

Kendra shook her head. "And risk Aunt Meg's disapproval? Never. She was the only family I had. How about you?"

"I have a couple of aunts and uncles and lots of cousins. And, yes, Wolfe and I played hooky plenty of times." He smiled reminiscently. "That's the fun of having a twin—what trouble you don't think of to get into, the other one does." Gradually his smile faded. "I miss Wolfe. It's like a part of me is gone, never to be recovered. And yet sometimes I feel he's near me—the shadow you've seen once or twice."

She'd seen Dewolfe's ghost? His spirit? The thought made Kendra uneasy.

''Wolfe shows himself to you because he knows,'' Hart added.

''Knows what?''

''What's between us.''

What *was* between them? A few kisses, a shared goal and a tenuous bond that had drawn her to him from the first. Nothing more. Why was she so sure she loved him? Why did she feel that without Hart she'd never be whole?

''Under the circumstances I can't promise you anything,'' Hart said. ''I can't even be sure of keeping you safe. I wish I could.''

''No one can ever be sure of keeping another safe,'' she countered. ''It isn't like a gift you can give someone.'' Which reminded her of the topaz.

''When I was sorting through things in the south attic,'' she said, ''I found an old miniature portrait of a woman wearing a a topaz lavaliere on a heavy gold chain. Gregory says the topaz is a family heirloom my father had given to his first wife, Collis's mother. Gregory and Leda packed it away with her belongings after she died.

''He insisted on giving me the lavaliere, claiming the topaz belongs to me regardless of the codicil to Collis's will, because the lavaliere was a Tremaine possession and I'm the last of the Tremaines. I'm not so sure.''

''Does the jewel make you uncomfortable when you hold it in your hands?''

What an odd question, she thought. ''As I recall, the topaz felt warm. I don't remember any other feeling except admiration for its beauty.''

''Then keep it.''

"But the topaz is huge. Though I'm no expert, I know it must be worth thousands of dollars. Maybe even hundreds of thousands."

"The value isn't important. Have you worn the— What the devil is a lavaliere, anyway?"

"An old-fashioned name for a pendant. This is an old-fashioned piece of jewelry we're talking about. I haven't put it on yet."

"Do. Then see how you feel. You'll know after that whether to keep the topaz or to sell it. Either way, the jewel belongs to you. Morel was right about that. The estate belongs to you as well, but Morel doesn't intend you to have it. Somehow he maneuvered your brother into that restrictive codicil, quite possibly by playing on your brother's childhood jealousy of you."

She frowned. "I can see where he might profit if I don't remain in the house until Midsummer Day but, since I'm abiding by the terms of the codicil, what does Gregory have to gain?"

"Everything. If you don't survive, the entire estate is then his, as next of kin."

She stared at him, stricken.

"He doesn't intend you to survive," Hart continued. "Why do you think he refuses to tell you about Tola until it's too late? He loses nothing by offering you the topaz because he expects it to come back to him."

"I guess Gregory would be my next of kin," she said slowly. "There's no one else. But you're making him out to be a—a monster."

"In human form, yes. Why do you think I've been pleading with you to go back to the city? I've suspected him from the first."

Her mind roiled in confusion. "You mean you think he killed Dewolfe?"

"No, not directly. Quite likely Morel never so much as set eyes on my brother. But not all the monsters on Tremaine property are in human form. Don't forget Tola. I believe Mishibezo and Tola are one and the same. And I know that Tola and Morel make a formidable combination."

"Wait—don't jump to conclusions about real monsters. This has just now occurred to me and I'm still putting it together. Both Leda and Gregory admit someone named Tola does exist. He must be hidden somewhere—probably on the island. But does that automatically make him a monster? Isn't it more likely he's defective in some way—mentally or physically or both—and the Tremaines chose to keep him hidden rather than sending him off to an institution?"

"If this is true, why not tell you immediately?"

"Leda claimed my father and my brother should have told me about Tola. Since they didn't, she said she couldn't."

"Morel should have explained the situation as soon as you arrived. He didn't. Why does he insist he must wait until after Midsummer Eve? It sure as hell isn't because you don't inherit the estate free and clear until then. One way or another, Morel has never intended for you to inherit the estate."

Was Gregory as terrible as Hart believed him to be? She didn't trust Gregory, but it was difficult to accept Hart's bleak view of him. "I don't know what to think," she admitted.

Hart shot her a frustrated look but said nothing. They rode in silence until he abruptly swerved left onto a rutted, overgrown track. He drove about a hundred yards before coming to alder saplings growing across the track. He stopped and parked next to an ancient Jeep.

"Looks like we hike in from here," he said.

"Let's make a pact," she said. "No mention of your brother or anything to do with the Tremaines until we reach Yettman's cabin."

Looking at his scowl, she thought he meant to refuse, but after a moment he smiled and reached to give her a quick hug. "You're right. As you reminded me once before, we're alive, we're together and it's a beautiful day."

Once out of the truck, Kendra took a deep breath of mountain air. It *was* a beautiful day, the best kind, warm with a cool breeze. Her heart lifted and she flung her arms into the air and twirled around.

"Is that some kind of Celtic dance?" Hart asked.

"Only we of Celtic blood know the steps," she said with mock haughtiness.

"Is that so?" He grasped her hands and swung her around and around, circling the tiny clearing where the trucks were parked until she grew dizzy, as well as breathless from laughing. Clinging to him, she begged him to stop.

"I'm about to spin off the face of the earth," she protested.

"No," he said, pausing and drawing her to him, holding her as they swayed as though dancing to slow, sweet music no one else could hear. "No, we're not ready to spin away. Not yet. But we will. Soon. I promise."

A thrill trickled through her, settling low and deep inside. Hart released her and they stood gazing at one another, the glow in his dark eyes warming her more than the June sun.

"Very soon," he whispered, touching the curve of her upper lip with his forefinger.

Turning away, he strode back to the truck and removed a wicker basket. "Guess what I found stowed away in the garage," he said.

"It looks like— Can it really be an old-fashioned picnic hamper?"

"You win the grand prize, my Celtic beauty."

"And what might that be, O Prince of the Blood?"

Hart grinned. "The chance to share the contents of the hamper with me, plus a surprise bonus gift to be announced later. Now all we need is to find the perfect spot for a picnic."

"I'll help you search if you'll point out the trail."

They pushed through underbrush and saplings at first, climbing steadily, following a trail so obscure Kendra wasn't sure she could have kept to it without Hart in the lead.

They walked and walked until she finally asked, "Just how far is 'beyond,' anyway?"

"Not quite so far as 'beyond the back of nowhere,'" he assured her.

After what seemed hours to her, they came to a large stand of mature trees where the underbrush thinned and then disappeared. Soon the ground dipped down into a glen where a stream gurgled invitingly.

"I don't know what it says to you," she told him, "but that stream is telling me that its sole purpose in flowing past this particular spot is so I can take my shoes and socks off and plunge my aching feet in its wonderfully cool water."

"I hear the stream murmuring to me about that grassy clearing beyond its far bank."

"The picnic spot!"

He shook his head. "The *perfect* picnic spot."

Once they'd waded barefoot through the stream to the glade, Kendra decided it really was perfect. Pines circled a tiny clearing where a deadfall, its needleless branches angling across the glade, allowed just enough room to lay the red-and-white Hudson's Bay blanket Hart had brought over the new green grass.

He insisted she sit on the blanket while he arranged the contents of the hamper in front of her, saying, "He who brings the food calls the tune."

When he finished, he joined her on the blanket. Kendra picked up what looked like a tortilla, bit into it and was immediately surprised. Instead of the peppery Mexican concoction she'd expected to find inside, she tasted a mixture of corn, lima beans, and small pieces of meat she couldn't identify, subtly flavored.

"This is delicious, but what is it?" she asked.

"Absolutely authentic Native American."

"Chippewa?"

"Not exactly. I borrowed a little here and there from others of the blood."

"Ah, Nouvelle Native American Cuisine. What's the meat?"

"Venison. Here, have another."

An outcropping of rocks provided a backrest for them, and the soft murmur of the stream offered a musical accompaniment while they ate.

As he handed her a soft drink, he said, "I was tempted to bring a thermos of coffee, but recalling your unkind remarks about my lack of brewing talent, I refrained.''

She waved a half-eaten venison tortilla—her third—at him. "Any man who can put together something this good can learn to make a decent cup of coffee."

"Who'll teach me?"

"Well, I don't like to brag, but when I make coffee people always ask for a refill."

"How about a deal? You teach me to brew decent coffee and I'll share my secret recipe with you."

She licked a dollop of the tortilla mix from her forefinger and held out her hand. "Deal."

Instead of shaking her hand, he raised it and closed his lips around her forefinger. "Mmm, tasty," he murmured. "I think I'll try another."

A frisson of unexpected pleasure ran along Kendra's spine as he tasted her fingers one by one. No man had ever done such a thing to her before, and she'd never dreamed it would feel so erotic. But maybe that was because the man was Hart.

"If I don't stop now," he said, releasing her hand, "we'll not only never get to Yettman's, but I'll forget why we were going there in the first place."

Kendra sighed. He'd almost made her forget already. "You provided the food," she said, "so that means I'm the cleanup committee."

While she was packing the hamper, Hart climbed the rocky outcropping behind her. She was zipping the blanket back into its plastic carrying case when he called to her.

"Come and look!"

Still barefoot, she scrambled cautiously up the rocks to where he stood at the top. He pointed. At first she saw nothing more than another large cluster of rocks below a sheer cliff face. Then shading her eyes against the sun, she made out a dark shadow on the cliff just above the rocks.

"A cave!" she cried. "If we're going to explore it, I'd better put my shoes on."

"I think the cave might have been home to some of my long-ago ancestors," he said. "I'd like to take a closer look, but we'd better push on."

As they clambered back down to the picnic site, she said, "I didn't know the Chippewa ever lived in caves."

"Many of the early eastern Algonquin tribes did, and the Chippewa are of Algonquin stock. I'll be back to take another look at that cave when I get the chance."

Not wanting to spoil her lighthearted mood, she tried to put from her mind the reasons why he couldn't take the time now, but she failed. The picnic had been fun but it was only a brief interlude. The real reason for their excursion was to question the former Tremaine grounds keeper.

Leaving the blanket and hamper behind to be retrieved on their return, they hiked on and, as if in response to her shadowed thoughts, a cloud covered the sun.

Hart glanced at the sky and increased his pace. "The weatherman was right—there'll be some rain later. We'll try to beat it."

"Hey, I'm a city girl, remember?" she protested as she tried to keep up with him. "We might walk fast, but we don't walk fast far."

Luckily for her stamina, the cabin they were looking for turned out to be no more than a mile away.

A hound puppy raced to meet them, barking and wagging his tail.

A bewhiskered fortyish man stepped from behind a woodpile, shotgun in hand, though not aimed at them. Hart halted and so did she. The puppy ran up to Hart.

"He ain't got the watchdog idee yet," the man said, studying Hart as he patted the little brown-and-white hound. His gaze flickered over to her, then back to Hart. "I never did hold much truck with ghosts and like that, but if you're who I think you are, maybe I'd best start believing."

"I'm not Wolfe, I'm his twin," Hart said, giving the man his name. "This is Kendra. You're Pete Yettman, right?"

"Could be."

"Matty Cusick told me where you lived. I'd like to talk to you."

Pete Yettman nodded, laid the shotgun against the side of the woodpile and walked toward them. "How is old Matty?"

"He claims if it weren't for his knees getting so damn stiff, he could still outwalk you."

Yettman smiled. "That's Matty. Well, if we're going to natter, I reckon you might as well come sit on the porch." He clapped his hands at the pup. "Come here, Spot. Come here I say."

Spot took one last lick at Hart's hand before obeying. They settled themselves on the cabin's small porch, Kendra in the rocker, the two men in Adirondack chairs, the pup lying at his master's feet.

"You're the spitting image of your brother, headband and all," Yettman said.

"I'm wearing his headband," Hart said. "It's the only trace I've found of him. So far."

"I can guess why you're here." Yettman glanced at Kendra, then focused on Hart.

"I know you used to be the grounds keeper for the Tremaine estate," Hart said. "How well did you know my brother?" Hart asked.

Yettman shrugged. "Didn't know him at all, hardly. Saw him on the grounds, he asked me some things. Ordinarily I wouldn't've given him the time of day if that damn thing hadn't've got old Curly the week before. That dog and me'd been together ten years. Best dog I ever laid eyes on, Curly was."

"What got Curly?" Hart asked.

"That thing in the lake. Never saw it clear 'cause it was dark at the time. You ain't supposed to go ramming around those grounds at night, and I never did afore then." Yettman pulled a pipe and a nearly empty pouch of tobacco from the pocket of his red plaid shirt and began filling the pipe. "See this here, don't you? Like a fool I left my pipe on the chopping block outside the back door of the Tremaine house. Never missed it till after supper. My quarters was over the garage, as maybe you know. Night was dark as pitch, but I figured I'd take a chance on running over there and getting my pipe 'cause I sure did crave a smoke.

"I tried to keep old Curly from coming with me, but he slipped through the door. Anyway, I ran like hell and got the pipe okay. Was crossing the drive coming back when Curly started growling and whining at the same time. That old dog got in front of me—" Yettman blinked and his voice grew hoarse. "Never knew it at the time, but he was trying to protect me.

"I swear I didn't see the damn thing till it was looming over me and Curly. The dog went for its throat, and I took off for my quarters to get my shotgun and flashlight, but I was too late. Nothing to see but the trail where it dragged Curly's body to the lake."

"Did you ever find any other trace of the dog?" Hart asked.

Yettman shook his head. "I figure that thing ate him—fur, bones and all."

Kendra grimaced. Surely a human, no matter how grotesquely malformed in mind or body, wouldn't do such a horrible thing. But if Tola wasn't human, what was he?

"Mad as I was," Yettman continued, "I never said a word to Tremaine. Weren't no use—he'd warned me not to leave my quarters at night or to let the dog out. While I was worrying over whether to quit or not, your brother showed up and began asking me questions about the lake and the island. Like I said, he hit me at the right time—I told him about Curly.

"The next day Mrs. Morel comes to find me and says I'm to run a trespasser off the grounds right away. So I moseyed around till I saw your brother, told him what she said and asked him to leave. He didn't give me no trouble—climbed over that broken wall right away and took off on his motorcycle. But what he must've done was come back at night. Mind you, he already knew it was dangerous to be on the grounds after dark, 'cause of what happened to Curly.

"I ain't real clear on what happened that night 'cause I didn't get in on it till toward the end. I ain't no coward, but I wasn't willing to tangle with what got Curly, so I kept close to home come dark. I was sort of dozing when I hear a lot of commotion, shouting and yelling and some awful strange noises I didn't like at all down by the lake. Took me a while to decide I better take a look.

"I headed out with my shotgun. Didn't need no flashlight—the moon was pretty near full. When I got close, I see that lawyer fellow, Morel, running hell-bent for the lakeshore, yelling like a madman at Tremaine. 'Collis!' he shouts. 'Come back. Don't be an idiot, you can't control him. Not when he's feeding.' I can't see Tremaine, and he don't say nothing. All this time there's a lot of splashing and a sort of grunting that raises my hackles.

"When I finally can see the lake clear through the trees, all the ruckus has died down. Morel's dragging something out of the water to shore, and there's ripples, like something swimming toward the island. I know I ought to offer to help, but it's like I'm frozen where I am. Then I get a look at what Morel's brought to shore and bang, up comes my supper.

"I can gut deer and skin rabbits—nothing like that bothers me. But this weren't no animal. I ain't going into no more detail, but it was what was left of Tremaine."

Kendra covered her mouth with her hand.

"Sorry, miss, I didn't mean to upset you," Yettman said. Turning to Hart, he added, "What I figure happened was Tremaine tried to stop the thing from killing your brother and got hisself killed, too. Anyway, I quit the next morning. Afore I left, though, I took a gander at where your brother used to hide his bike outside the wall, and there it was.

"Didn't like to take the bike straight off, in case I was wrong about what happened to him, so I went over to Matty's and stayed a couple days with him afore I snuck back to check on that bike. It was still there—hadn't been touched. So then I knew. I got the bike here in back of the cabin and the stuff he left with it. Didn't figure I was stealing the bike—more like I was keeping it safe in case somebody came after it sometime." He shrugged. "'Course, if no one had, I reckon the bike would've been mine."

"Show me," Hart said tersely.

Still dazed by the horror of Yettman's story, Kendra remained on the porch when the two men left, the pup trailing them. Poor Collis—what a ghastly fate. Evidently he'd tried to save Dewolfe, thinking he could reason with Tola, or control Tola in some way. As he apparently had done in the past, according to what he'd scrawled in the diary. He'd misjudged, and his failure had cost him his life. She hugged herself, mindlessly rocking back and forth in the rocker. Whatever Tola was, he was dangerous.

When Hart returned, he carried a small backpack. "Wolfe's things," he said. "Nothing in them that sheds any light on what happened."

"That's mighty big of you letting me keep the bike," Yettman said to Hart.

"I'll send you the papers when I get the registration straightened out," Hart told him.

"I surely do thank you." Yettman turned to Kendra. "You still look a mite peaked, miss. Sorry you had to hear what you did."

"It's always best to know the truth." She held out her hand and, after a moment, Yettman shook it. "Thank you," she told him.

"Be glad to offer you folks some coffee and a bite to eat," Yettman said, glancing up at the gray clouds overhead. "Weather looks pretty chancy."

"We'll try to beat the storm," Hart said.

The pup ran after them when they left, and they had to stop and wait until Yettman coaxed it back. Hart then set such a rapid pace that Kendra soon found herself gasping for breath. She'd thought she was in fair shape, but evidently not for mountain hikes.

The sky grew ever darker. Lightning zigzagged and thunder rumbled. Though distant at first, each bolt and boom seemed closer, until at last the rain began, a patter at first, then a slashing, drenching downpour. Fighting her way through the storm took all her concentration, wiping the horrors Yettman had told them from her mind.

Hart backtracked and grabbed her hand, saying, "We'll make for the cave."

Completely disoriented in the storm's fury and darkness, she kept a tight grip on his hand. How he could tell the right way to go was a mystery to her. By the time he pulled her up and into the cave, they were both soaked to the skin. Her hair was plastered to her head and across her face and her dripping wet clothes clung to her, unpleasantly clammy.

Though she wondered how he could possibly have found them, before reaching the cave Hart had managed to retrieve the hamper and the blanket, still zipped in its plastic carrying case. "Welcome to my ancestors' home," he told her, gesturing around the cave.

They didn't have to enter through a maw, as this cave was open on three sides, really more like a deep overhang than an into-the-side-of-a-mountain cave. Though the cave was large enough, the overhead rock didn't provide much headroom—Hart couldn't stand upright.

Kendra pushed her wet hair from her face, wringing the water from it as she watched him drop to his knees and carefully unzip the plastic holder.

"Dry!" he said triumphantly, lifting out the blanket. He looked up at her and smiled. "As host, I'm happy to be able to offer you the finest accommodations," he said, "but you'll have to strip to take advantage of my offer."

CHAPTER ELEVEN

Hart watched Kendra slide off her denim jacket, but she turned her back to him before tugging off her wet jeans and T-shirt. By the time he'd finished stripping, she had wrapped herself in the red blanket and stood staring at him. He freed one edge and pulled the warmth of the dry blanket around both of them.

Discovering she was shivering, he put an arm around her, drawing her closer against him, and she laid her head on his chest. He wanted this woman with a hunger that transcended any desire he'd ever known, and yet he also felt a protective tenderness toward her. How did *she* feel? Did the same burning need simmer inside her, a need threatening to boil out of control? Or was she so chilled and tired that she merely wanted to rest in his warm embrace?

"C-can we s-sit d-down?" she asked through chattering teeth.

Attempting to ease onto the rock floor while still wrapped in the blanket, they tried to coordinate their movements and failed. Hart found himself flat on his back with Kendra sprawled across his chest. She wore nothing but her panties, and the soft pressure of her bare breasts against his chest aroused him almost beyond reason.

"You feel so good," he murmured, shifting her until they lay facing one another, his arms around her.

"Does that mean 'soon' has arrived, like you promised?" she whispered, her breath warm and sweet against his lips. "Personally, I think it's one of the longest soons I've ever waited for."

He touched her lips with the tip of his tongue, tracing their enticing curves. She sighed, her lips parting as she edged closer. Accepting the invitation, he kissed her long and hard and deeply, his hands molding her to him.

Her fingers caressed his nape, threading into his hair, then hesitating. After a moment he realized she'd encountered the headband. Freeing one hand, he reached up and pulled off the band. He'd vowed to wear the headband until he'd avenged his brother, but Wolfe, he knew, would understand why he removed it to make love with Kendra.

"I knew I wanted you as soon as we met," he whispered into her ear. "Then I discovered what I really wanted became much more. I'm just beginning to realize *how* much more."

"More..." she murmured.

He wasn't certain whether she was agreeing with him or asking for more. Either or both suited him. As far as he was concerned, this was only the beginning of their being together. If he had anything to do with it, there'd always be more.

She moaned as he cupped her breasts, turning onto her back and arching into him while he caressed her nipples, first with his thumbs, then with his lips and tongue. He longed to taste every inch of her beautiful body and had eased her panties off and begun his journey when her seeking fingers closed around him, making him groan in anguished need.

"Now," she whispered against his lips.

He rose above her and she guided him into her moist heat. Though he'd meant to take it slow and easy, her ardent response melted his resolve, making him plunge deep within her.

She called his name over and over in a rising crescendo that stoked his passion, as together they found the thrusting, fiery rhythm of life.

Her cry of release tipped him over the edge. Locked in each other's arms, they floated slowly back into reality. He didn't want to let her go, he wouldn't let her go, but eventually enough reason returned so he remembered the hard rock bed beneath her. Holding her close, he flipped over so she lay on top of him.

"Now it's your turn," he murmured.

She raised her head to look at him. "You mean you're not satisfied?"

"I'll never be satisfied, not where you're concerned."

She was silent for a few moments before asking, "Do you suppose they approve?"

"Who?"

"Your cave-dwelling ancestors. After all, I'm the enemy."

"Not *my* enemy." He ran a caressing hand over the sweet curve of her hip. "And certainly more than a friend." *My love,* was on his lips, but he held the words back, suddenly apprehensive, as though saying them aloud might jeopardize their truth.

"You shivered," she said. "Are you cold?"

He pushed away his sense of foreboding. They were safe for now, safe here in the cave. But the storm had almost passed, the rain was lessening. Within an hour the sun would be shining and they'd have no excuse to linger in the cave. His arms tightened around her, an almost desperate need adding urgency to his kiss.

When Hart kissed her, the swift heat of desire sizzling through her surprised Kendra. He'd taken her to such heights, she hadn't expected to feel such a driving need—at least, not so quickly. She rubbed her breasts against his chest, savoring the wonder of his skin against hers, murmuring in pleasure as she felt him stir within her.

"Never," he whispered against her lips. "I'll never get enough of you."

His words, the incredibly erotic feel of him inside her, blanked her mind, shutting out everything else. She pushed herself up until she sat astride him and, eyes closed, began a sensual rocking that made him groan and raise his hips.

And then he rolled her over, thrusting hard and fast. She matched his frenzy, sparks of pleasure shooting through her, igniting a deep explosion that flung her out of control and into an ecstatic release.

He cried out, clutching her to him, with her all the way.

When they lay spent, still holding one another, a strange sensation stole over her. Though they were no longer united flesh to flesh, she felt linked to Hart, a part of him. In the same way, he was a part of her.

"Woman of my spirit," he said softly.

She sighed, so deeply moved she couldn't speak.

The hike back to the road and the ride up the mountain to where she'd left her car were anticlimactic in every sense of the word. Uncomfortable in her soggy clothes, depressed at having to return to the house and fearful of what might happen there, Kendra sank into gloom. Wonderful as their time together had been, it was over, at least for the near future.

She glanced at Hart, wondering how he felt, and found him looking at her.

"I think you should leave before tomorrow night." Anger tinged his voice. "You don't want the estate, anyway—give up the idea of immediate possession. What the hell good is it going to do you if you're dead?"

She clenched her hands together in her lap. "I gave you my terms. We still have time before dark to pack and drive down the mountain together, never to return."

"You know I can't make that promise."

"Then the discussion is over."

"Don't be a fool! If you—"

She glared at him. "I *said* I didn't want to hear any more about it. Not unless you change your mind."

He muttered something about stubborn females that she ignored and they rode in silence.

"You heard Yettman," he said after a time. "Tola's no simpleminded member of the family being kept hidden. He's a monster, a monster who killed both our brothers. Killed and ate Wolfe, if Yettman's correct. And very likely killed and ate Patrice, as well."

Kendra swallowed convulsively, tasting bile. "Gregory might have been telling the truth about seeing her safely off the grounds."

Hart's grunt managed to indicate both disgust and disbelief. "Morel lied to you about your brother's death. He wasn't killed by falling rocks—he was killed by Tola. If he never saw him face-to-face, Morel may not realize the trespasser Tola killed was my brother, but, from Yettman's account, Morel certainly knew the man died. Why does he continue to conceal this murderous monster?"

She shook her head, chilled to the very marrow of her bones by his words.

"The steel trapdoor in the cellar indicates Morel and his mother are determined to keep Tola out of the house," Hart said. "They even lock the cellar door."

Kendra drew in her breath. "That reminds me. Gregory asked me to put back the brass key to the vault door. I forgot."

"You mean you kept that key?"

"I think so. I'll have to search for it in my room. It's not the only one—he has another."

"Keep the key. It'll give you some control."

She nodded in understanding. Possession of the key meant she could do her best to make certain the door to the vaults was kept locked.

But something he'd said about Leda troubled her. "Do you think Leda is aware Tola killed my brother?"

Hart shrugged. "I suspect she does. And I'm certain she knows Tola killed Wolfe. It explains her fainting when she saw what she thought was a dead man's ghost coming out of the cellar."

"Yet I do believe Leda likes me and is worried about me," Kendra said musingly. "Maybe she wrote that anonymous warning note." Something else occurred to her. "Wolfe's headband. If Collis died when Wolfe did, he couldn't have hidden the headband. And Gregory would surely have destroyed it if he'd found it. That leaves Leda. She must have found the headband and hidden it in Collis's closet. I wonder why."

"Who knows? I can't fathom Mrs. Morel's motives. But you're probably right in thinking she left you the note. I wish you'd take her excellent advice and leave while you can."

"Let's not begin another argument."

Hart didn't reply. Almost immediately he pulled off the road, and she realized they'd arrived at the place where she'd left her car.

He parked and walked with her to the car. As she was about to slide under the steering wheel, he held her back, kissing her quickly. "I couldn't bear to lose you," he said as he released her.

The warmth of his kiss and his words lasted until she reached the gates. Pausing, she activated the opener. Was she imagining things or did the gargoyles decorating the barred iron actually leer menacingly at her as she drove through?

When she entered the house, Leda popped out of Gregory's office. "Gregory told me I was wrong, but I thought maybe you might not be coming back," she said. "He had to leave for Albany. His case is first on the court docket tomorrow morning."

"Why did you think I—?" Kendra began but was interrupted by Leda's gasp.

"Goodness, you're soaking wet!" Leda exclaimed. "You must have gotten caught in the storm. You'd best take a nice hot shower and put on dry clothes right away." She gestured toward the stairs. "Go on, now. Hurry before you catch cold."

When Kendra came downstairs in dry jeans and a sweatshirt after her showering, she found Leda in the kitchen.

"I've made you some nice hot cocoa," Leda said. "My mother always believed hot cocoa was the best way to ward off a cold."

Kendra thanked her and sat on a stool to sip the cocoa.

"I thought you and I could have soup and a sandwich for our evening meal," Leda went on. "There's a bit of baked ham left, and I used the bone to make pea soup."

"I'll make the sandwiches while you heat the soup," Kendra told her, expecting to have to override Leda's protest. But the old woman merely nodded.

Kendra was cutting slices of rye bread when she heard the back door open. She paused, knife in hand, letting her breath out in a sigh of relief when Hart appeared. Since Gregory's gone, who else could it be? she chided herself.

"I noticed Mr. Morel's car wasn't in the garage," he said. "When will he be back?"

"He said before sunset tomorrow." Leda, standing by the stove, stirring the pot of soup, didn't look at him as she replied.

"Did he leave any instructions for me?"

"No, he did not." Leda spoke dismissively.

"In that case—"

"Can we offer you a bowl of soup and a sandwich?" Kendra put in. Leda might wish to be rid of Hart, but she felt far safer with him in the house.

Hart smiled at her. "Did I ever tell you that feeding me's the way to my heart?"

She slanted her eyes at him. "The only way?"

Leda turned, giving them each a sharp glance.

Oh, great, Kendra thought ruefully. If she didn't before, now she certainly suspects there's something between Hart and me, and she'll be watching us.

"Maybe you could take a look at the front door after you eat," Kendra said to Hart, improvising hastily to give him a chance to go upstairs while she kept Leda busy in the kitchen. "Gregory mentioned he was going to have you lubricate the night bolt because it was becoming difficult to slide open."

"We must be certain all the doors are locked and bolted tonight," Leda said.

"I'll double-check them," Kendra promised.

"Yours, too, young man." Though Leda addressed Hart, she didn't look directly at him.

"I fully intend to sleep behind locked doors tonight," he assured her.

Leda raised no objection when Kendra set three places at the kitchen table. Though the pea soup was hot and delicious, the atmosphere during the meal was cool and forbidding. Kendra poured the after-supper coffee with a sense of relief that supper would soon be over.

She noticed with dismay how Leda's hands shook when she lifted her cup to sip the coffee. And didn't her lips have a bluish tinge?

"I want you to rest," she told Leda firmly. "Hart and I will clean up."

"He can't be out after dark," Leda said.

"I won't be, ma'am," Hart replied.

Leda sighed. "I tire so quickly these days. And lose my breath, too. It's getting so I hate to face climbing the stairs."

"I'd be glad to lend you a hand," Hart said.

She shook her head. "I'll manage on my own, thank you." Even the tartness in her voice seemed weaker to Kendra. "I do think I will retire early, though. Kendra, you be careful to lock up after he leaves."

Leda rose from her chair and walked slowly to the back stairs. Before reaching them, she paused and turned. "Don't worry about any noise you might hear during the night. We're safe enough."

"Noise?" Kendra asked, suddenly tense.

"From falling rocks. Because of the storm. Gregory thinks storms bring on rock falls in those underground caverns."

Not certain she believed in the rockfalls, but unwilling to upset the ailing Leda by saying so, Kendra didn't reply directly. "Why don't you let me make breakfast in the morning?" she asked. "You deserve to sleep in now and then."

"I'll be myself after a night's rest," Leda insisted. But her tread as she climbed the steps was slow and uncertain.

"She looks ready to keel over," Hart said in a low tone.

"I know. But she insists on making the meals. I can't lock her in her room to make her stay there. Come on, let's get the dishes done."

As Hart carried the dirty dishes to the sink, he said, "Any truth to the stiff bolt?"

"Actually Gregory did mention it, but not as a task for you—I made that part up in case you needed an excuse to seem to be leaving by the front door."

He nodded. "Mrs. Morel might be old and frail but she's not stupid. She felt the vibes between us." As Kendra ran water into the dishpan, he came up behind her and wrapped his arms around her, hugging her against him for a long, delicious moment.

When he let her go, Kendra felt abandoned, though he was no more than a few feet away. Yet she knew she couldn't spend the night in his arms. Not in this house.

"Tainted," she said.

He nodded, aware, without her telling him, what she meant. "I agree. Not that sleeping in the same room with you without sharing your bed is my idea of a night to remember," he said.

"We might risk one chaste good-night kiss."

"When have I ever given you a kiss that was even remotely chaste?"

She smiled, warmed by remembering. "How about a good-night handshake?"

"We might risk that."

As she squeezed detergent into the dishwater, Kendra wished she and Hart were somewhere else, anywhere else, cozily doing the dishes together before going to their bedroom, a bedroom where they'd feel free to make love.

"Before I forget," Hart said, reaching into his pocket, "I'd prefer you kept this." She glanced sideways and saw he was holding Patrice's double-heart gold pendant.

"My hands are wet," she said, masking her reluctance to touch the hearts. "Put it on the sill for now—" she nodded toward the window over the sink "—and I'll take it when I finish."

The pendant reminded her of the frightening scene she'd watched from her window the night Patrice disappeared. Much as she wanted to believe Gregory had seen Patrice safely through the gates, she'd been forced to admit to herself that his explanation didn't match what she'd seen from her bedroom.

Even if she couldn't quite accept Hart's theory that Gregory didn't mean her to survive tomorrow night, she still knew she couldn't trust Gregory.

"I'm glad he's not here," she said aloud.

"Morel?" Hart said. "Yes, it fits my plans."

"What plans?"

"I won't have to worry about him chasing me out of your room in the middle of the night."

She gazed at him suspiciously. "I don't think that worries you much. Are you hiding something from me?" A horrible thought flashed into her mind. "You can't be thinking of going into the vaults and opening that steel trapdoor!"

"Relax. I've no intention of touching the steel door. Even if I was crazy enough to risk opening it, the kitchen door to the cellar is locked, and I don't have a key."

Kendra bit her lip. She kept forgetting. "I promise I'll try to find the key. But if I do, I'm keeping it."

He put a hand over his heart, his expression exaggeratedly wounded. "You don't trust me!"

"Let's say I can't quite conquer my suspicion you're up to something you don't want to tell me about. Which means it's dangerous. I'm warning you, I'd better not wake up in the middle of the night and discover you've crept out on some perilous mission. If that's what you have in mind, you may as well take me with you right from the start, because I'll come looking for you, anyway."

"Perilous mission," he echoed, grinning. "That has quite a ring to it—straight out of a CIA thriller. But I don't plan to embark on any missions in the middle of the night, perilous or otherwise. Honest."

Later, in her bedroom, Hart unrolled his sleeping bag. Kendra, barefoot, in jeans and a T-shirt, rummaged in the closet, going through all her pockets, finally unearthing the brass key in the pocket of the knit dress she'd worn the night they investigated the vaults.

She set the key on her vanity table beside the velvet jewel box containing the topaz.

A Tremaine jewel, one her mother had never owned and probably had never seen. Why, then, did she have the strange sensation that her mother hovered near her now?

On impulse, she opened the jewel box and fastened the lavaliere around her neck, staring at herself in the mirror, entranced by the beauty of the stone and feeling, oddly enough, that her mother approved of her wearing it.

She was startled when Hart's mirror image, naked to the waist, appeared behind hers. Seeing him drove everything else from her mind.

He reached around to touch the gem lying between her breasts. "Nice resting place," he murmured. "Are you turned off or on?"

"On. But now I can't tell whether by the jewel or by you." She reached to unfasten the clasp.

"Let me."

His fingers brushed her nape as he undid the chain, and she closed her eyes briefly, savoring his touch. As he leaned over to lay the lavaliere into its box, she rested her cheek against his arm, murmuring his name.

Gripping her shoulders, he urged her up from the stool, turning her into his arms. His lips came down on hers. His taste was more potent than any wine, and she found his masculine scent such a powerful aphrodisiac that her surroundings began to blur and fade as she gave herself up to the passion only he could evoke.

This was the wrong place, and yet she wanted so desperately to continue making love with him, wanted to feel once again the thrill of his caresses, wanted to be held in his arms all night long.

"I must have been mad to think I could be with you and not touch you," he whispered against her lips. "Tell me to stop."

How could she? Her fingers traveled up from his nape to tangle in his hair and bring his mouth to hers once again. She touched the headband, Wolfe's headband, and jerked her hand away, reminded of the surroundings she'd momentarily forgotten.

"We can't," she lamented, pulling free.

As she watched Hart sigh and run his fingers over the beaded band, her regret suddenly vanished, erased by something that continued to puzzle her.

"I still can't understand why Leda would have saved the headband. Doesn't it strike you as odd?"

"I'm not sure. My guess is she was and is powerless to stop what's going on here, but the killings trouble her. Perhaps because she was unable to save Wolfe, she couldn't bring herself to get rid of the only thing left of him. She must have been afraid that if her son found it, he'd dispose of the headband, so she hid it. I feel Leda's the key to all that's wrong here, that she knows the answers, but—" he paused and turned up his hands "—she's an old, sick woman. Did you notice how blue her lips were at supper? I'm afraid if we put any pressure on her to tell us, she might have a fatal heart attack."

"We mustn't cause her harm," Kendra agreed.

"So we're no further ahead." He reached for her hand, grasped it firmly in his and shook it. "Good night. I'm heading for the sleeping bag before I lose both my resolve and my good intentions."

Kendra smiled wanly as she echoed his good-night. He was right, she knew. She didn't have to like it, though. Since her oversize T-shirt was comfortable for sleeping, she pulled off her jeans, crawled under the covers and flicked off the bedside lamp. A sliver of moonlight slanting through a gap in the curtains gave the room a pale, eerie glow.

"Will-o'-the-wisp," Hart said after a time.

She realized he was commenting on the moonlight and said, "I'm almost positive that's *not* what I saw the night Patrice vanished."

"It wasn't, even though those flickering phosphorescent lights do exist. Among my people it's called the bearwalk, because a will-o'-the-wisp means a man is walking the night in the guise of a bear—a shapeshifter, in other words. Since only men with powerful medicine can change their shapes, it's dangerous, and often fatal, for an ordinary person to get close to such power. At best, to see a bearwalker is a bad omen."

After a moment, she asked, "Do you believe in bearwalkers?"

"Two months ago, I might have said no. Even after I first arrived here, knowing Wolfe was dead, I might have hedged. Since then I've come to realize that bearwalkers might well exist—as well as many other things taught to me as a child that my adult self dismissed as superstitions."

Feeling a sudden chill, she pulled the covers closer around her.

"Wolfe was always more of a mystic than I, more interested in Grandfather's teachings. He was drawn to the mythology of other peoples because of his fascination with the beliefs of his own. He stayed in Michigan and regularly visited the place where we'd been raised. On the other hand, I deliberately studied science to counter what I learned as a child, and not only moved far away, but stayed away from the reservation.

"The last time I saw Grandfather, he related a vision dream concerning my brother and me, a dream where he saw our spirit animals, mine the deer, my brother's the wolf, meet beside a woodland lake under a full moon.

"A white owl, perched in a nearby pine, called to them, saying, 'Tonight, because you have come to this lake, I will show how each of you will die.' The deer and wolf, knowing the owl is a death-bringer, believed he could do what he said. Nevertheless, they defied him.

"'My brother will save me from death,' the wolf said.

"'Once but not twice,' the owl agreed.

"'I will die saving my brother,' the deer said.

"'You will not die the first time you save him,' the owl told him. 'The second time you cannot save him, though he will try to save you.' He flapped his wings and flew silently into the night.

"The deer and the wolf laughed, for they were young and not afraid of death. As one, they bent to drink from the lake, but before their tongues touched the water, the moon slid behind a cloud, plunging the world into menacing darkness. The waters of the lake churned violently, causing the deer and the wolf to draw back, startled and afraid.

"And when the moon next appeared, only one remained."

CHAPTER TWELVE

Kendra waited for Hart to go on, to tell her who was left beside the lake in his grandfather's dream. When he didn't, she asked, "Was it the deer or the wolf?"

"Neither," Hart replied. "Grandfather saw himself. But instead of the cool waters of a woodland lake, he stood beside the flaming lake that lies halfway along the path to the Land of Spirits, the lake that burns the evil from each passing spirit so only what is good goes on. His vision showed his own death was near. It was a true dream—I never saw him again."

Having no idea what to say, she remained silent.

"I did save Wolfe's life once," Hart said after a time. "And I did fail the second time. The lake is—" He stopped.

Is Lynx Lake, she said to herself. More impressed by the eerie similarities than she wanted to be, Kendra tried for a lighter touch. "I've never seen a white owl outside of a zoo," she told him.

"They're not that uncommon—you have a white owl on the grounds. I'm surprised you've never heard him hooting. If you like, I'll show you the pine he roosts in."

Owls, she knew, hunted at night. Imagining the bird, great white wings outstretched, floating silently overhead like one of the pitiful wraiths in her own frightening dream, Kendra shuddered. "No, thanks. I'll take your word that he's there."

She wished Hart wasn't across the room from her, lying on his sleeping bag. She wanted him next to her in her bed. She needed the comfort of his warm presence. If only—

The first clang froze her, the second thrust her bolt upright. "Hart!" she cried, as the clanging grew frenzied. "Tola's trying to get out!"

"He can't." Hart spoke as he crossed the room to her. Sitting on the bed, he said soothingly, "Whatever he is, he won't get past that steel trapdoor. Remember what the workman who installed the door said—not even an elephant could get through."

Comforted by the remainder, Kendra reached for his hand and gripped it. "Leda knew he'd try," she said. "That's why she mentioned the falling rocks."

"Yes." He eased her down, tucking her in. Lying on top of the covers, he smoothed her hair. "There's nothing we can do but wait out the noise."

Reassured by his words and more by his nearness, she let out her breath in a long sigh. But when the clanging ceased abruptly, the renewed silence, rather than a relief, seemed strangely ominous. Even with Hart's hand against her cheek, it took a long time before she finally drifted off to sleep.

When she woke in the early morning, she saw Hart, fully clothed, standing by her dresser with the brass key in his hand.

"I thought I'd check the cellar before I leave," he said. "If everything's all right, as I expect it will be, I won't come back upstairs. I'll just leave the key in that blue vase in the entry on my way out the front door."

He bent, kissed her quickly and left while she was still forming her protest.

Go down into the vaults? She grimaced. Safe or not, she hoped she never had to descend those stone stairs again. Rising, she opened her bedroom door and stood waiting and listening. Not until she heard the front door open and close, assuring her Hart hadn't come to any harm, did she relax.

She showered before dressing in new black jeans and a bright yellow T-shirt, but, even though she didn't hurry, Leda was not in the kitchen when she came downstairs. Still, it *was* early. Kendra ate a quick breakfast, all the while watching for Leda, who didn't appear. Was she all right? Knowing the old woman would resent being checked on, Kendra decided to mask her intentions by taking a breakfast tray up to Leda—nothing fancy, just coffee and toast.

Leda's voice, when she knocked at her door, sounded normal enough. As soon as she noticed the tray, she said, tart as ever, "I don't need to be pampered!"

Nevertheless, though she was sitting up, she hadn't yet gotten out of bed and her lips still had a bluish tinge.

"Everyone should be treated to breakfast in bed once in a while," Kendra said firmly. "It's one of those little luxuries that makes life worth living." Paying no attention to Leda's muttering, she arranged the tray—an old wicker bed tray that she'd found in the pantry—in front of the old woman.

"I've already eaten, and Gregory's not here," she told Leda, "so there's no reason you can't take it easy this morning. Or the rest of the day, for that matter."

Leda frowned but took a sip of coffee. "I didn't sleep too well," she admitted.

"I'm not surprised, what with all that clanging. And please don't tell me I heard rocks falling."

"Gregory says rockfalls cause the noise, and I do not dispute what my son insists is true."

Maybe you should, was on the tip of Kendra's tongue, but she held the words back. "I'll plan the evening meal," she said instead.

"You don't need to," Leda informed her. "I'll be coming down a little later." She sat up straighter. "I may feel slightly indisposed but I'm not in my grave yet, you know."

"Oh course not. I'll see you later, then." Kendra paused at the door when Leda called her name.

"Gregory says you have the Tremaine topaz," Leda said.

"Yes, I do."

"Wear it today. And tonight."

Glancing down at her informal garb, Kendra asked, "Dressed like this?"

Leda waved her hand impatiently. "Your clothes don't matter. Think of it as humoring a slightly addled old woman. Will you wear the topaz for me?"

"If you want me to, naturally I will."

"Thank you, my dear. You've been very good to me, little as I deserve it."

Impulsively, Kendra returned to the bed, leaned down and kissed Leda on the forehead before leaving.

Stopping in her own room, she removed the lavaliere from the jewel case and fastened its thick gold chain around her neck, then shook her head at the image of the shimmering golden topaz against the prosaic background of her cotton T-shirt. Recalling how she'd imagined that her mother approved of her wearing the jewel, she smiled. At the same time, she realized that the noticeable weight of the lavaliere, rather than annoying her, felt strangely comforting.

Once more downstairs, she resisted her impulse to go outside and look for Hart. She certainly didn't want him to feel she was trailing him like that hound puppy had yesterday. Resolutely entering the kitchen, she began sorting through the contents of the pantry and the freezer while trying to decide what to serve for the evening meal.

Finding a hefty chunk of already-cooked pot roast in the freezer, she decided to thaw it out for hot roast-beef sandwiches. As she removed the remnants of the roast, she remembered the other, larger freezer in the storeroom and what Patrice had said about the contents. Setting the roast on the counter, she entered the storeroom to see for herself what was inside.

She discovered a sheet of black plastic covering the contents, exactly as Patrice had described. She folded back the plastic and stared at an unwrapped side of beef halfway down, the topmost item. She remembered Patrice saying the freezer was full to the brim. Not any longer. Telling herself not to be alarmed by what it might mean, she replaced the plastic, closed the freezer and left the storeroom.

After pouring herself a cup of none-too-warm leftover coffee, she sat on a stool in the kitchen sipping it while she tried to make sense of what she'd seen, at last, making up her mind that if Leda seemed improved when she finally came downstairs, she was going to have to answer a few questions.

Kendra wandered into the dining room and noticed that the pink roses in the dolphin vase decorating the dining room table had shed most of their petals. It was past time to pick fresh flowers. Once in the garden, secateurs in hand, she hesitated at a bush of crimson buds but shook her head and walked on. White? No, not white. At last she paused by a pale yellow bush, snipping off buds that promised to open into full, beautiful blooms.

She heard Leda's slow footsteps descending the back stairs while she was arranging the roses in the vase at the kitchen sink.

"Oh, no," Leda said when she came into the kitchen. "The roses should be white. We always pick white roses for Midsummer Eve."

Kendra continued to arrange her roses, saying mildly, "I prefer yellow. In any case, what does it matter?"

"Gregory will be displeased."

"At the moment he's not here to be displeased. If he decides to dash out and cut white roses when he returns, that's his privilege. I've chosen yellow." Kendra lifted the vase from the counter and marched toward the dining room, determined not to be swayed.

It was more than a whim—she didn't want a single white rose in the house, didn't want to be reminded of her unpleasant dream about the lost brides. She'd just set the vase on the dining room table and was contemplating her arrangement when she heard Leda give a strangled scream.

Rushing back, she saw Leda, her face drained of color, clutching at the edges of the kitchen sink. Hurrying to her, Kendra put an arm around the old woman, supporting her.

"That—" Leda raised a trembling finger and pointed to the window sill over the sink. "That belongs to Patrice."

Glancing at the sill, Kendra saw the double heart where she'd absentmindedly left it last night after Hart had given the entwined hearts to her. She picked it up with her free hand. "Yes, this is Patrice's," she said. "Hart and I found it near the pines."

Leda turned to her, tears swimming in her eyes. "He told me he'd seen her out the gate," she whispered.

She meant Gregory, not Hart, Kendra realized.

"He told me someone was waiting to give her a ride," Leda went on. She gripped Kendra's arm. "The chain—did you find the chain?"

"No. Just the double heart."

Leda's face crumpled, her weight sagging against Kendra. Alarmed, Kendra half dragged, half carried her to the nearest couch, a setee in a small room off the dining room, referred to as the morning room. Easing Leda onto the setee, Kendra knelt beside her. Alarmed by her bluish color and the way she gasped for breath, Kendra began to unbutton the old woman's high-necked dress.

"No," Leda mumbled, lifting a shaking hand to stop her. "Don't."

Deciding that to go against Leda's wishes would do more harm than the good that might come of loosening the tightness around her neck, Kendra obeyed.

"Apron pocket," Leda said.

After a moment, Kendra understood what Leda wanted and reached into the pocket of the old woman's apron, removing a small brown medicine bottle. Nitroglycerin. Unscrewing the lid, she fumbled out an incredibly tiny pill and put it to Leda's lips.

"Do you need water?" she asked.

Leda shook her head. "Under tongue. For heart."

After long minutes that seemed to stretch into hours, Leda's skin began to look less blue, and she breathed easier. "Help me upstairs to bed," she said in a nearly normal voice.

"Don't you think you should rest right here a little longer?" Kendra asked apprehensively. "At least until after I call your doctor."

"No doctor!" It was a command. "The pill is working. I'm better."

It was true that she did look and act improved.

"I've had this condition a long time," Leda said. "I know what to do. Just give me a hand up the stairs to bed so I can rest."

Reluctantly, hoping she was doing the right thing by allowing Leda to move, Kendra helped her to sit and then stand. When the old woman didn't collapse in her arms, she breathed a sigh of relief. Maybe Leda did know what she was talking about.

The journey up the stairs was slow, as much because Kendra was afraid to hurry as from Leda's weakness. After she pulled down the covers and eased the old woman onto her bed, Kendra once again tried to open the tight collar of Leda's dress. She got her hand slapped for her effort.

"I prefer to undress myself," Leda snapped. "Thank you for helping me upstairs, but I don't need any more assistance."

"I don't like to leave you alone," Kendra demurred.

"Very well then, you'll find a silver dinner bell in a compartment of the dining room sideboard. Fetch the bell and I'll ring it if I need you."

By the time Kendra returned with the bell, Leda had changed into her nightgown and propped herself up against the pillows. The gown's neck was not especially low, but for some reason she'd wound a white silk scarf around her throat so that no skin was visible. It was difficult for Kendra to imagine anyone being so modest.

"Put the bell on the nightstand and leave my door open. If I ring, I assure you the sound can be heard very clearly downstairs. Ring it and you'll see."

Kendra obeyed, producing clear, high notes that she could well believe carried far.

"So you see it's perfectly safe to leave me by myself, which I much prefer," Leda said, flapping her hands in a shooing motion.

Feeling more comfortable about Leda being alone now that she had a method to summon help, Kendra nodded. "I'll look in on you around eleven," she said. "Are you sure you don't want me to call your doctor?"

"Must I say everything twice? No doctor."

"All right, not unless you get worse," Kendra temporized. "I do hope Gregory won't be—"

"My son is well aware of my heart problem and he knows I am capable of judging my own condition. He won't fault you for doing as I ask. Please stop dithering about in my room and let me rest."

It wasn't until she'd gone downstairs that Kendra remembered what had caused Leda's collapse. Seeing Patrice's entwined hearts on the window sill. Going over in her mind what the old woman had said, she realized that the sight of the hearts had made Leda doubt her son's story. More than that, Kendra felt it had convinced Leda that something terrible had happened to Patrice.

* * *

Hart, wearing jeans in lieu of a breechclout—he didn't own one—slipped on his moccasins. Carrying the knife with the deer-horn handle sheathed at his waist, he examined himself in the mirror over his bathroom sink. He'd gathered part of his shoulder-length hair into a scalp lock. Though it wasn't long enough to make a proper braid, he'd wound the hair around a piece of basswood bark so that the scalp lock stood erect, the ends of the hair spraying out at the top.

A thick white line drawn from his forehead and down his nose to below his chin divided his face in half. The left side, the heart side, he'd painted completely black to mourn his brother. The right side was painted red to show, as the scalp lock did, that he was a warrior heading into battle. He nodded, turned away and crossed to the door.

In the garage, he removed the canvas from the fiberglass canoe and carried it out. The sun had dipped behind the pines. The sky was clear. There'd be few if any clouds to conceal tonight's moon, full for Midsummer Eve. Before dark he had to trace the monster to its lair.

He knew little about what he would be facing except that the creature hunted at night, possibly because of intolerance to the sun's rays. So it followed that the monster probably slept during the day. Since it never seemed to go far from the lake, perhaps the monster couldn't remain out of the water except for short periods of time. Hart hoped to surprise it.

Inverting the small, light canoe over his head, he tipped it slightly so he could see where he was going. As he trotted along the path to the lake, he was reminded of how often he and Wolfe had portaged when they were teenagers, hauling a canoe around river rapids or from lake to lake.

"I wish you were with me now, brother," he said aloud.

A moment later he sucked in his breath, staring. Ahead of him, just off the path, a gray shadow weaved in and out among the pines.

Though it appeared to move on four feet, what he saw was too insubstantial to be a real animal. Could it be Wolfe's spirit, in the guise of a wolf? If he'd had the time, he could pause to open his mind and his heart, then maybe he'd know for sure.

But he had no time to spare. He had to paddle to the island not only before dark, but also before Gregory returned home to stop him. He was certain that whatever was to be found on the island would provide answers to all the dark questions roiling in his mind. If he was successful, he'd avenge his brother and save Kendra from deadly danger. Muscles tightened in his jaw. He *had* to succeed.

He was no shaman, like Grandfather. He had no special Mide power to call on. But, using what he'd learned from Grandfather, he'd done all he could to transform himself into a warrior, both outwardly and inwardly. Like the old-time warriors of his people, he would face death without flinching. He would face death—and win.

Lynx Lake lay dead ahead, its water glittering in the late afternoon sun, the island sitting serenely in the lake's center. When he reached the lake, he set the canoe half in the water, half on shore and unhooked the paddle from its fastening.

Before he could wade into the shallows to float the canoe, the gray shadow sprang in front of him, obviously trying to urge him back.

Don't try to stop me, he told the wolf spirit silently. *I have no choice. I must find Mishebezo now, before dark. Find him and kill him.*

The gray shadow retreated, vanishing into the trees. Hart waded into the water, floated the canoe, then eased into it, pushing off with the paddle. The canoe skimmed lightly over the water, almost flying toward the island, or so it seemed to him.

"Ninsa," he intoned, speaking his native tongue to strengthen his spirit, *"mingagwedjisia. Gocu nindanibosi."* I will test my power. I am not going to die.

He'd ceased to think of the creature he sought as Tola. The warrior he'd become hunted Mishibezo, ancient and evil, a monster who must be destroyed. To avenge his brother. To save the woman he loved. He knew how it could be done because Grandfather had whispered the secret to him in a dream just before he woke this morning.

"Mishibezo's scales turn back the sharpest knife," Grandfather had warned. "You must strike where he has no scales."

The island loomed before him; he could see its pebbled beach and the rocky outcropping at its center where, no doubt, lay the entrance to the underground, to the tunnels and caverns leading to the house.

Soon, he told himself. Soon now.

Without so much as a warning ripple, the canoe was suddenly lifted into the air, flipping over, flinging Hart into the water. Something clutched at his foot, but he kicked free and surfaced. Well aware of what had attacked, knowing Mishibezo had the advantage in the water and quite likely would drown him, Hart swam desperately toward the island shore.

For a moment he thought he might make it. Then something gripped his ankle, sharp claws digging agonizingly into his flesh and, despite his struggles, he was inexorably pulled under the water.

Leda had refused any supper, and Kendra, worried about her, had little appetite. After she finished the last of the pea soup, she decided to make oatmeal cookies to keep busy. She was removing the last batch of cookies from the oven when, from upstairs, she heard the chime of the silver bell. Pausing only long enough to turn off the oven, she hurried up the back stairs.

She found Leda slumped back against the pillows, clutching at her chest. "Feels as though I'm being crushed," Leda whispered. "Pill."

Kendra fumbled one of the tiny white pills from the bottle, inserted it in Leda's mouth and hovered anxiously. When she noticed Leda, fighting for each breath, fumbling at the silk scarf around her neck, Kendra bent down and unwound the scarf, exposing Leda's throat.

She drew in her breath. Instead of normal skin, an iridescent growth that appeared to be scales covered the old woman's neck, extending down onto her upper chest to where the neck of the nightgown began. No wonder Leda always wore high-necked dresses.

Leda clutched at her hand. "Don't leave me," she gasped, her hand wavering toward Kendra.

"I won't." Doing her best to ignore the strangeness of Leda's skin, Kendra sat on the edge of the bed and grasped the sick woman's hand. "Is the pill helping?"

"Give me one more," Leda said.

Kendra obeyed. After a time, Leda's tight grip on her hand eased. "Not so bad now. I can breathe," she said. But her lips were still blue.

"I think you ought to be in the hospital," Kendra told her. "I'm going to call an ambulance."

Leda's grip tightened again. "I don't want to go. I won't."

"At least let me try to reach your doctor. Is that his name on the medicine bottle?"

Leda nodded. "You can call him," she said, releasing Kendra. "But no hospital."

"I'll just be a minute." Kendra, with the medicine bottle bearing the doctor's name and phone number clutched in her hand, hurried down the front stairs to the one and only phone in the house, in the entry. When she put the receiver to her ear, she heard no dial tone. She clicked the buttons on the holder several times without results. Replacing the phone and picking it up again didn't help, either. The phone was dead.

When she returned to Leda's bedroom, the sick woman gave her a questioning look.

"I'm afraid there's something wrong with the phone," she said. "Why don't you let me drive you—"

"No! I'm not going anywhere until after I speak to my son. He'll be home before dark."

Kendra glanced at her watch. Almost seven. It might be an hour before Gregory's return. What was she to do about Leda in the meantime? She could hardly force her into the car. "I'll try the phone again in a few minutes," she said. "It may be a temporary problem."

"Sit beside me," Leda urged. "I feel better with you here."

Not knowing what else to do, Kendra obeyed.

Leda closed her eyes, her hand resting lightly in Kendra's. "You saw, didn't you?" she mumbled. "Saw Tola's mark. We all bear it in one place or another. All the Morel bloodline. Gregory is fortunate, for his is small and well hidden, being on his back."

Kendra swallowed. The scales were Tola's mark? And Gregory had them, too? "My half brother—?" she began.

"Collis had the mark, oh yes, and more. His left leg ended in a webbed flipper instead of a foot. You must have noticed his limp."

Kendra stared at Leda in horror. As a child she'd watched Collis limp but she hadn't known what caused it. She'd never seen him with his shoes off.

"You shan't be Tola's bride," Leda went on. "It's not right."

Still horrified by what she'd heard about Collis, Kendra blurted, "The lost brides."

"Lost," Leda echoed. "Tola shouldn't have taken Collis's wife. That was wrong, that was evil. I told Gregory something must be done, I told him and Collis both that Tola was beyond control. Collis believed me. He turned against Tola and made up his mind there'd be no more deaths. That's why he tried to save the trespasser wearing that headband. But he failed. Tola—" Her words trailed off.

"Tola killed Collis as well as the trespasser," Kendra put in, burdened now with the certain knowledge of how both Dewolfe and her brother had died.

"Though it's true Tola upset the boat and frightened your father into a heart attack," Leda said, "he'd never harmed one of the true bloodline before he attacked and killed Collis. Why, this is his family."

An icy trickle ran down Kendra's spine. What did Leda mean by *his family?* The Tremaines?

"I've warned Gregory evil has come to possess Tola, but he won't listen," Leda said sadly. "Gregory still believes he can control Tola. He can't. No one can. Not anymore. Poor little Patrice..." Tears trickled from under her closed eyelids.

Kendra, though appalled by the revelations, patted the sick woman's hand. How could she blame Leda, so old and sick?

"Tonight is Midsummer Eve," Leda said brokenly. "I meant to try to help you, but my heart—" She fisted her free hand between her breasts, pain twisting her face. "I'm dying, Kendra. I'm useless to you. Find your young man and flee—flee before it's too late."

Startled, Kendra protested, "I can't leave you here alone."

Leda disengaged her hand from Kendra's. "You can do nothing more for me. Save yourself."

Kendra stood up, her gaze on Leda's ashen face. "I won't abandon you. I'll find Hart and come back. We'll bring you with us when we—"

"Go!" Leda cried. "It's already after seven. Hurry!"

"But why? Please tell me why!"

"Tola. He'll come for you."

"Hart won't let that happen," Kendra said firmly, denying her mounting apprehension.

"Tola can't be stopped. If ever he was—" Leda shuddered. "We'd all die. The house would collapse around us. It would be the end of every Morel. Every Tremaine. But Tola isn't easy to kill. Go while you can. Now!"

CHAPTER THIRTEEN

Impelled by Leda's urgency, Kendra ran down the stairs and out the front door, calling Hart's name. After getting no answer, she hurried to his apartment. He wasn't there, but his truck was parked next to the garage so she knew he must be somewhere on the grounds. Glancing apprehensively at the red-in-the-west evening sky, she thought in despair of the estate's many acres. Since she had no idea where Hart might be working, it might take some time to locate him, time she didn't have. How could she make him realize she needed him?

Not only must they leave the grounds before dark but also before Gregory returned home. While she might be wrong, she strongly suspected Gregory wouldn't let her leave, that he'd find some means to keep her here so he could carry out his plans for Midsummer Eve.

Tola's bride. She shuddered at the thought.

Opening the door of the truck, she sounded the horn, loud and continuously. No matter where on the grounds he was, surely Hart would hear the insistent clamor.

After several minutes, she left the truck, looking hopefully in all directions. There was no sign of him. But among the trees she saw a shifting gray shadow. As she watched, the shadow drifted toward the lake, moving on four feet, then paused, as though waiting for her to follow.

Kendra swallowed, aware that Hart believed this might be his brother's spirit. "Dewolfe?" she whispered.

There was no response, but then she hadn't really expected one. The shadow remained stationary, waiting. Since Hart had neither appeared nor given any response to the horn blowing, Kendra decided she had nothing to lose by following where the shadow led. If it was really Dewolfe's spirit, perhaps the shadow would take her to Hart.

As soon as she started toward it, the shadow moved on, slowly at first, then, as she kept pace, faster and faster, until she had to run to keep it in sight. When at last the shadow halted at the verge of Lynx Lake, she caught her breath in dismay. No! Hart couldn't have gone into the water.

Why had she been led here? Was the shadow something other than Hart believed? Was it a malevolent manifestation, a projection of the monster?

Kendra cringed away, but the shadow made no move toward her, merely loping back and forth along the shore of the lake, behaving, she fancied, a bit like a distraught dog who'd lost its master.

She stared out over the lake and tensed when she noticed something in the water not far offshore, something floating. Poised to flee, she held. What she saw was no monster. In fact, it looked very much like an overturned boat.

Oh dear God, Hart's canoe! She'd forgotten about the canoe, forgotten he'd bought one. When had he retrieved it from Matty Cusick's cabin? She answered her own question. Yesterday, after he'd dropped her off at her car and before he returned to the estate. He'd gone to get the canoe in secret because he knew she'd object.

And here it was. Here was Hart's canoe, overturned in the water, but where was Hart? She could hardly believe he'd been foolhardy enough to try to paddle to the island, yet the evidence was in front of her. No wonder the shadow—she no longer doubted it was Dewolfe's spirit—had led her here. Something dreadful had happened to Hart.

He must still be alive—he had to be alive or Dewolfe wouldn't have come to fetch her. She was the only one who could or would help Hart. She must save him—but how?

She could think of only one thing to do, and the mere thought of attempting it scared her half to death. But there was no one else to call on, there was no one but her. If she didn't try to retrieve the canoe, she might be signing Hart's death warrant.

Taking a deep breath in an effort to quell her rising terror, she yanked off her shoes and waded into the water, determined, despite her fears, to recover the canoe and go after Hart. To find him. To save him.

The lake's bottom sloped rapidly downward, forcing her to swim in the chilly water. With each stroke she took, she expected the monster to erupt from the water or, worse, to attack her stealthily from beneath. She was gasping from fright as much as exertion by the time she reached the overturned canoe.

Since everyone at her summer-camp sessions had been taught how to right an overturned canoe and get back into it, Kendra was able to flip it over, grateful the boat was so light. Spotting an oar floating nearby, she collected it and dropped it into the boat.

Now came the hardest part—climbing in without upsetting the canoe all over again. She managed on the third try and immediately began paddling toward the island, casting apprehensive glances at the darkening sky.

Likely enough the island was no safer than the lake so she must reach it before dusk, find Hart, paddle back to shore with him and flee the estate. He must be on the island; she refused to believe he might be drowned.

Though the summer twilight would last for about another hour, the top curve of the full moon was already rising over the pines. Full darkness wouldn't settle in until after nine but the uncertain light was fading. It was no longer day, it was definitely Midsummer Eve. Time for Tola to claim his bride....

When Mishibezo grabbed his leg, attempting to pull him under, Hart made a desperate lunge for the paddle floating nearby. His maneuver didn't break the monster's grip, but the unexpected movement pulled the beast up instead of Hart going under. Hart swung the paddle at the top of the monstrous scaled head, all that was visible, connecting with a solid thwack that jarred the oar from his hand.

Feeling the beast's hold on his ankle loosen, Hart jerked free and swam as fast as he could toward the island. When the water grew shallow he thrust himself erect and scrambled onto the shore, racing for the outcropping of rock he'd noticed earlier. A glance over his shoulder showed something huge and silvery rising from the water, rising onto two legs.

As Hart had hoped, he found the dark maw of a cave and plunged inside, stumbling over what he belatedly realized were bones as he ran toward the back of the shallow cave where he saw a smaller opening.

He crouched and entered the cleft, hoping he'd reach the maze of caverns and tunnels he believed lay under the lake and led to the house. His best chance for survival was to hide from the beast in the tunnels and wait to try for a surprise attack. And he had to survive. Had to kill the monster. Kendra's life depended on it.

Had Mishibezo trailed him? Hart wasn't sure. He'd heard a strange shuffling behind him when he ducked into the cave. Now he heard nothing but the drip of water somewhere ahead. He felt his way along in the intense darkness, running his right hand along the rock wall as he pushed slowly on. Time ceased to have meaning.

There was a smell of mold and of something else— the same alien scent he'd detected once before in the cellar of the house. The air was damp, with a chill that made him wish he'd pulled on a shirt. His left leg hurt with every step he took. Reaching down to investigate, he found the leg of his jeans in ribbons and the torn skin of his ankle sticky with blood.

Mishibezo's claws were lethal. Hart hoped they weren't poisonous, as well.

What was this strange amphibious beast? Though he hadn't had more than a glimpse, Hart thought it was covered with scales, like a snake. Kendra had wondered if what she called Tola might be a misshapen human, but he didn't think that was possible. The fact that it stood on two legs didn't make it human—some animals, such as bears, often stood on their hind legs.

Recalling the bones he'd tripped over in the cave, Hart grimaced, realizing in dismayed anger that some might be his brother's. Mishibezo ate what he killed, making no distinction between animals and humans. Among primitive peoples, humans may once have eaten their own kind, but they no longer did.

Except for windigos. The hair rose on Hart's nape and his steps faltered as he remembered the windigo tales he'd heard as a child. "Long ago, in the time of our ancestors," the stories usually began, "giants lived among us and they were cannibals called windigos...."

Eventually all the giants were killed, but their spirits still roamed the earth and in the snowbound winter, during Hungry Moon, these evil spirits sometimes entered a human and tempted him to become a cannibal.

"Even today," the storyteller would warn, "beware the lone man you meet in the woods when the snow is thick and frost chills the air. For he may be a windigo...."

Hart had shed his belief in windigos with his childhood, but now somewhere behind him lurked a dangerous beast that meant to kill and eat him. A beast who was far more familiar with this dark underground labyrinth than he was.

The wall under Hart's right hand made an abrupt turn. He edged forward cautiously, passing, he realized when he found he could stand upright, from the tunnel he'd been following into a cavern. He had no idea of its size. Listening for any sound of pursuit, he heard a faint murmur of running water.

Was he about to come to an underground stream? If so, did it connect with the lake? If it did, had the beast been able to swim to the cavern to waylay him? That might explain why he hadn't heard any noises behind him—the beast didn't need to follow him through the tunnel if it could get to the cavern by swimming.

Going back is likely to be fatal, Hart told himself, so I'll have to continue on and take my chances. Let's hope Mishibezo can't see in the dark any better than I can.

As he edged along the wall, something suddenly brushed against his legs. Even as he leapt back, Hart realized what had touched him hadn't been solid. Not the beast, then. But what?

Hope flooded his heart. Wolfe? he asked silently. Are you with me, brother?

A sense of completeness settled over him, a feeling he hadn't known since Wolfe died. His brother *was* with him in spirit.

Danger ahead.

He might have believed the thought was his own except he had no way of sensing what lay ahead. Wolfe was warning him.

The darkness was absolute; he had to have some guide in order to go on, had to feel his way along a wall. If continuing this way was dangerous, there was no choice but to retrace his steps to the tunnel opening and try the left cavern wall.

Wait—what was that faint greenish glow? A tiny light hovered before him, dancing like a will-o'-the-wisp. Leading him astray?

Follow.

The word echoed in his mind. Certain the command came from his brother, he took a deep breath and obeyed, walking into the unknown darkness, his gaze fixed on the flickering light that, though too weak to illuminate the surroundings, beckoned him forward.

The sound of running water grew louder and louder. At last the light paused. Hart stopped, then slid one foot forward until he felt the rock floor disappear. As he'd suspected, they'd come to the underground stream. Now what? Could he jump? He had no way to know how wide the stream was.

Swim across? Yeah, sure, he thought. Just me and Mishibezo in the water.

Follow.

The light dropped lower, waiting. Hart shrugged, sat down and eased forward, his left ankle throbbing painfully, until his legs were over the edge and his feet in numbingly cold water. To his surprise, his right foot touched a hard, irregular surface. He stood, finding himself ankle-deep in water. Either the stream was very shallow or, more likely, this was the site of a recent rockfall.

Moving with caution, he followed the light, sliding each foot ahead to prevent stepping off into deep water without warning. He'd reached the opposite side and was scrambling onto the cavern's rock floor when he heard an ominous splashing in the stream.

Quick.

The light bobbed ahead of him and he limped hurriedly after it. A pause. He halted, holding his hands in front of him and touched rock again. A cavern wall.

Climb.

Up, up the light rose. He felt for handholds in the rock, found them, and found footholds as well. Slowed by his injured ankle, he clambered laboriously up the rocky wall, eventually reaching a ledge. When he hauled himself onto the ledge, the light winked out, but he still felt his brother's presence.

I hope you know what you're doing, bro, he said silently, because I sure as hell feel like a sitting duck up here.

Below, the splashing ceased. Hart heard the same squishing noises he'd listened to earlier and pictured Mishibezo easing from the water and slithering over the cavern floor searching for him. Since he wasn't making a sound, the search had to be by sight or by smell or both.

Straining his ears, Hart tracked the monster as it slithered closer and closer to where he perched, high above. The noises ceased. After long moments of silence, claws scrabbled on the rock face directly below Hart. He tensed, knowing it had located him. Could the creature climb? Gripping the horn hilt of his knife, he crouched, waiting.

If my bones are meant to molder in this cavern, he vowed grimly, I'll make damn sure Mishibezo's bones mingle with them.

Remembering his dream in which Grandfather warned him the knife wouldn't penetrate the creature's scales, Hart felt along the ledge with his free hand for a loose stone. Locating one slightly larger than a softball, he grabbed it. Knife in one hand, stone in the other, he poised himself, ready to attack.

The greenish light that had led him to the ledge blinked to life, faintly illuminating a groping, taloned and webbed hand about to fasten on the lip of the ledge. Raising the stone, Hart brought it smashing down on the hand.

The hand disappeared, and Hart heard a bellow of pain, a clatter of rock fragments ripping loose, then the thunk of a heavy body slamming onto the rock floor. The light winked out, leaving Hart in total darkness once more.

There came a slithering, a splash, then fainter splashing sounds. After that, nothing but the gurgling of the underground stream. Had Mishibezo fled? Or had the creature cleverly pretended to swim away while in reality it lay in ambush below?

Hart was sure it would take more than a rock smashing his webbed fingers to discourage Mishibezo. On the other hand, he had no way of knowing how much time had passed since he'd entered the tunnel. For all he knew, the full moon rode high, summoning the monster to Midsummer Night.

When at last the light appeared again, dancing down to floor level, Hart was ready to risk leaving the ledge. Facing the rock wall, he eased over the edge, searching for footholds. Finding them. But as he lowered himself, his wounded left ankle gave way and, despite his frantic clutching at the ledge, he plunged down, landing on his back with a jarring jolt. His head struck the rock floor and he slipped into unconsciousness.

In the blue twilight, with the moon not yet high enough to add its pale light to the summer evening, Kendra dipped her oar in and out of the water, falling into the long-ago paddling rhythm she'd learned as a teenager. Water dripped unnoticed from her wet shirt and jeans as she propelled the canoe toward the island. She was only vaguely aware of the weight of the topaz lavaliere dangling from its chain around her neck.

She was completely focused on Hart. He had to be somewhere on the island, maybe hiding from Tola. Or injured. Should she call to him? No, she didn't dare. What if Tola heard her?

Hart had to be alive. He must be. In the few weeks she'd known him, she'd come to love him. She loved him wholeheartedly; they were connected to one an-

other by an indissoluble bond. If anything happened to
him—

No, she wouldn't think about it. Hart lived. She
knew he did. And she was determined to rescue him.

From Tola. The monster in the lake. In this very lake
she paddled across. Panic tightened her chest, rising in
her throat until she could taste its metallic tang on her
tongue. Leda's voice echoed in her head, crying, *Flee!*
In her mind's eye, she saw Patrice's double-heart pendant lying among the pine needles.

Tola had killed. He would kill again.

Her rhythm faltered; the oar grew still in her hands.
Why wasn't she in her car, speeding down the mountain to safety instead of paddling toward the island,
toward the center of danger?

If she turned back, away from the island, she'd be
deserting Hart. Leaving him to the merciless Tola.
Kendra shuddered, her gaze fixed on the island. Never!
Gripping the paddle with renewed determination, she
dipped it into the water, and the canoe shot ahead once
more.

Suddenly, directly in front of her, something broke
through the surface in a tremendous rush of cascading
water. Something huge that, touched by the moon's
rays, gleamed with a silver sheen. Not a human, not an
animal. And certainly not a fish.

Silver eyes fixed on her, their glare freezing her as she
stared at the grotesque and terrifying monster. Panic-
stricken though she was, she recognized the monstrous head as the same one she'd seen on the toy boat.
Tola! Paralyzed with horror, she couldn't move,
couldn't scream, couldn't think.

Hart opened his eyes to darkness. He was lying on
his back, and his head throbbed painfully. Where was

he? He stared at a quivering greenish glow, inadequate illumination for seeing his surroundings.

Rise.

The command blazed in his mind. Without pausing to wonder where it came from, he tried to obey. When he put weight on his left leg, pain arrowed through it, homing in on his ankle. As he shifted most of his weight to his right leg, the light circled him, bobbing up and down as if in agitation.

Wolfe, he thought, remembering. Wolfe's spirit had been leading him through the underground passageway. He'd climbed to a ledge to escape from Mishibezo and then fell and knocked himself out as he tried to climb back down.

Follow.

Once again united with his brother, he nodded and hobbled after the beckoning light, doing his best to ignore the stabbing pain in his ankle.

He couldn't judge how long he might have lain unconscious. How much time had passed since he entered the passageway? Hours, surely. What, he wondered, had lured Mishibezo away from him, back into the lake? Moonrise? Or Kendra?

Surely she wouldn't have the left the house. She'd be safe as long as she remained inside the locked doors. Or would she? What would happen when Gregory returned? As he must already have done.

Hart gritted his teeth against the pain and increased his pace, watching the dancing light. When it dropped lower, he crouched, knowing the cavern must be narrowing into a tunnel once more. He had to reach Kendra before the monster harmed her. He had to save her.

She was the woman he loved, the woman whose spirit matched his.

Damn it, they belonged together and no monster from hell was going to take her from him!

She couldn't be out there under the moon, the helpless prey of Mishibezo. No, not exactly prey. A bride. Tola's bride.

Hart's roar of anguished rage echoed along the tunnel. At the same time, his guiding light vanished.

Kendra watched in helpless horror as the monster swam toward her canoe, moonlight glinting off its silvery scales. The same scales she'd seen on Leda's neck. She gasped when a taloned hand with webbed fingers reached out and fastened on the prow of the canoe. Webbed. Like her half brother's foot had been.

Tola. Coming to kill her.

The creature's name rang in her ears. It took a few moments for her to realize someone was actually calling to the creature. A man. Tola turned away from her to look at the shore. Released from the monster's hypnotic gaze, Kendra found herself able to move, and she glanced shoreward.

Though she couldn't identify him in the dusk, a man she knew must be Gregory stood at the waterline. "Tola," he called. "Don't harm her, Tola. She's your bride. Tola's bride."

The creature looked again at her, its gaze fastening on the topaz she still wore. It grunted, and the webbed fingers slid away from the canoe. Kendra, whimpering with fright, forced herself to dip the paddle into the water again, one thought convulsing her panicked mind—Get away! Flee!

Bringing the canoe about, she paddled frantically
toward shore, toward Gregory, expecting never to set
foot on dry land, expecting at any moment to be
dragged overboard by Tola. She could hardly believe
it when she finally felt the canoe scrape bottom.

Flinging down the paddle, she leapt into the shallows and splashed toward shore. Gregory lunged at her,
and she swerved to avoid him. "No!" she cried.
"Don't touch me!" He wasn't to be trusted; he expected her to become Tola's bride.

Hart, his right hand following the wall for guid-
ance, hobbled along in the darkness, hoping for his
brother's return. Why had Wolfe's spirit abandoned
him? Knowing Kendra needed him, he cursed in a
rambling monotone at his inability to protect her.

He'd never felt so alone or so helpless. He was some
warrior, wasn't he? Wounded, trapped in blackness,
below ground in a monster's labyrinth.

He stumbled over an obstacle in his path and fell
forward onto an elevation of some kind that blocked
the tunnel. In his despair, it took him a few moments
to understand he'd found stairs cut into the rock.
Climbing them cautiously—all but dragging his left
leg—he counted eight steps before his head brushed
against something. Reaching up, he felt cold, hard
metal under his fingers. The steel trapdoor! His heart
lifted.

Climbing higher, Hart shoved against the trapdoor
with all his strength. It didn't budge. Locked, as he'd
half-expected. He eased down the stairs until he could
sit without his head hitting the door. He was strong but
he knew he wasn't as powerful as Mishibezo. If the
monster hadn't been able to force the steel door open,

there was little point in him wasting any more effort. Or
even banging on it. If anyone heard him, they were
likely to believe he was the monster and ignore the
noise.

With the door locked against him, he was still
trapped. Still helpless.

CHAPTER FOURTEEN

Splashing in and out of the water at the lake's edge, Kendra did her best to dodge Gregory's attempts to grab her. If he succeeded, she'd have no chance at all to escape becoming Tola's bride.

Suddenly the gray shadow appeared, thrusting itself between her and Gregory. He staggered back, mouth gaping in shock. She darted past him, running toward the house, the shadow loping ahead of her. Was Gregory pursuing her?

Glancing over her shoulder, she saw far worse. A huge silvery shape slithered rapidly after her. Tola! She could see scales gleaming in the moonlight, see that the monster was all too obviously a male.

Renewed terror sped her along. Reaching the house, she yanked open the door, slammed it behind her and shot the bolt before flicking on the light. She hadn't noticed the gray shadow slipping through the door with her, but when she turned, the shadow stood beside one of the tables in the entry.

Kendra started for the kitchen, planning to bolt the back door. The shadow moved to intercept her and blocked her way. She paused, afraid to try to bypass it. Though so far it hadn't harmed her, she worried about coming too near.

"Let me past," she said desperately. "If I don't hurry and lock all the doors, Tola will get in."

A loud banging on the front door, so forceful the heavy wooden door quivered in its frame, increased her fear, making her try to dart past the shadow. As she brushed against it, an unpleasant chilly tingling quivered through her. She jerked back.

"Please!" she cried.

The shadow shifted, wrapping itself around the table. As she stared in confusion, the table shook wildly and tipped over, the blue vase on top smashing onto the parquet floor. Among the shattered shards gleamed the brass of the key to the vaults. She'd totally forgotten about Hart dropping the key into the vase.

At last understanding what the shadow wanted, she retrieved the key. Since the shadow no longer blocked her passage, she ran toward the kitchen, turning lights on as she passed, still determined to lock the other doors. She'd no more than reached the kitchen doorway when all the lights winked out, plunging her into darkness.

Kendra froze, aware the fuse box was in the storage room. Had Gregory gotten into the house through the back door? Forcing herself to move, she felt her way across the room, located the utility cupboard by the sink and fumbled inside until she grasped the flashlight Leda kept there.

What now? She resisted her impulse to turn on the flashlight, knowing she'd be exposed. A faint greenish glow suddenly materialized by the door to the vaults, making her draw in her breath. It wasn't an ordinary light—what could it be? At the same time that she realized the glow centered on the lock, she felt a tingle coming from the brass key in her hand.

The shadow had wanted her to find the key. Did it now want her to unlock the door to the vaults? Why?

Before she could decide, she heard a sinister slithering coming from the direction of the storeroom and she tensed, poised to flee.

But in what direction? Where did safety lie? Only outside the grounds. Her car keys were in her shoulder bag upstairs. Too far away. The only hope she had was the shadow. For some reason, it wanted her to go into the vaults. Gritting her teeth to hold back the whimpers of fear that clogged her throat, she crept toward the door to the vaults. Her fingers shook so badly she had trouble fitting the key into the lock, despite the faint greenish illumination.

As she frantically rammed the key home and turned it, a rank odor seeped into the kitchen. Not from the vaults but from behind her. From the storeroom. Tola!

Kendra yanked the key free, flung open the vault door and stepped onto the stone stair. Slamming the door, she locked it from the vault side, leaving the key in the lock. Flicking on the flashlight, she rushed down the stairs, the green glow bobbing ahead of her, leading her to the steel trapdoor.

Reaching the trapdoor, she stared down at the shiny metal. Obviously the shadow wanted her to unbolt it. She swallowed and crouched down, but even though she was almost certain Tola was upstairs, she couldn't force herself to draw the bolts. What if she was wrong?

"I can't," she said aloud, cringing from the echo of her own voice as it bounced off the stone walls of the vault.

"Kendra?"

Hart's voice came to her faintly. He was alive! But where was he?

"Kendra, let me out!"

Underneath the trapdoor! All but sobbing in relief, she hurriedly reached for the first bolt, flipping it up from the bar and ramming it open. At the same time, she heard the clatter of metal on stone from behind her. The brass key, she realized with fright, had been forced from the lock and had fallen onto a stone step. She drew in her breath, remembering that Gregory had another key.

Frantically she fumbled with the second bolt, finally freeing it. The trapdoor was flung open, and Hart scrambled up from the darkness below. She clung to him momentarily, reassuring herself he was really there, really flesh and blood and not another phantom.

"They're coming," she gasped. "Tola and Gregory. Coming down the stairs from the kitchen."

Hart grabbed the flashlight. Its beam glinted off the silvery scales of Tola, already halfway down the steps, so huge he had to crouch because he lacked headroom. Behind him, Gregory stood framed in the open doorway.

Hart returned her flashlight. "Wolfe," he whispered. "Are you with me, bro?"

Kendra tore her terrified gaze away from Tola and saw the gray shadow at Hart's side. She watched as Hart gripped the horn handle of the knife sheathed at his waist, freed the curved blade and advanced toward the monster, chanting. To her dismay, she noticed he was limping. Then she saw the torn jeans and the bloody gashes on his left ankle.

How could any man, armed only with a knife, prevail against such a dreadful creature? And Hart was already injured—what chance did he have?

In the story he'd told her, Manabozho had conquered Mishibezo, the evil water monster who'd killed his brother. But Hart was no supernatural Chippewa hero, he was a mortal. While Tola was—What was he?

He walked on two feet like a man but he couldn't be human. Not covered with scales as he was, not with webbed and taloned feet and hands, not with that all but chinless head. The pupils of his silver eyes were slitted like a reptile's and his sharp, pointed teeth were sharklike. She'd never set eyes on anything more repulsive. Or more terrifying.

Tola towered over Hart—taller and broader, more massive. A monster unlike anything else in this world.

"Kill him, Tola," Gregory urged. "Kill him quickly and take your bride."

She shivered, her gaze flicking toward Gregory, now at the foot of the stairs. Like hers, his flashlight beam focused on Tola and Hart.

With a shout, Hart leapt at Tola, the blade of his knife flashing in the light as he stabbed the monster. Kendra cried out when Tola's claws slashed at Hart, missing him by a hair as Hart flung himself sideways. Though she'd been sure the knife had struck Tola's chest, she could see no wound. Were his scales armorlike, protecting him from injury?

"His knife can't hurt you," Gregory said, edging closer to the pair. "Nothing can. You're invulnerable. Kill him. Now!"

A flame of pure rage directed at Gregory burned away some of the fear clogging Kendra's mind. Why, she asked herself, did Tola half close his eyes? When she'd seen him outside in the moonlight she was certain his eyes had been fully open. Did the flashlight's beam bother him? Quite possibly, since he hunted only in darkness.

Testing her theory, she directed her beam into the monster's eyes and was rewarded when he blinked, turning his head from the glare. Hart took advantage of Tola's momentary distraction by lunging at him again, knife upraised.

Though Hart drew back unscathed, once again his attack failed to wound Tola. As Kendra shifted position to better direct her own flashlight attack, she noticed from the corner of her eye that Gregory was also moving. Toward her.

She'd be no match for him. He was bigger and stronger. She shifted her light so she could cast a quick glance about, searching for a weapon. But the vaults were empty except for old tools near the furnace, leftover from former days when it must have been coal-fired.

As she edged sideways to avoid him, Gregory said, "There's really no point in trying to get away from me, my dear. No point at all. It's as futile as Hart's battle with Tola. The Morels will prevail. We always have. Because years ago we dared to choose a path the Tremaines refused to follow."

She stared at him, confused by his words. "Are you saying Tola is a Morel?"

"You've got it wrong side to. We Morels are part of Tola."

Kendra, trying to keep track of Hart while evading Gregory, was shocked speechless. She'd seen Leda's scaly neck and Leda had told her about Collis's webbed foot, but she hadn't really believed either to be more than abnormalities. Human abnormalities. Finally she gestured toward Tola and blurted, "Your Morel ancestors mated with—with that?"

"No one knows for certain what drove the first woman of the family to defy old Ezekial and become Tola's bride but once she bore his child and Tola's blood mingled with ours, we understood. He's more than human—and so are we!"

Kendra shuddered at the glitter in Gregory's silver eyes, so like Tola's, as well as at the thought of any woman voluntarily submitting to that monster. "How could she? And why didn't Tola kill her?"

"Because she was a Tremaine," Gregory said. "Old Ezekial discovered Tola lived in the lake after he purchased the land. Finding Tola hard to kill but surprisingly intelligent, he made a pact. In return for the Tremaines feeding him and providing him with a bride each year, Tola agreed never to harm one of the family. Mid-June is the only time Tola can mate so finding brides wasn't too much of a problem."

She stared at him in horror. "You mean that ever since Ezekial's time the Tremaines have deliberately sacrificed a young woman to Tola every June?"

Gregory shrugged. "You might put it that way. But, of course, when a Tremaine woman answered his mating call, she wore the topaz to identify herself as family so she wasn't eaten afterward. Ezekial didn't approve of Tola's blood mingling with Tremaine blood and so he disinherited and exiled the Morel branch of the family." He took a step toward her. "But we've returned. And we intend to remain."

Tola's roar echoed through the vaults, terrorizing her anew as well as momentarily transfixing Gregory.

Looking at the monster, Kendra saw blood trickling from a gash near one of his eyes. He lunged at Hart, who sidestepped, avoiding the talons, but she caught her breath when she noticed Hart's injured ankle give way. Though he managed to recover his balance before Tola could reach him, she feared for his chances the next time. What had happened to the gray shadow? And why, if it was Dewolfe's spirit, wasn't the shadow helping Hart?

Suddenly a loud rumble startled them all. Kendra found herself staggering over the cement floor, almost dropping her flashlight as she fought to stay on her feet. What had happened? She fetched up against the unlit furnace and braced herself there, belatedly realizing the floor was shuddering under her feet.

"Underground rockfall," Gregory muttered. "A bad one."

She saw Hart was now behind the momentarily distracted monster. Transfixed, she watched as he leapt into the air, landed on Tola's shoulders and jabbed at the monster's face with his knife. Tola screamed in pain, twisting around and dislodging Hart, who jumped free of him, landing on his injured ankle. His desperate attempt to stay on his feet failed. He fell heavily and lay unmoving.

"No!" Kendra cried as Tola flung himself at the downed man, his talons reaching for Hart's throat.

"Kill!" Gregory shouted.

The gray shadow materialized, seemingly standing on Hart's body. Tola's claws dug into the shadow. The monster roared in pain, drawing back, then slashing at the shadow again. Another roar and retreat. Behind the shadow, Hart rose to one knee, shaking his head as though dazed.

Engrossed in the battle, Kendra forgot about Gregory until he gripped her arms, holding her fast despite her attempt to jerk free of him. She dropped her flashlight and still lit, it rolled away.

"Tola," he called, "forget the fight. I'll take care of Hart. Here's your bride. Come and get her. Come here, Tola. Come to me."

Tola's head began to turn toward Gregory. Kendra screamed, redoubling her efforts to get away. She tore one of her arms from his grasp but failed to free herself. In the process, she kicked over the old coal shovel that had been leaning against the wall beside the furnace. As it clanged onto the cement, she remembered seeing a long, straight poker beside the shovel. After making a frantic lunge, she felt her fingers close over the cold iron of the poker. She swung it at Gregory, hitting his side.

He grunted from the blow, staggering back, then rushing at her again. Wielding the poker like a sword, jabbing and swinging, Kendra stood him off, keeping a wary eye on Tola as Gregory forced her away from the furnace.

The monster's back was to her and, stalked by the gray shadow, he slithered slowly on his webbed feet, as though injured. The shadow, she noticed, drove Tola inexorably toward the gaping trapdoor. Hart pushed himself to his feet.

Another subterranean rumble shook the floor. Kendra stumbled sideways, holding tightly to the poker. Hart limped across the floor and lunged at Gregory. Gregory, his gaze fixed on Hart, yanked a gun from his coat pocket and aimed carefully.

"No!" Kendra cried. She hurled the poker at him, hitting him across the back. The blow staggered Gregory and his shot went wild. Unable to regain his balance, he fell against Tola.

The monster roared, half turned, grasped Gregory in his taloned hands and, clutching him, leapt down into the dark pit of the open trapdoor. Hart flung himself onto his knees, slammed the steel door shut and locked the bolts.

Before he could rise, a third crashing rumble from below quivered through the vaults. Kendra dropped onto her knees beside Hart. He held her to him while the floor shuddered beneath them. Huge cracks gaped in the cement around them and dust sifted down from overhead. Kendra's lost flashlight, which had been providing the only illumination, went out.

She clung to Hart in the darkness. When at last the underground rumbling ceased, he rose, pulling her up after him.

"We'll try for the stairs," he said. "Slide your feet ahead so we don't fall into one of those cracks."

Hand in hand, they began groping their way slowly across the vaults, and the greenish light appeared ahead of them. "It's Wolfe," Hart said. "Follow him."

The stone stairs were intact, but when they reached the top, the door, jammed askew in its frame, refused to open. Hart's efforts to force the door open finally made a large enough gap for them to squeeze through into the kitchen.

By the flickering light of a kerosene lantern on the table, they saw Leda lying facedown on the kitchen floor with shards of china and glass surrounding her. Hart lifted her into his arms.

"She's alive," he said.

"It's her heart," Kendra told him. "We'll take her with us. Take her to a hospital." She glanced apprehensively over her shoulder at the open door to the vaults. "Hurry!"

"My truck?"

She shook her head. "Not enough room. Put her in my car." Taking the lantern, she lit his way as he carried Leda across the littered kitchen and through the back door.

Before they reached Kendra's car, she saw that the porte cochere had collapsed onto it. Coming closer she shook her head in dismay as she stared at the car's smashed top and shattered windows.

"My keys were upstairs, anyway," she told Hart. "I don't know if I could have made myself go back inside after them."

"It'll have to be the truck," he said, angling off toward the garage, limping markedly.

Holding the lantern, Kendra walked beside him, darting nervous glances to the right and left. "What if they've reached the lake?" she asked. "What if they're already stalking us?"

"I got Tola with my knife," Hart said. "He's badly hurt. Maybe not fatally—who knows what it takes to kill a monster?"

"Gregory has a gun," she reminded him.

She relaxed slightly when they reached the garage and Hart laid Leda onto the front seat of his truck. Then she tensed all over again when he left her with Leda to hurry up the stairs to his apartment. It seemed forever before he returned carrying a shirt. And accompanied by the gray shadow.

Hearing a distant rumble, Kendra looked past him toward the house. She blinked in disbelief. "Hart?" she quavered. "Am I seeing things?"

He whirled to stare at the house, and she grasped his hand, holding it tightly as together they watched in awe while the stones of the structure broke away from each other, tumbling in crashing disarray as the mansion slowly disintegrated, falling in on itself.

"The ground underneath the vaults must have been honeycombed with caverns," Hart said. "And the rockfalls we heard and felt were those caverns collapsing. The collapse pulled the house down."

Leda had warned her. Leda had said: *When Tola goes, the end will come. The end of all of us.*

As she turned back to the truck, Kendra realized she felt neither relief nor sorrow at the loss. She'd never really belonged in Lynx House, just as she had never really owned it. But it frightened her to think there might be more to come.

Working in silence, they propped Leda between them on the seat, her head on Kendra's shoulder. With the shadow loping beside the truck, they drove toward the gates. As they neared, she noticed headlights focused on the gates from outside, headlights that didn't move. Who was there? Hart pressed the opener. Nothing happened. The gates remained closed.

"Jammed by the underground shaking," Hart muttered. "I was afraid of that." Stopping the truck, he got out.

She watched him limp toward the barred gates and wondered how he expected to open them by hand. The gray shadow flowed after him, blocking his path before he reached the gates. Hart paused and crouched, his hand hovering over the shadow as though he longed to touch it but knew he must not. He inclined his head—listening, she thought, to silent words.

After a moment the shadow vanished. Hart rose and limped to the gates. "You out there," he shouted at the lights. "It's over and done with. The house is gone and the monster's dead. So is Gregory Morel. I can't open the gates. Please help us get out of this damned place."

No one answered. But Kendra heard a door slam. Joey stepped into the glare of the headlights.

"Where's Patrice?" he demanded. "What've you done with her?"

"I'm afraid the monster got her."

"Oh my God." Joey's face puckered up.

"I'm sorry about Patrice, but I'm glad you're here," Hart said. "You know I'm no Tremaine—please help me get out of this hell. You can do it with that tow truck."

The glare of the headlights had prevented Kendra from seeing Joey's truck. With her arm around the unconscious Leda, she prayed that the monster really was dead. Unless he and Gregory had been crushed in the rockfall, how could Hart be certain they were dead?

As Kendra cast an uneasy look through the window of the pickup, dreading that she might see Tola slithering toward her, Leda stirred, moaning.

"I'm here," Kendra soothed. "You're not alone. Soon we'll all be safe."

But would they?

She heard the roar of a motor and the headlights outside the gate shifted, turning away. Was Joey deserting them? How would they ever get out?

"He's going to latch the hoist hook to the gates," Hart called to her. Moments later, the tow truck, motor laboring, pulled away. With a protesting screech, one of the gates jerked free of the other and clanged onto the road, opening a gap wide enough for the pickup. Hart eased the vehicle through, then stopped to thank Joey who was freeing his hook from the battered gate.

Joey stopped and peered in at Kendra. Seeing Leda, he asked, "Is the old lady dead, too?"

"She's very sick," Hart said.

"What about her?" Joey asked, jerking his head toward Kendra while speaking to Hart as though she wasn't present. "She coming back here?"

"No!" The word burst from Kendra. "No, I'm never coming back."

Joey nodded. "We've had more'n our fill of Tremaines," he said bleakly before turning away.

Hart drove a short way down the road, then stopped and waited until the tow truck headed in the opposite direction, toward the village.

"I have to go back," he told Kendra. "There's something I've left undone."

"No!" she cried. "Oh, no, please!"

"I'll be as quick as I can."

He slid from the pickup and limped back to the open gate where, just inside, the shadow waited. Together they trotted across the grounds until they reached the broken stones of what had been Lynx House. Using dried twigs for fuel, Hart coaxed a tiny fire into existence.

He stood and raised his head, gazing up at the full moon whose brightness hid the Milky Way from his sight.

"My brother," he said, "I have made a fire to light your way. It is time for you to leave me. You have completed your final task, you have finished your journey here. You are free to travel to that land where our forefathers have gone. You go alone, you go before me, it is not yet my time to follow...."

Warmth surrounded Hart, almost as though Wolfe embraced him. Then the shadow shifted, elongating as it began to rise from the ground, drifting like smoke, up, up toward the night sky. An eerie howl echoed through the darkness, and then the shadow vanished.

His brother's spirit was finally at rest.

Leaving the fire to gut itself out, Hart ran back to the pickup.

Kendra gasped with relief when he climbed into the cab. "I heard this fearful howling and I feared—" she began.

"There's nothing to be afraid of," he said, giving her hand a quick squeeze. "That howl was Wolfe's farewell."

They drove in silence down the mountain until he asked, "How's Mrs. Morel doing?"

"She's still unconscious."

"I'm afraid she doesn't have much left to live for," he said. Reaching across, he touched Kendra's cheek. "We do."

Kendra moved away from his caress. She didn't respond to his words.

Hart glanced at her, frowning. "What's the matter? I thought it went without saying we'd be together when this was over."

She turned her face from him. "You thought wrong. We can never be together. Never, never."

CHAPTER FIFTEEN

Kendra sat beside Leda's hospital bed, exhausted. Though there were no windows in the small intensive-care unit, she knew the sun must be rising. She'd had no sleep. Leda had been admitted sometime after midnight and Kendra, having convinced the hospital Leda had no other known relatives, had been allowed to remain with the old woman.

"It's against our ICU rules," the nurse had told her, "but what the hey. You sure won't do her any harm sitting there."

Kendra realized the nurse had bent the rules because she thought Leda would die before sunrise. But the squiggly lines on Leda's heart monitor still went up and down.

"Gregory," Leda murmured without opening her eyes.

Kendra leaned close. "This is Kendra. Gregory's not here."

Leda seemed to struggle to open her eyes, as though even that tiny movement took more energy than she had available. Her gray gaze fixed on Kendra. "You're safe," she whispered. "The topaz saved you."

Kendra had forgotten about the lavaliere she still wore.

Before she could reply, Leda said, "But Gregory's dead. My son is dead."

Kendra decided Leda deserved the truth. "I'm afraid so."

Leda sighed. One lone tear trickled from the corner of her eye and rolled down her cheek. "Even as a boy he was never satisfied," she murmured. "Always wanting something more." After a moment she added, "So many dead. Because of Tola."

"We think Tola was crushed in a massive rockfall."

"I hope so. I pray he's dead. He destroyed the Morels."

"And the Tremaines," Kendra said sadly.

"No, no. You're a Tremaine and you live."

"And you, a Morel, are still alive."

Leda half smiled. "My heart and I are old. It's past our time to go. We've lived too long as it is. But you're young."

Kendra bit her lip. "With my monstrous heritage, what do I have to live for?"

"But you're a Tremaine."

"So was my half brother. You told me about his webbed foot yourself."

"Oh, my dear." Leda closed her eyes momentarily. "Come closer. I have so little breath to waste."

Kendra hitched the chair up against the bed, bending her head so her ear was next to Leda's mouth.

"Didn't you understand what I meant when I told you only the Morel line was tainted?" Leda asked. "Collis was half Morel. Your mother was not a Morel."

"But my father was a Tremaine."

"The Tremaines never carried the taint. Not until Collis."

Kendra pulled back to stare at her. "Are you certain?" Tola's frightful image loomed in her mind, making her shudder.

"Your blood is as pure as your young man's. Tell him I'm sorry I couldn't save his brother. It's another sin I must answer for, among all the rest. But I loved my son, so how could I betray him? And now he's gone and I have no one. No..." Her words trailed off.

Kendra watched Leda's eyes droop shut and glanced apprehensively at the monitor. The lines still went up and down. Leaning close again, she whispered in Leda's ear, "You're not alone. You have me. We have each other. Don't die and leave me, Leda, because then I truly will have no family."

Alone in the waiting room, Hart stood when Kendra entered. "How is she?" he asked, holding out his arms.

"Still alive," Kendra said as she nestled against him. "I wonder if it's because I begged her not to die? Maybe it was selfish, but I didn't want to be alone."

"Alone? How can you be alone with me here?" Hart demanded.

She freed herself and looked at him. "I meant family. You have aunts and uncles and cousins, but Leda is all I have left."

"Aunts and uncles and cousins I don't visit. Wolfe was better than I at keeping in touch." He sighed. "I learned the hard way how important family really is. Now I have to try to find a way to go home."

She smiled slightly. "I understand it's possible to drive from New York to Michigan."

"I meant, go home for good. Wolfe was right. No one stands alone. I've been selfish. Like Gregory Morel was. I need to find some way to help my people instead of just looking out for myself."

"You couldn't be like Gregory," she said indignantly. "Not in a million years. You're everything he wasn't. You're brave and good and—"

"And in love with you." Hart drew her into his arms once again. "Speaking for my aunts and uncles and cousins, they'd be more than happy to become your aunts and uncles and cousins."

"How do you know?"

"Because my wife is a part of my family."

She took his face between her hands, gazing somberly into his eyes. "I'm a Tremaine. Leda says my family doesn't carry the bad genes like the Morels, but can we ever be sure?"

"*I'm* sure. And so was Wolfe. Otherwise you never would have seen his spirit. No one else did, you know. Just you and me."

A thrill arrowed through her. If Dewolfe's spirit had accepted her, maybe she was free of the taint.

"And if Leda lives," Hart added, "she'll be a part of my family, too."

Kendra stood on her tiptoes and kissed Hart.

"I'll take that as a yes," he murmured.

His lips slanted over hers, gentle at first, then more demanding, more passionate, his kiss filled with the promise of unfailing love.

CHAPTER SIXTEEN

Deep under the ruins of Lynx House, something stirred. Rocks rattled, scattering in all directions as a massive figure slowly and painfully crawled free of the fall. Sensing a still-warm body near him, he worked it free of the rocks and, dragging the body behind him, slithered on his belly through a narrow opening. The man was dead, but Tola never left food behind.

His skin prickled, dry from the rock dust and from being out of the water too long. He was blind in one eye where the other man had hurt him and he ached from his bruising by the rocks and from the strange shadow that had attacked him.

Those in the house were gone. The house itself was gone. But others would come. They always had.

Finally he eased into the welcome water of the underground stream that led to the lake. Those who fed him might be gone, but Tola lived.

As he always had. As he always would.

EPILOGUE

Mary Hole-in-the-Sky gazed down at the naked dark-haired baby lying on a blanket on her kitchen table. "He's one of us, no doubt about that," she said, grinning at Kendra. "Not that there ever *was* any doubt. You're too bemused by that worthless nephew of mine to even notice other men exist." She glanced at the old woman seated in the rocker. "Isn't that true, Leda?"

"Well, I don't know that he's worthless," Leda said, "but there's no doubt the pair of them are pretty well wrapped up in each other."

Kendra smiled as she slid a fresh diaper under her son's bottom. Aunt Mary and Leda got along just fine.

Little Wolf waved his hands and kicked, gurgling at his great-aunt as if to add his own comments.

"Well, I admit Hart's improved since he got himself a wife," Aunt Mary said. "Sort of brought him to his senses, I'd say."

She laid a friendly hand on Kendra's shoulder. "If Grandfather were still alive, I think he'd approve of you. I know the rest of us do. We figured Hart would find a fancy woman to go with that fancy job of his in California. But we got lucky—he picked you and here he is back home teaching in an Upper Peninsula high school. It's too bad—" She broke off and reached down to tickle the baby under the chin until he laughed in delight.

Kendra knew what she'd meant to say—it was too bad Dewolfe wasn't alive to welcome his brother's return to the fold.

"But this little Rainwalker here," Mary went on, her gaze on the baby, "is my nephew's greatest achievement." She glanced up at Kendra. "That's not to say you didn't contribute your share."

Kendra laughed. "You mean, little Wolf has my brown eyes. The rest of him is certainly pure Rainwalker."

"I quite agree," Leda chimed in. "Pure Rainwalker and purely wonderful."

Kendra smiled at Leda. Only Leda really understood her long months of worry, her apprehension when she lay on the delivery table. Even when the doctor had assured her she'd borne a perfect little boy, she didn't really believe it until she saw for herself. Wolf had inherited no taint.

As she fastened the baby's diaper, warm arms encircled her from behind. "Keep practicing on this one," Hart murmured in her ear. "Something tells me next time—say maybe a couple years from now—it'll be twins."

She handed the baby to Mary and turned to face Hart. Cuddled against him, she said, "Something tells me that if you're right, more than one of us had better keep practicing with this one."

Mary spoke up. "Something tells *me* that if you don't stop nuzzling each other, those twins are going to arrive sooner than you expect, like, hey, exactly nine months from now...."

* * * * *

SILHOUETTE® *Shadows* ™

Welcome To The Dark Side Of Love...

AVAILABLE THIS MONTH

#15 FOOTSTEPS IN THE NIGHT—Lee Karr
Anxious to learn about her true family heritage, Maurie Miller traveled to Ireland, only to land in a nightmare. Someone had mistaken her for another woman—a woman who shared the same face—a woman in grave danger.... Maurie had but one chance of survival—Daylan O'Shane, the handsome neighbor who watched her every move.

#16 WHAT WAITS BELOW—Jane Toombs
When Kendra Tremaine inherited her family's estate, she also inherited the menacing legend of Lynx Lake. People had ended up missing or dead at the hands of a mysterious entity, and Kendra wanted some answers. Would she find an ally in Hart Rainwalker, the enigmatic groundskeeper who harbored a secret agenda as well as a blatant attraction?

COMING NEXT MONTH

#17 THE HAUNTING OF BRIER ROSE—Patricia Simpson
With her twenty-first birthday quickly approaching, Rose Quennel vowed to break the chain of dark possession that had cursed both her mother and grandmother. But a midnight shadow threatened to fulfill the legacy by arousing forbidden desires. Could mysterious Taylor Wolfe help end the nightmares, or was he responsible for the midnight madness?

#18 TWILIGHT PHANTASIES—Maggie Shayne
Tamara Dey never knew about her connection to the undead; her guardian kept it a secret to advance his research. Now Eric Marquand appeared in Tamara's life, inspiring an irresistible attraction and haunting feelings of remembrance. But could their love transcend the curse of immortality?

OFFICIAL RULES • MILLION DOLLAR SWEEPSTAKES
NO PURCHASE OR OBLIGATION NECESSARY TO ENTER

To enter, follow the directions published. **ALTERNATE MEANS OF ENTRY:** Hand print your name and address on a 3"x5" card and mail to either: Silhouette "Match 3," 3010 Walden Ave., P.O. Box 1867, Buffalo, NY 14269-1867, or Silhouette "Match 3," P.O. Box 609, Fort Erie, Ontario L2A 5X3, and we will assign your Sweepstakes numbers. (Limit: one entry per envelope.) For eligibility, entries must be received no later than March 31, 1994. No responsibility is assumed for lost, late or misdirected entries.

Upon receipt of entry, Sweepstakes numbers will be assigned. To determine winners, Sweepstakes numbers will be compared against a list of randomly preselected prizewinning numbers. In the event all prizes are not claimed via the return of prizewinning numbers, random drawings will be held from among all other entries received to award unclaimed prizes.

Prizewinners will be determined no later than May 30, 1994. Selection of winning numbers and random drawings are under the supervision of D.L. Blair, Inc., an independent judging organization, whose decisions are final. One prize to a family or organization. No substitution will be made for any prize, except as offered. Taxes and duties on all prizes are the sole responsibility of winners. Winners will be notified by mail. Chances of winning are determined by the number of entries distributed and received.

Sweepstakes open to persons 18 years of age or older, except employees and immediate family members of Torstar Corporation, D.L. Blair, Inc., their affiliates, subsidiaries and all other agencies, entities and persons connected with the use, marketing or conduct of this Sweepstakes. All applicable laws and regulations apply. Sweepstakes offer void wherever prohibited by law. Any litigation within the province of Quebec respecting the conduct and awarding of a prize in this Sweepstakes must be submitted to the Régies des Loteries et Courses du Quebec. In order to win a prize, residents of Canada will be required to correctly answer a time-limited arithmetical skill-testing question. Values of all prizes are in U.S. currency.

Winners of major prizes will be obligated to sign and return an affidavit of eligibility and release of liability within 30 days of notification. In the event of non-compliance within this time period, prize may be awarded to an alternate winner. Any prize or prize notification returned as undeliverable will result in the awarding of that prize to an alternate winner. By acceptance of their prize, winners consent to use of their names, photographs or other likenesses for purposes of advertising, trade and promotion on behalf of Torstar Corporation without further compensation, unless prohibited by law.

This Sweepstakes is presented by Torstar Corporation, its subsidiaries and affiliates in conjunction with book, merchandise and/or product offerings. Prizes are as follows: Grand Prize–$1,000,000 (payable at $33,333.33 a year for 30 years). First through Sixth Prizes may be presented in different creative executions, each with the following approximate values: First Prize–$35,000; Second Prize–$10,000; 2 Third Prizes–$5,000 each; 5 Fourth Prizes–$1,000 each; 10 Fifth Prizes–$250 each; 1,000 Sixth Prizes–$100 each. Prizewinners will have the opportunity of selecting any prize offered for that level. A travel-prize option, if offered and selected by winner, must be completed within 12 months of selection and is subject to hotel and flight accommodations availability. Torstar Corporation may present this Sweepstakes utilizing names other than Million Dollar Sweepstakes. For a current list of all prize options offered within prize levels and all names the Sweepstakes may utilize, send a self-addressed, stamped envelope (WA residents need not affix return postage) to: Million Dollar Sweepstakes Prize Options/Names, P.O. Box 4710, Blair, NE 68009.

The Extra Bonus Prize will be awarded in a random drawing to be conducted no later than May 30, 1994 from among all entries received. To qualify, entries must be received by March 31, 1994 and comply with published directions. No purchase necessary. For complete rules, send a self-addressed, stamped envelope (WA residents need not affix return postage) to: Extra Bonus Prize Rules, P.O. Box 4600, Blair, NE 68009.

For a list of prizewinners (available after July 31, 1994) send a separate, stamped, self-addressed envelope to: Million Dollar Sweepstakes Winners, P.O. Box 4728, Blair, NE 68009.

Silhouette Books
is proud to present
our best authors,
their best books…
and the best in
<u>your reading pleasure!</u>

Throughout 1993, look for exciting
books by these top names in
contemporary romance:

DIANA PALMER—
Fire and Ice in June

ELIZABETH LOWELL—
Fever in July

CATHERINE COULTER—
Afterglow in August

LINDA HOWARD—
Come Lie With Me in September

When it comes to passion,
we wrote the book.

BOBT2

MEN MADE IN AMERICA

Fifty red-blooded, white-hot, true-blue hunks from every
State in the Union!

Beginning in May, look for MEN MADE IN AMERICA!
Written by some of our most popular authors, these
stories feature fifty of the strongest, sexiest men, each
from a different state in the union!

Two titles available every other month at your favorite
retail outlet.

In September, look for:

DECEPTIONS by Annette Broadrick (California)
STORMWALKER by Dallas Schulze (Colorado)

In November, look for:

STRAIGHT FROM THE HEART by Barbara Delinsky
(Connecticut)
AUTHOR'S CHOICE by Elizabeth August (Delaware)

You won't be able to resist MEN MADE IN AMERICA!

**And now for
something completely different
from Silhouette....**

SPELLBOUND
R O M A N C E

Every once in a while, Silhouette brings you a book that is truly unique and innovative, taking you into the world of paranormal happenings. And now these stories will carry our special "Spellbound" flash, letting you know that you're in for a truly exciting reading experience!

In October, look for *McLain's Law* (IM #528) by Kylie Brant

Lieutenant Detective Connor McLain believes only in what he can see—until Michele Easton's haunting visions help him solve a case...and her love opens his heart!

McLain's Law is also the Intimate Moments "Premiere" title, introducing you to a debut author, sure to be the star of tomorrow!

Available in October...only from
Silhouette Intimate Moments